CARMEN CAVANAGH

Annie Smithson

CARMEN CAVANAGH

Foreword by Alan Hayes

ARLEN
HOUSE

CARMEN CAVANAGH

is published in 2022 by
ARLEN HOUSE
42 Grange Abbey Road
Baldoyle
Dublin D13 A0F3
Ireland
Email: arlenhouse@gmail.com
www.arlenhouse.ie

978–1–85132–278–7, paperback

International distribution by
SYRACUSE UNIVERSITY PRESS
621 Skytop Road, Suite 110
Syracuse
New York 13244–5290
United States
Email: supress@syr.edu
www.syracuseuniversitypress.syr.edu

Digitisation by Susan Bennett and Alan Hayes

Typesetting by Arlen House

Cover artwork: 'Motley' (1936) by Lillias Mitchell
is reproduced courtesy of the artist's estate,
with thanks to Margaret Greeves and Geraldine Mitchell

Foreword
ANNIE SMITHSON
THE PUBLISHING PHENOMENON

Alan Hayes

Annie Smithson (1873–1948) was Ireland's biggest selling and most widely read author from the 1920s to the 1940s. Her publisher, The Talbot Press, of 85–89 Talbot Street, regularly reissued and reprinted her novels, often with new dust jackets. They knew their market. In the 1920s alone, there were at least two, if not three, colour dust jackets created for *Carmen Cavanagh*, though unfortunately none appear to have survived. The first edition was a co-publication with the prestigious London firm, T. Fisher Unwin, who had a lucrative business relationship with Talbot Press.

Carmen Cavanagh is Smithson's third novel, first published in September 1921, and regularly reprinted over the coming decades; the 10th edition appearing in 1951. But there were more printings than that. Her books were sold internationally, they were serialised in newspapers and journals for decades. Phoenix Publishing, a mass market publisher of cheap editions, headquartered on O'Connell Street, sold her books nationwide door to door by salesmen on bicycles. Her brilliantly-savvy publisher made huge profits from "Annie M.P. Smithson", the author they developed, nurtured and promoted, yet she lived frugally and failed to benefit from the enormous sales her books achieved. For some inexplicable reason, she continued to sign contracts for each book that gave her a modest fee, and she waived her rights to ongoing royalties on sales. Many of her 25 books were reprinted annually, with some going into biannual prints. Her books were a phenomenal success the general public couldn't get enough of. For people who couldn't afford to purchase them, they could be borrowed from lending libraries that were scattered everywhere, often consisting of a few shelves in the village grocery store. In *Dancing at Lughnasa*, Brian Friel's play about his five impoverished aunts in Donegal in 1936, Smithson's novel *The Marriage of Nurse Harding* (1935) is brought to the cottage for his aunt Agnes to read. Boston College have a 1921 first edition of *Carmen Cavanagh*, inscribed by Lily Yeats, sister of W.B., and gifted to Cuala Press typesetter Molly Gill. Annie Smithson was read widely, and well regarded in her day. The lack of significant literary or feminist engagement on her enormous output over the past 70 years is noticeable, bar scholars such as Oonagh Walsh, Danae O'Regan and Caitríona Clear. The dismissal of her work as romantic nationalist Catholic fiction fails to reveal the true story.

A self-taught writer, with no delusions of grandeur in her writing abilities, who stated she found writing easy and enjoyable, Smithson was also one of the first proponents of magic realism in her fiction. Her novels are well-written and entertaining, with lots of drama, intriguing plot points and clever character development. Her female characters are always well drawn, and, in *Carmen Cavanagh*, so too are the numerous, distinctive, male characters.

From her first novel, *Her Irish Heritage* (1917) to her final, *Paid in Full* (1946), Smithson developed a massive and loyal readership – though mainly women – of all ages. Some of these women became leaders of the second wave feminist movement in the 1960s and 1970s and have cited Smithson's female characters as positive role models in their socialisation and political formation.

Her books were well reviewed, though it is not always clear whether reviewers actually read the books they were reviewing. By this quirk of dismissing Smithson with faint praise and mislabelling her as a lightweight romantic novelist, her books appear to have been ignored by the censor. Thus Smithson was able to address numerous controversial subjects in her fiction such as rape, infanticide, illegitimacy, domestic violence, infidelity, sex before marriage, revolutionary violence, coercive control, dysfunctional marriages, separation and divorce, murder, depression, bigotry, class barriers and suicide.

Smithson, surprisingly, was not a member of the Irish Women Writers Club which ran from 1933–1958, when she was at her commercial peak. Possibly po-faced, she may not have been liked by sister writers, or even felt the need to network with them. Smithson had a busy day job running the national nursing organisation, and her free time would have been spent on her onerous writing output, managing to produce a new novel either yearly or biennally.

Reviewing *Carmen Cavanagh*, the *Irish Independent* said Smithson:

> has now her public, and deservedly so, and that public will
> relish her latest book as keenly as it relished her other books ... it
> helps one to spend a pleasant evening – it is interesting, and
> there is nothing in it to offend the adult mind ... there are scenes
> which touch the heart – unless the heart is a hardened sinner.
> The descriptions of the peasants are not too flattering; at the

same time they are earnest and sincere; and if there were more intimacy in them the book should have a value beyond that of the usual novel. (12/09/1921).

Clearly, this reviewer missed so much, as you will see when you read the novel. *Carmen Cavanagh* is set largely in the wilds of Donegal, in Gleann Cholm Cille in 1911, and the story explores the exacting lives and work of two district nurses, Marcella Campbell and Carmen Cavanagh, and dispensary doctors in a region where medical duties had to be carried out under very trying and harsh circumstances. Much of Smithson's writing is thinly disguised biography – as will be revealed when Marie Bashford-Synnott publishes her full-length study, *Annie Smithson: Revolutionary Novelist and Nurse*. She only stayed in Donegal for twenty months, and it is likely she left, or was forced to leave, due to a shocking event she describes in this novel. Contrastingly, the scenes set in Dublin are full of joy at a city she loves, and some of the characters are clearly based on family members. One surprising plotline, of an entire family escaping their psychotic head of household and emigrating overnight to Canada, while he lay in a drunken stupor unaware that when he would awake his family and furniture would be disappeared forever, is actually true, as Bashford-Synnott has discovered. I shall not spoil any more plotlines, save to say that by the end of the novel Carmen Cavanagh is a powerbroker in charge of her own destiny. She chooses her redemption. How so? Read on.

Different editions of *Carmen Cavanagh*, 1921–1951

1920s–1940s dust jackets from Talbot Press and An Gum

Her Irish Heritage (1917), novel

By Strange Paths (1919), novel

Carmen Cavanagh (1921), novel

The Walk of a Queen (1922), novel

In Times of Peril: Leaves from the Diary of Nurse Linda Kearns (1922), editor

Nora Connor: A Romance of Yesteryear (1924), novel

The Guide (1925), short stories

The Laughter of Sorrow (1925), novel

These Things: The Romance of a Dancer (1927), novel

Sheila of the O'Beirnes (1929), novel

Traveller's Joy (1930), novel

For God and Ireland (1931), short stories

Leaves of Myrtle (1932), novel

The Light of Other Days (1933), novel

The Marriage of Nurse Harding (1935), novel

The White Owl (1937), novel

A Dúthchas Gaedhealach (1938), *Her Irish Heritage* as Gaeilge

Wicklow Heather (1938), novel

Margaret of Fair Hill (1939), novel

The Weldons of Tibradden (1940), novel

Katherine Devoy (1941), novel

By Shadowed Ways (1942), novel

Tangled Threads (1943), novel

Myself – and Others (1944), memoir

The Village Mystery (1945), novel

Paid in Full (1946), novel

CARMEN CAVANAGH

I

THE BACK OF BEYOND

In the dusk of the September evening the shabby country car, with the lean horse between its shafts, came slowly down the rough mountain road. Two people were on it besides the driver – a middle-aged woman sitting beside him viewing the passing landscape with looks of grim disapproval, and on the opposite side a girl of about twenty-five, pale and tired-looking, but whose big eyes twinkled with amusement when they encountered the disgusted glances of her companion.

It was certainly a wild part through which they were driving, and to those unaccustomed to such scenery it must indeed have appeared too wild to be beautiful – for its beauty was of that grand yet lonely and isolated type which appeals to certain temperaments. The road, if such it could be called, was in a terrible state, for though the evening was fine, there had been a continuous rain during the last few days and the horse's hoofs and the wheels of the car sank deeply into the soft soil, while at frequently-recurring intervals here and there great holes would suddenly yawn in the path before them – holes which, however, the driver and his skinny animal managed in some extraordinary manner to avoid, literally by a hair's breadth, as it seemed to Marcella Campbell.

On their right nothing was to be seen as far as the eye could reach but miles of flat, moist bogland; and on their left a sheer declivity of rock led down to where a mountain torrent dashed over its stony bed. Not a human being was in sight, and, except for the occasional call of some seabird flying over the bog, there was absolute silence – silence, that is, save for the sound of the shaky car as it crawled and jolted along and the husky voice of the consumptive driver wheezing forth remonstrances and admonitions to his dejected animal.

It was all very cheerless and depressing, and to the two travellers, tired after their long railway journey, it seemed inexpressibly dreary. Even the girl, who had been cheerfully optimistic up to this, began to feel lonely and more or less wretched and homesick – homesick for the lights and stir of the city, for the bustle and noise of the pavement. She glanced around her at the seemingly endless vista of bog, and shivered involuntarily. Dusk was closing in rapidly, adding to the loneliness of this isolated region. How different from the streets of Dublin at the same hour!

However, she must not let her thoughts run away with her in that fashion, and, with a valiant effort to try and take an interest in her present surroundings, she leant over the well of the car and addressed the jarvey.

'It's very quiet here,' she said. 'Is it always the same?'

'Aye.'

'The road is in an awful state,' she continued. 'I wonder they don't try to put it in better repair.'

The driver made no answer to this, and Marcella relapsed into silence, However, after a few moments during which he had evidently been considering the gist of her remarks, Con Doherty volunteered the statement that 'a couple of them Congested District men had been down from Dublin a few weeks back to have a look at the roads.'

'Well, what did they do?' asked Marcella, as the driver paused again.

'Do? Sure they did nawthing! What good would the likes of them do anyway? The man that was driving them was a stranger and a foreigner to the roads, and, signs on it, he went and let the horse break his fore leg in that very hole we're after passin'.'

'Oh! The poor brute!' exclaimed his listener. 'Surely after that they settled something about getting the road repaired?'

'Divil a bit!' was the stolid answer, 'and what ails the same roads anyway? Ain't they the same as they always were, and won't they last our time widout strangers and foreigners comin' and interfarin'?'

Abashed, Marcella retired into silence once more. She sighed rather wistfully and drew her wraps more closely around her. It was nearly dark now and decidedly chilly, and the girl felt suddenly very tired and weary. Reaching over the well of the car she laid her hand on the elder woman's arm.

'Ellen,' she said, 'isn't it an *awful* journey? Will it ever come to an end?'

'God knows, Miss Marcella; it's what I'm wondering meself,' replied the other. Gloomily she swept the darkening horizon as she spoke, as though trying to pierce the dusk in a vain endeavour to find out whither they were journeying. But the road remained the same – on one hand the measureless bogland, and on the other the cliffs and roaring torrent below. Not a human habitation or sign of life was near, save only the curlews, with their mournful cry, and the sound of the rickety car which was taking them – where?

Ellen Doyle – Dublin born and bred – sighed heavily.

'It's the back of beyant, Miss, that's what it is,' she said, and would talk no more.

It seemed to Marcella like a dream journey – a nightmare in which she would never reach her destination – never be able to get off that horrid car and to stretch her weary and cramped limbs.

She must have dozed for a short while, for the next thing of which she was conscious was a suppressed shriek from Ellen Doyle, and at the same time the car seemed to be suddenly shot up in the air.

'Oh! May God help us! We'll be killed altogether! Miss Marcella, dear, are you all right?'

'Yes, yes, Ellen, I'm all right! What's wrong?'

'Wrong? Sure nawthing's wrong,' answered the slow accents of Con Doherty. 'Have sense woman,' he continued to the indignant Miss Doyle, 'have sense and don't go leppin' and scramin' like a two-year-auld, frightenin' the mare like you!'

The car was going down a very steep hill – so steep that it gave Marcella the impression of being driven down the side of a house. She would have given a great deal to have left the car and walked, tired as she was, but did not venture even to suggest such a thing to their driver, especially as he seemed so utterly indifferent and stolid. To him this awful drive was evidently an everyday affair, and his attitude towards the two strangers on the car was one of ill-concealed contempt.

And after all the journey was not a nightmare – it was real – no dream. And being so, like everything else in this old world of ours, had to come to an end sometime. And, therefore, just as Marcella was giving up hope, she saw in the distance a revolving, flashing light, and at the same moment Con Doherty pointed his battered old whip in that direction.

'Yon's the island,' he said briefly.

'The island?' repeated Marcella, curiously.

'Aye, that's the light from the lighthouse at Glenbeg.'

'And is that where we are going?' asked the girl.

'Yerra, not at all! Sure your house is in Glenmore, just beyant there at the foot of the hill. There's the lights now.'

And, peering into the darkening night, Marcella could see a light twinkling steadily here and there at intervals.

'Oh, Ellen!' she cried joyfully, 'we really *are* nearly there at last!'

But Ellen only responded by a grunt; she was older than her young mistress by many years, and age had given her a more pessimistic outlook on life.

As they drew nearer, the lights were seen to be coming from the windows of the small cabins which they were passing, but Marcella tried in vain to take stock of her surroundings. It was now too dark to decipher objects even near at hand, and so she gave up the attempt and waited with what patience she could muster until she should reach her new abode. And after a few moments the car suddenly stopped with a jerk, and Con Doherty stolidly announced, 'Ye're there now.'

Marcella, in her relief, jumped quickly down from the car, and so stiff and cramped was she after her seven hours' drive, that her knees seemed suddenly to become of no use to her, and she almost suffered the humiliation of measuring her length on the hard road. She managed to recover herself, and, going round to the other side of the car, she helped Ellen to descend. This was no easy task, for Ellen was fat and, if not fair, was certainly forty, and well over it. But as their morose jarvey showed no signs of coming to her assistance, Marcella was compelled to do so.

Both travellers then looked around them curiously, but they could not see any house.

'Yon's the gate, at the side,' said Con, 'there's a cart track up to the back door, and I'll lead the horse up.'

'Is there no other gate?' asked Marcella.

'Aye, ye're standin' by it, but it's locked and the key is in the house. The big gates are open.'

Marcella put out her hand gropingly and felt a small gate, but on each side big bushes seemed to be growing, although she could not be sure of anything in the dark. 'Come, Ellen, we had better follow the car,' she said, 'we will never find the house by ourselves.'

And so, stumbling and slipping, they followed Con Doherty up the uneven cart track which led round to the back premises.

They found him turning a huge rusty key in the lock of the back door.

'Mr Strong gave me the key,' he volunteered, 'and he tould me to tell ye that the key of the front door is hanging in the kitchen.'

The door swung back, creaking on its hinges, and they entered the kitchen. At first all that Marcella noticed was the damp musty smell and a feeling of intense cold – it appeared to be colder here than it had been out of doors. Then Con struck a match and producing a bit of candle from his pocket held it aloft while he looked for some place on which to deposit it, and by its flickering light Marcella Campbell surveyed her new home.

And what she saw was enough to depress the most optimistic of women.

The kitchen floor was flagged and the flags were uneven and broken in places, and just now green with damp. A large deal table stood in the window, and there was also an old dresser and a few wooden chairs; and all these, like the floor, were covered with damp and mildew. The grate was very large and antiquated, and red with rust, while underneath it yawned the big hole for the turf ashes – the 'pit' in local parlance.

By now Con Doherty had fixed the candle on the dresser by the simple expedient of sticking it on to some of its own grease. He turned then and asked, 'Which of yez will give me a hand with them boxes? It isn't meself could lift the like of them down off the car. I have tubercular in the chest ever since the last time the travelling Health Show was here – that's what they told me anyway.'

Ellen Doyle, seeming too dazed to speak, followed him outside, and Marcella, feeling utterly miserable, sank down in a chair and, in spite of herself, let a few tears find their way from her big grey eyes to her clasped hands.

But at the sound of returning footsteps she hastily brushed them aside and went forward to help the other two with the boxes.

'Oh! Just leave them there – anywhere – till the morning,' she said hastily. 'We must get the fire lit, I'm so cold – and to think that this is only September. I wonder is there any coal, or even sticks – there must be, for the Superintendent in Dublin told me all would be ready for us. Perhaps you know where the coal house is?' turning to Con.

He gazed back at her stolidly.

'It's not coal that ye will be using here,' he said then, 'there's none of that nearer than Sligo. And there's no turf saved for ye this year, because we didn't know whether another nurse was coming or not, and Nurse Brady is gone these three months. But I'll step across to Andy Walker – that's their house in the field forninst ye – and see if maybe he will bring over a creel.'

As his footsteps died away, the other two looked at one another, and Marcella, who had just been almost in despair, suddenly found herself laughing, for the picture which Ellen Doyle made – standing rigid with disapproval in the midst of such chaos – was indeed comical to one possessed of the saving sense of humour. And Marcella Campbell possessed such a sense in a marked degree, and tonight it was to prove a real boon to her.

'Oh, cheer up, Ellen dear!' she cried. 'Don't look so doleful. Let us pretend that we are out for a picnic somewhere and make the best of things. What a blessing it is that we brought groceries and other necessaries with us. Get that box open and we will get a whole candle and see what the rest of this mansion is like.'

The kitchen led into a narrow hall, and crossing that they opened the door of the sitting room – long and low-ceilinged and full of musty, dusty furniture. Upstairs they found two bedrooms in fairly good repair, and several other rooms with the ceilings open to the heavens and the plaster coming off the walls. There was a bed in each of the habitable rooms and sheets and blankets – these being so damp that they seemed literally wet in their hands.

'We must bring these down and air them at the fire – when we *get* a fire!' said Marcella. 'Oh! I hear footsteps – it must be the man with the turf!'

And such it proved to be. Andy Walker, the younger, a great hulking young giant of about twenty, was standing awkwardly in the kitchen. He proved, however, to be much more sympathetic than the dour Con, and, after the latter had been paid his exorbitant charge and dismissed, Andy volunteered to 'put down a fire', an offer thankfully accepted, and in an incredibly short space of time a huge turf fire was blazing cheerily in the grate.

'I brought ye a wee sup of sweet milk,' he said then shyly, 'I thought ye might be wanting it for your tay.'

'Oh, thanks so much! It's very kind of you,' said Marcella gratefully.

'I'll bring ye over another creel in the morning,' he said, preparing to take his departure, but waiting to ask if there was anything more he could do for them.

'No, thank you,' said Marcella, 'we are all right now that we have this fire, and thank you again.'

So, with an awkward 'Goodnight' their good Samaritan took himself off, leaving the two wanderers feeling different beings as they sipped their hot tea and warmed their cramped limbs by the cheery blaze.

The next morning life once more seemed worth living, and very much so. Marcella had slept well, for she had been tired out, but, being always a light sleeper, she awoke early. Like most people awakening first amidst strange surroundings, she forgot for the moment where she was, and lay looking around her at the unfamiliar room, rather bare and comfortless-looking, with part of her luggage strewn around as she had left it, through sheer weariness, the night before. Then suddenly remembering, she jumped out of bed and ran to the window.

'Now at last I can see where I am,' she thought.

And, gazing out, she got her first glimpse of the beauty of Donegal.

Her window looked out on the front towards the little iron gate which she had struggled unsuccessfully to open in the darkness of the preceding night. She saw it now, in the near distance, a long path leading to it from the hall door – a path which was bordered on both sides by a great hedge of veronica bushes. Fuchsias were growing everywhere – at the front door, at the gate, and away by the roadway itself – growing wild, as they do all through Donegal. To the left of the house was another small gate leading into the vegetable garden, which was in a state of terrible neglect, the weeds, indeed, as Marcella afterwards discovered, being breast high. A roadway ran by the front gate, and whitewashed cabins were dotted here and there, while on her right hand she could make out the cart track up to the side of the house along which she and Ellen Doyle had groped and stumbled in the darkness.

But the greatest beauty of all was the sea. Such a sea! So heavenly greeny-blue in colour, and shining and flashing now in the light of the morning sun. It was Marcella's first sight of the Atlantic, and she drew a deep breath of sheer delight as she looked upon it. Away in the distance was the island on which stood the lighthouse – a splash of dazzling light against the vivid green – warning unwary mariners to beware of one of the most dangerous coasts in Ireland.

Between the sea and Marcella's house was a wide expanse of bog, from which steep rocky cliffs led down to the sparkling waves beneath. The cold and damp were gone; it was an ideal morning, and as she hastily dressed, bent on more voyages of discovery, Marcella wondered how she could ever have felt depressed or disheartened. She knew that she was in a new world, amidst people and surroundings to which so far she had been a stranger, and the very novelty of her surroundings aroused her interest and stimulated her energies. She had come amongst these people as their district nurse – she was therefore bound to get to know them intimately; she would share their joys and sorrows, see them under all sorts of conditions – at their best and at their worst. She honestly wished to help them, to be of use to them – one on whom they could depend at all times. And yet she felt some very serious qualms and doubts as to her reception by these people in whose midst she now found herself.

When she had been informed where her district was to be she had begged the Superintendent not to send her there. She had never been in any isolated part before, and she had felt really nervous about going so far from all that was familiar to her. However, the fiat had gone forth from the Head Office, and Marcella Campbell had said farewell to the aunt with whom she had found a home since the death of her parents, many years ago, and to all her friends and acquaintances in dear old Dublin, and, in the faithful company of Ellen Doyle, who had been a housemaid to her mother years before, she had fared forth to see what fortune had in store for her amidst the bleak bogs and hills of far Donegal.

As she descended the stairs, she could hear Ellen talking to herself – a sure sign that things were going wrong with her – and so on entering the kitchen Marcella was not surprised to find her handmaid engaged in trying to blow the turf into a blaze. Of course neither of them had dreamt the night before of 'raking' the fire into the pit and covering over the turf with the hot ashes. If they had done so, the turf would be red hot in the morning and the fire would have been easily lit. But they knew nothing of the way of turf, and to Ellen the task of lighting the fire, without either sticks or coal, was a herculean task. She thought of her kitchen range in Dublin and nearly wept.

'Miss, dear, I don't know when I'll have even a cup of tea for you,' she said, pausing for a moment to get breath from her strenuous blowing, to Marcella. 'How I'm ever going to manage with only turf fires I can't imagine! If there was even a gas cooker itself!' – and she threw a speculative eye around the kitchen as though by any chance such a useful article might have been overlooked.

'A gas cooker here! Oh, Ellen!' cried Marcella, and her ringing laugh brought a reluctant smile to the other's woebegone countenance.

But the turf was conquered at last, and they got tea – smelling, of course, strongly of turf – and Marcella made a hearty breakfast of bread and butter – 'all turfy, too' – as she remarked resignedly.

There is nothing so disagreeable at first to those who are unused to it as this peculiar clinging odour of turf. Every bit of food which one eats seems to be impregnated with it, and for first week or so strangers often have to fight against a positive nausea when eating. But after a while it is no longer noticeable, and in the days to come Marcella used often to wonder at her dislike to it in the beginning, just as Ellen Doyle, when she had become learned in the art of turf fires, and of cooking all sorts of delicious things in the despised pot oven, used to wonder how she had ever found these things difficult.

Their breakfast was hardly over when the back door latch clicked and without either knocking or asking permission, a woman entered.

Both Marcella and Ellen looked at her in surprise, and indeed Ellen's face expressed very strongly her disapproval of such cool proceedings. It was, however, merely the custom of the district, and Mrs Gillespie, as she entered smilingly, had not the least notion that her advent could be anything but welcome.

'Well now, and how are ye?' she exclaimed cordially, stepping up to the table and shaking both warmly by the hand. 'So ye have got your breakfast? I was just saying to my man that I had better step up and see what the nurse would be wanting in the way of things – ye being strangers and all! It's me that keeps the shop at the crossroads up above, and Nurse Brady always left me her custom, and I hope that you and I will get on finely too! 'Deed but I'm sure we will, and God knows but we're all glad to see the nurse's house taken agen!'

She paused for breath, and Marcella muttered some suitable reply, while Ellen continued to eye the visitor with cold disapproval.

'Ye will be wanting some goods immediately, I'm thinking?' insinuated Mrs Gillespie, with that keen business instinct which had made her one of the richest women for miles around.

She was a sharp-featured and sharp-tongued little woman, of middle age, married to a man very much her junior, and they had one child – a boy of seven, very ugly, and frightfully precocious, but in the eyes of his doting parents he was a 'thing of beauty and a joy for ever.' They lived in a very small cabin at the 'crossroads' only a few yards from the nurse's house. It consisted indeed of only one room, and a curtain divided it into house and shop – the shop being the front and larger part, where every conceivable article, from 'a needle to an anchor' could be bought – at about three times their proper price.

The house part – religiously concealed behind the curtain – was but a few feet in area, practically all of which was taken up by the bed. Where the Gillespie family cooked or washed or did anything else was always an unsolved problem to Marcella. Their meals they partook of in the shop itself, generally on an old fish barrel, turned upside down, behind the counter.

Mrs Gillespie had over seven hundred pounds in the bank – in her own name, her husband being an absolute nonentity – but to look at her or to hear her talk, one would get the impression that she found it a hard task indeed to make ends meet, and that, more often than not, she was shamefully robbed by all her customers. The latter, however, told a different tale.

'Och! God knows she's awful hard – sure she'd skin a flea for its hide!' was the verdict of those poor creatures who brought their sprigging to 'Arabella', as she was universally called. Marcella often wondered why she had been christened Arabella – a name which somehow always seems to conjure up a good-natured 'sonsy' woman, with rosy cheeks and innocent eyes, the very antithesis to the present possessor of the name.

'We brought some groceries with us from town,' said Marcella now, when she could get a word in edgeways.

'Och! They'll not be lasting ye long; ye'll be wantin' some fresh goods in surely. Take a stroll up to my place when ye're ready this evening, and ye can have whatever ye may fancy' – this in the tones of one who was conferring a free and munificent gift – 'and,' she added, rising at last, 'I'll show ye both round the town afterwards. Ye will be wantin' to get to know your way around and to know the people too.'

'Oh,' said Marcella with interest, 'I didn't know that there was a town here.'

'A town!' cried Mrs Gillespie shrilly, "deed then and there's as fine a town as ye could wish to see from here to Derry City itself.'

When she had gone Marcella looked at Ellen.

'Well! I'm glad there's a town of sorts anyway,' she said, 'and there are evidently shops around here too. We will want bread this evening, Ellen, so we will stroll over, as she said, and see what there is to be seen.'

'Which won't be much, I'm thinking,' said Ellen, with the scornful indifference of the Dubliner exiled from her beloved city, as she endeavoured to hang the kettle straight on the hook over the fire.

Marcella spent the day in unpacking, and Ellen started house cleaning. They partook of a nondescript dinner at midday, and, after a cup of tea at half-past five, they sallied forth to find Mrs Gillespie's shop at the crossroads and to be taken around on their tour of inspection. It was a lovely evening, quite mild and warm – a great contrast to the preceding one – and as they walked down the front path between the scented veronica bushes where the bees were humming busily and came out on the roadway, Marcella drew in a deep breath of the pure air, feeling almost intoxicated by its salty sting.

'Oh, Ellen, it's lovely here!' she cried.

The other did not reply – the beauties of Nature had little appeal for Ellen Doyle.

A few yards further on they came upon the Post Office – but only that it had 'Glenmore Post Office' painted on a board nailed over the door they would not have recognised it as such. It was simply an ordinary white-washed cottage – very pretty – with the late roses still climbing up its walls. The half-door stood open in the usual way, and Marcella entered with the intention of purchasing some stamps, but really more from curiosity than because she wanted the articles in question. The Post Office was in the kitchen, down one side of which under the window ran the counter. A turf fire was blazing on the open hearth, and the kettle was singing on the crook, but there was no one to be seen, except a huge tabby cat which sat on the counter and blinked lazily at Marcella.

'And they call this a Post Office!' exclaimed Miss Doyle. At that moment the back door, which was facing them, opened and two people entered – a middle-aged woman, with a bucket of water, and a young girl carrying a large can of buttermilk. She was a very pretty girl – lovely, indeed, she might have been called – although her type, slender, dusky haired, blue eyed – was common enough in those parts. Her colouring was that of the wild rose; her whole appearance had something flower-like about it, although she wore the home-spun skirt, coarse apron and little shoulder shawl of the district. She wore neither boots nor stockings, and her feet were shapely and well formed – feet which were a pleasure to look at, and which are only found amongst those women who are used to walking in their bare feet.

Marcella took note of all these details with the quickness of the trained nurse, even while the girl stood hesitating on the threshold with the can of buttermilk in her hand, surveying the newcomers with frank curiosity. In the meantime, the woman had put down the bucket and, first hastily wiping her hands in her blue-checked apron, she advanced smilingly.

'Ye're welcome,' she said, shaking hands vigorously with both her visitors.

'Mary Ellen!' to the girl, 'here's our new nurse. Come and bid her welcome.'

The girl came forward shyly and shook hands. She did not speak, but her smile was a welcome in itself.

'Sit ye down – sit ye down,' said Mrs McNeilis, drawing forward chairs to the fire, and completely ignoring the idea that her visitors had called on any other business except to chat with her. She was a handsome, dark-eyed woman, inclined to be stout, but although she had doubtless been very good-looking in her youth, still Marcella thought that she could never have had the beauty of her daughter.

In the course of their conversation the wanderers from Dublin gleaned some rather startling details about the postal arrangements. It appeared that Glenmore was only a sub-office to that of Ardglen, which was three miles away. The mail car from Kilbeg – the nearest railway station, twenty-five miles distant – reached Ardglen about midday and Mrs Strong, the postmistress there, had to sort the letters and give them to 'Paddy the Post', an elderly, slow-going individual, who owned a cart and a white pony, nearly as old and quite as slow-going as himself. Between them these worthy pair conveyed the letters for Glenmore to that place, delivering them to Mrs McNelis, who, on her part, gave them over to 'Maggie the Post', or 'Maggie John', as she was frequently called, according to the local custom of discriminating certain individuals by the Christian names of both parents – rendered quite necessary sometimes in a district like the one we are writing about, where marriages frequently occur between individuals bearing the same family name.

'Maggie the Post' was a tall, gaunt woman, with very large feet, on which she generally wore men's boots. In the winter she was completely enveloped – head and all – in several large shawls; but in summer she blazoned forth her official dignity by wearing a sailor hat with a red band – a hat that must have done duty for many years, as proved by the faded V.R. still to be deciphered on it.

After delivering the Glenmore quota of letters, which, except on American mail days, was almost *nil*, 'Paddy the Post' proceeded to Glenbeg the next village, three miles further on, with the remainder. There he lived, and the next forenoon on his way to Ardglen he emptied the Glenmore letterbox.

'But then,' said Marcella, puzzled and bewildered, 'can we not answer letters by return? In case of an important letter to which one wished to reply at once – what could be done?'

Mrs McNelis glanced at her with what appeared to be good-natured pity. 'It's quare and strange,' she said then, 'how fond all the city people do be of writing letters! Sure what harm would it do any letter to be left unanswered for a day? All the same if ye *did* want to reply by return, ye would just have to go over to Ardglen and post it there. There's a post car that leaves there for Kilbeg late in the evening.'

Only one daily post, which arrived at 2.30pm, and none on Sunday, and no means of posting by return, except one walked or cycled three long miles – and how long and dreary those same three miles could be Marcella was to find out very soon.

She was still pondering on her postal discoveries, when she reached 'Arabella's' at the crossroads.

The 'shop' was full, overflowing, in fact, on to the roadway. Mrs Gillespie's voice could be heard within talking rapidly in Irish, but no sooner did she perceive her visitor than she relapsed at once into the English tongue, and literally swept her other customers aside as she emerged from behind the counter and led Marcella into the shop, the rather scornful Ellen following.

'Come ye in, come ye in,' she cried, 'and how do ye find yerselves this evening? Bravely, I hope? James!' calling shrilly to an invisible being behind the mysterious curtain – 'bring out two chairs here for the Nurse and Miss Doyle,' for Arabella immediately took her stand as a lifelong friend of both the newcomers, a pose which was meant to establish her superiority over the others in the shop, some of whom indeed were only 'those poor mountainy ones' living all the same only a few miles distant from Arabella's superior residence, and closely allied to her either by birth or marriage.

A tall, red-haired young man of about twenty-six emerged, blushing awkwardly, with two chairs.

'This is my man, now, Nurse,' announced Mrs Gillespie, beamingly. It was as well that she said her *man*, as otherwise Marcella would most certainly have thought he was the lady's son, which indeed he could very well have been, as far as years went.

The son, however, was now to be produced, Mrs Gillespie calling vociferously for 'John Joseph!' There was, however, no reply, although the cry was taken up by the customers in the shop and passed on to those outside, like the name of a witness wanted in court.

'Let ye go look for him, James, and bring him back wid ye,' commanded Mrs Gillespie, and the obedient James departed, as one used to obey and question not.

Having seen Marcella and Ellen seated in state, in which position they found themselves the cynosure of all the eyes that could possibly be focussed on them, Arabella, with an elaborate apology for leaving them, retired once more behind the counter, where she resumed her bargaining and haggling with two girls who had brought several dozen handkerchiefs which they had been 'sprigging' as the exquisite embroidery of the Donegal peasant is called. Mrs Gillespie held the important post of local agent for a well-known Belfast firm, but she was only the local agent. The middleman, who of course made the most profit out of the business, living at Carragh – a village some ten miles inland between Glenmore and Kilbeg, supplied her with the work to be done; blouses, frocks, pillowslips, handkerchiefs, etc., and she in turn doled it out to the people around. The pay they received was miserably small – as low as four pence a dozen for the handkerchiefs, which would be sold for very high prices in the Northern city. Small as the payment was, the workers seldom received it in cash, Arabella preferring, for very obvious reasons, to pay them in kind, and the people themselves, being entirely ignorant of prices or business outside of their own small area, were quite content to get their 'grain of tay and sugar' in return for some of the most beautiful embroidery that could be seen anywhere.

When at last the shop was cleared, and Arabella turned to her visitors, Marcella asked her a question that had been in her mind since she entered the shop.

'Were you not speaking in Irish when we came in?' she asked.

Mrs Gillespie turned an unbecoming brick-red – a sure sign of annoyance with her.

'Irish,' she repeated, "deed and it's not much of *that* I know; but of course wid those quare mountainy folk I have to be trying to make meself understood – and it's little English they have, God help the poor, ignorant craturs.'

Marcella's eyes opened wide in astonishment. Arabella's English was at its best a poor, broken thing, and little as Marcella knew of the Gaelic tongue, yet she had noticed that the shop woman seemed to speak it with an ease and fluency to which she never attained when speaking English. Marcella Campbell was nothing if not outspoken; she was frank almost to a fault, a trait which could possibly be traced to some Quaker ancestors.

'But why should you not speak Irish?' she very logically inquired, 'it is the language we should all be speaking by right, and I only wish that I knew it properly, and I intend to learn it while I'm here. I wish you would help me, Mrs Gillespie?'

'Help you with the Irish! Is it me? Sure it's only a word here and there that I know; it's only used now by the poor mountainy people! It's not what I would be talking at all. Sure James would kill me outright if he caught me spakin' it.'

Clearly Mrs Gillespie considered herself insulted at being asked to speak her native tongue, whose very idioms she was translating into broken English.

Fortunately at that moment the useful James returned, as if the mention of his name had conjured him forth, and with him was the renowned John Joseph.

Instantly Mrs Gillespie was all smiles again, and as the adoring mother she took her offspring by the hand and led him forward. 'Now, Nurse,' she announced in tones of calm triumph, 'this is my boy, and I'll engage ye seldom saw his like in Dublin city itself.'

And Marcella, looking upon him, agreed with his mother. John Joseph was a small, undersized boy of nearly seven; he had his father's red hair and sallow complexion, and his mother's small foxy eyes and thin lips. He was very dirty and also sticky, being engaged in his usual occupation of sucking sugar-stick.

Throwing truth boldly to the winds, Marcella duly admired the Gillespie progeny. Not so Ellen Doyle. She remained silent – too silent for Mrs Gillespie's satisfaction, so she enquired at last:

'Well, Miss Doyle, what do *you* think of John Joseph?'

Ellen Doyle surveyed his unhealthy, putty-coloured face for a moment, and then – 'I think he's full of worms!' she said curtly.

Arabella Gillespie was her deadly enemy from that hour. Without even deigning to reply to such an insult, Mrs Gillespie turned with wounded dignity to Marcella.

'Well, Nurse, if you're ready we'll go round the town,' she said.

Marcella never forgot her first tour of the 'town' of Glenmore.

'Ye'll have seen the Post Office?' inquired Arabella as they stepped forth, speaking in the tones of one who said, 'You have seen the Vatican in Rome!'

'Oh yes,' replied Marcella checking a smile, 'we have seen the Post Office.'

The 'town' consisted of about fourteen little white-washed cabins, each one very like its neighbour. They were all clean inside and out. All had big turf fires on the open hearths, generally with the inevitable pig's pot hanging from the crook, and very often with an old grandmother sitting on the 'wee creepy forninst the fire' and stirring the great saucepan of stirabout for the family supper.

The work outside and within was nearly over for the day, but women's work is never done, and the girls and women in most of the houses were all at their embroidery frames, sprigging for dear life, and continuing to do so even while they talked to their visitors.

From house to house they went, and Marcella received the usual welcome in each. She was very tired and glad beyond words when at last Arabella retraced her footsteps. A long, low terrace of white houses standing by themselves on a steep incline, and having a rather modern appearance about them, attracted her attention.

'Oh them?' sniffed Arabella, 'them's the coastguards. Very respectable, some of them, and friendly enough; but they're all English.'

This last remark, spoken in tones of pitying contempt, greatly amused and puzzled Marcella, coming as it did from the lips of one who was evidently ashamed to be found speaking her own tongue.

'Ye'll have to go and see the Walkers,' Arabella presently announced. 'They'll expect it. They live foreninst ye in the fields – 'deed I'm thinkin',' cocking an inquisitive eye sideways, 'that young Andy brought ye over turf and sweet milk last night?'

'Oh yes,' said Marcella, 'and his sister called today to tell us that Nurse Brady used to get her milk there. I suppose that I had better do so too?'

'Yerra yes – sure ye might as well,' replied Mrs Gillespie with condescension. 'Of course the Walkers are Prodestans,' she continued, as they walked up the road, past her own gate, and crossed a stile into the field opposite. 'This is the Prodestan end of the town, once ye pass the Post Office,' she explained.

'I see,' said Marcella, but she did not really understand very well.

'Ye'll be a Prodestan yerself!' inquired Mrs Gillespie, but more in tones of one stating a fact than asking a question.

'Oh yes,' replied Marcella indifferently, 'but my housekeeper here is a Catholic.'

But even the bond of similar religion could not bridge over the gulf that Ellen Doyle's outspoken remark had put between herself and Arabella, who only murmured a cold 'indeed' in reply.

Never having been in the Northern province before, Marcella was quite oblivious of the importance attached to religious differences there. Religion of any kind troubled her little. Having been brought up in that branch of the Anglican Church located in Ireland which has designated itself as the 'Church of Ireland', she was nominally one of its members, but as far as any real feeling went her spiritual nature was yet quite unawakened.

Ellen Doyle was different. She was a devout Catholic, a trifle narrow, and perhaps more than a trifle bigoted, but her faith was a living thing and dominated her life.

As soon as she entered the Walkers' house, which was larger and more prosperous than any of the others she had seen, being in fact a small farmhouse, Marcella saw at a glance that she was certainly in a 'Prodestan' atmosphere. Instead of the Rosary beads, which hung over the fireplaces in the other homesteads, there was a large and highly-coloured representation of 'King William crossing the Boyne.' The river must certainly at that period have been of very narrow dimensions, as the immortal if plain-featured monarch was depicted seated on a horse, a veritable charger indeed, as far as flowing mane and staring eyes went, whose left fore leg was already firmly planted on the farthermost shore while his back legs were still on the bank that he was about to leave behind! In place of pictures of national heroes and Catholic saints were those of English generals and statesmen, and a large engraving of a very stout Queen Victoria, presenting a huge Bible to a rather under-clad savage, was hung in a place of honour over the door.

But Marcella's welcome was as kind and sincere as any of the others she had received, and not only the welcome for herself but for Ellen Doyle and Arabella also; and even Miss Doyle, who had, figuratively speaking, been drawing her skirts more tightly around her on entering such a hotbed of Orangeism, even she was thawed by their genuine kindness and cheery chatter.

And yet there was no more bigoted Orangeman in the County of Donegal than old Andy Walker. Tall and morose, he sat in the chimney corner and spoke little, although his hand clasp had been warm and sincere. His son resembled him in many respects, but, like most of the younger generation he had less bigotry and more broadmindedness in his character. The daughter was fairly good looking and very pleasant in her manner, and the mother was just a stout, buxom farmer's wife. Religion, of course, was not touched upon, for the Walkers would never forget that two of their guests were Catholics, but had Marcella been alone, they would probably have spoken to her freely on the subject, for they took it for granted that she was 'one of themselves' and consequently of their own way of thinking. Afterwards, when they got to know her better, her very slack and indifferent way of looking at such things horrified and amazed them. Tonight, however, it was getting late, and she did not stay long, glad of the excuse that she was still tired after her long journey.

'True for ye,' says Mrs Walker, coming to the door with them, 'and I hope ye'll not get a sick call tonight. Ye would be the better of a few days to rest and to get to know the people around.'

'Oh! I hope I won't be called tonight,' said Marcella to Mrs Gillespie as she reached her own gate and stood to say goodnight. 'Do you think it is likely?'

'Well, I couldn't rightly say,' replied the other. 'Goodnight' and adding in confidential tones, 'but there's a good few of the wimmen brave and near their time. Well, goodnight till ye anyway, and I hope ye will get a good rest!'

'Good night, and thank you very much, you have been so kind!' replied Marcella, her soft Dublin accents making a delightful contrast to Arabella's Northern tones.

'Oh for nawthing! Ye are very welcome,' was the gratified and condescending response of Mrs Gillespie, as the gate clicked behind her.

II

THE CURSE OF EVE

Marcella Campbell was not called from her rest that night, nor indeed for a week afterwards. During that interval all she had in the way of patients was a child with a cut finger and an old woman with the 'rheumatics'. So she had time to give Ellen a hand with the house cleaning, which, between the two of them, went on apace, and a few days afterwards the house was transformed. The kitchen seemed quite bright and cheerful, and in the sitting room Marcella had wrought a metamorphosis with a regular 'turn-out' followed by a deft rearrangement of the furniture, all being finished off by her own cushions, photos and books. Mrs Gillespie stared open-eyed when she 'looked in' one day towards the end of the week.

'Well, I must say it looks grand!' she said. 'Ye'll have to be giving us a big night once ye have all settled.'

'A big night?' repeated Marcella in bewilderment.

'Aye, a big dance. All the neighbours would come. Barney McNelis can play his fiddle. Nurse Brady had many a dance here in this kitchen – that's what wore the flags away there in the middle!'

Marcella said no more, but she was determined that there would be no 'big nights' in the Nurse's house in Glenmore while she was mistress there. Her predecessor had been of a different type, and a different class, and some rather queer stories about her doings in far Donegal had reached the Nurses' Home in Dublin. That had been one reason why Marcella Campbell had been elected as the next nurse for Glenmore – one who could be depended upon to keep her position and while fulfilling all her duties as nurse to her patients be still careful not to put herself on their level. She was, however, some months in the district before the people recognised this fact, but by degrees they came to realise that while their new nurse was always at their call, and was kindness itself in times of sickness, that still she 'kept herself to herself' and made no friends.

On the fifth day of that first week Marcella was standing at the gate about half-past-two watching for the post. It was the event of the day for her. No exile, shipwrecked on a desert island, could have watched for the smoke of a rescuing vessel with more intensity of gaze than that with which Marcella used to look for the first glimpse of Paddy the Post and his pony cart coming round the bend of the road from Ardglen, that narrow turning on the cliff path, in winter so hard to pass for man and beast that it was known locally as 'Hell's Gate'. Then, after an interval of variable length, according to the gossip or messages he had brought with him, Paddy would resume his way towards Glenbeg, and the tall figure of 'Maggie John' would presently emerge from the Post Office and come down the road towards the Nurse's house. It was her first stopping place, and since Marcella's advent she had never had to pass it.

'Some for you, of course, Nurse,' she observed, as she handed Marcella three letters. 'Ye do get a power of letters,

God knows! If ye answer them all, I'm thinkin' that ye'll have to be sittin' up half the night.'

Marcella only laughed as she seized her letters, and walked up the garden path to read them. There was one from her Aunt Mary – all fussy kindness, as usual; one from a cousin in London, a journalist, who wanted a full description of the 'Donegal native' for his special paper, and the last was a thick envelope addressed in a rather uncommon handwriting. Marcella's eyes brightened when she saw it.

'From Carmen,' she murmured. And standing there between the veronica bushes, amidst the peace of the garden, with no sound but the distant boom of the Atlantic, Marcella read her chum's letter – a letter breathing of another world and another life:

47 Hill Square, Rathmines, Dublin,

Sept. 15th.

Dear Old Girl

How glad I was to get your P.C. on your arrival at Kilbeg, and your long letter since. What an *awful* place you have got to! Oh Cella, dear, but I'm lonely for you. I never missed anyone so much, and all the household here miss you too. Cis sends her love and all good wishes; she is better again, but *he* is as great a fiend as ever! Phil and I were at the pictures last night, and he was sitting alone in the kitchen, with only the light of the fire, when we got in. He had locked poor old Sarah in her bedroom because she wanted to set out some supper for us; all the house was in darkness except Miss Fallon's room. He started to storm at us for being late, but I soon stopped him; so after calling me 'a brazen hussy' and a 'shameless, unsexed being' he informed us that he had turned off the gas at the meter, and after presenting each of us with a half-inch of a candle and one match, he went off to bed. I flung my bit of candle after him – I have a store hidden as you know – and it struck him right on his bald patch – 'the Bourke spot' as he calls it!

Well, enough of that old beast; you know all his beautiful characteristics as well as ourselves!

Eileen and Letty are all right; we are going to Bray next Sunday to visit the O'Carrolls, who have taken a house there for this month. I wonder how I'll like district nursing when I start it! But really, I'm fed-up with private cases – all the men make love to me and all the women bore me – although *you* know that I can be really fond of my own sex.

Just imagine if I enter the Home for my training next month I'll be a finished district nurse in six months – that will be next March – as I have had my Midwifery and I'll be ready for work at once. Oh if only I could get a district *near* you – and the next stop is America. You must indeed be at the edge of the world!

There is a Fancy Dress affair at the Mansion House next week, and I'm going – as *myself*, of course! You know I have the whole rig-out since that amateur thing at Xmas. Captain Stenhouse is taking me. I have told no one except Cis – you know how horrid Phil would be.

Dearest Girl, do take care of yourself! How on earth *do* you pass your time? Are there *no* men at all? – not that they appeal to *you* much! – not even a curate – and is your medico married? Have you met him yet? If he is *anything* in man's shape and not a lady M.D., you are absolutely *certain* to marry him! What else *could* you do in such surroundings? Could you imagine *me* in Donegal? Oh could you! *Could* you?

Au revoir, dearest, and write *soon* to your *so* lonely, Carmen

PS – Give Ellen my love, and tell her she is to marry a nice comfortable old farmer!

Marcella stood for a few moments when she had finished reading, with the letter still in her hand. Her eyes were looking straight before her, as if she were gazing at the broad Atlantic and the distant lighthouse. But, it was a different picture which they really saw – the picture of a girl, dark-eyed, dark-haired, dressed in an old Spanish costume. She was sitting on a table, idly swinging her shapely legs and smoking a cigarette. How often she had seen Carmen Cavanagh just like that. How she loved 'dressing up' and what an ideal 'Carmen' she made! The flashing eyes, the alluring smile, the song, the dance, she was just perfect at them all.

'If only she could have gone on the stage her fortune was made!' thought Marcella, and glanced at the letter again.

'The curate or the doctor!' she echoed with a smile. 'There is only a rector, and he is very much married, according to the local gossip; and as for the doctor, he is newly arrived here too – just like myself – and I have not as yet had the honour of meeting him. Ellen!' she cried, as that worthy appeared in the porch, 'Miss Carmen sends you her love, and says that you are to marry a nice old farmer!'

'Ah! bad scran to her!' cried Ellen delightedly. 'It's the tease of the world she is! But God knows I'd give a lot to see her pretty face coming in at the gate this blessed minute – she'd be the one to cheer me up a bit.'

Marcella caught her breath sharply.

'Oh, Ellen!' she said chokingly, 'I miss her so! I miss them all! Oh! This is a very lonely place!'

'Me poor lamb!' said Ellen, 'you may well say that. But after all, Miss Marcella, sure you're not *married* to it, thanks be to God, and you can leave it when you like. Come in now and sit in the kitchen awhile with me – and don't be fretting.'

The following day was Saturday and Ellen, who had been making enquiries in the village, came back horrified with the information that there was only one Mass on Sundays at Ardglen – the nearest church – and that was celebrated at eleven o'clock.

'Oh, Ellen! that is terrible!' exclaimed Marcella, who knew what a good practical Catholic her housekeeper was. 'only *one* Mass on Sunday, and that at 11 o'clock! If there is no early Mass, how can people receive Holy Communion?'

'They have to wait till that hour,' said Ellen gloomily, 'but it seems that very few here receive weekly. It's not the custom in these parts; they only go to their duty a few times in the year as far as I can make out, at Easter or when there's a Mission and at the *Stations*, whatever they may be!'

'The Stations?' repeated Marcella, blankly. 'What are they, I wonder? Oh Ellen, I'm so sorry,' she continued. 'I should never have brought you to this God-forsaken place.'

But the faithful soul interrupted her.

'Just as if I would have let you come alone!' she said. 'Don't you worry, Miss Marcella, dear; I won't attempt to get over to Ardglen for confession this evening, but I'll go to Mass there tomorrow, and then, please God, I'll know my way, and perhaps I'll get used to the long fast.'

But Marcella was doubtful about that. It was a long walk to Ardglen and back; it would be lunchtime and past it before Ellen could get her first cup of tea.

'I shouldn't have let her come,' she thought sadly, 'but I never thought that she would have the slightest difficulty about her religious duties here. Poor Ellen! That's the last straw with her!'

That night Marcella got her first midwifery case. She was sitting by the kitchen fire, for the evening had turned out wet and stormy, and she was wishing that it was bedtime. But it was only a little after nine, and she knew that she would not sleep if she went so early. Ellen Doyle was ironing, and the kitchen seemed very homely and cheerful in contrast to the wind and rain beating against the windowpanes.

'What a night!' said Marcella, 'and how suddenly it changed after such a lovely day!'

Even as she spoke she heard footsteps at the back door and immediately afterwards the latch was lifted and two men entered.

Ellen turned and surveyed them in angry astonishment; she could never get accustomed to the local fashion of not knocking.

'Wet night,' said one of the men, and they seated themselves on convenient chairs.

From the moment of their entrance Marcella had felt certain that they had come to call her to a case. So she waited expectantly, and still they did not speak, and the silence remained unbroken, save for the occasional bang of Ellen's iron on the stand.

Then, 'It's very wet,' said Marcella, tentatively, looking at the sodden figures before her.

'Aye, it is that!' said the man who had not yet spoken, and the silence began again.

She surveyed them in some bewilderment. Both were dressed in the usual rough homespun of the district; they had big sticks in their hands and they kept their hats on, for your Donegal peasant never uncovers except at Mass, and never raises his hat to anyone but his priest – for in manners Donegal is typically Ulsterian.

Fully twenty minutes went by, and then Marcella asked, 'Do you want me?'

'Aye' said the younger of the two, a tall young fellow of about seven-and-twenty. 'Herself wants ye, and,' he added slowly as an afterthought, 'she bid me tell ye to hurry.'

'Aye, she did that!' added the elderly man, who turned out to be the patient's uncle.

'Good gracious! Why didn't you tell me before?' cried Marcella, jumping up, while Ellen turned to gaze at the 'great gawks' in disgusted amazement.

'Where do you live?' asked the girl.

'At Auchnamanagh,' was the stolid answer conveying, needless to remark, not the slightest information to Marcella.

'Oh! Where is that? Is it far from here?' she asked impatiently.

There was a moment's pause, while the men looked at one another.

'It would be about twelve miles, I'm thinkin',' said the young man,

'Aye – about that, or maybe nearer thirteen,' retorted the other deliberately.

'Have you a car with you?'

'Naw.'

'Then how did you come?'

'We walked it.'

And Marcella, looking at them, saw that they looked like it, drenched and wet, and their boots and even their trousers caked with mud.

'Well, you can't expect *me* to walk it!' she said. 'How am I going to manage?'

'Andy Walker, beyant there, used to drive the other nurse on his car,' said the elder man then, 'maybe I had better step across and ask him to yoke?'

'Maybe you had indeed!' said Marcella, now fairly at the end of her patience.

The two men then left the house as slowly and deliberately as they had entered it.

Marcella turned to Ellen.

'Did you ever see such a pair of fools in your life?' she cried – 'instead of calling at the Walkers and asking Andy to yoke while they came up here for me! It's a wonder they spoke at all? I suppose if I had said nothing they would have sat there till morning!'

'Indeed it's very likely, the uncivilised creatures!' replied Ellen, adding, 'Oh Miss Marcella, dear, such a night for you to have to go twelve or thirteen miles on one of their old cars! It will be the death of you!'

'No fear, Ellen! Warm me some milk while I put on my bonnet and cloak.'

When Young Andy presently arrived with the car he explained to her that he and Con Doherty were in the habit of driving the nurse when she got a night call, or at any time when the bicycle was of no use, such as when she had a call to the 'mountainy people' or when the roads were extra bad. She was supposed to employ them turn about. Andy's horse and car were fairly good, but Marcella thought of Con Doherty's turn-out with misgivings.

The drive was very long and very severe – cold and wet and pitch dark. How Andy drove in such darkness was astonishing to Marcella, for the lights of the car did little more than 'make darkness visible.' After about two and a half hours hard going, against the storm, the car stopped and all dismounted.

'Ye'll have to walk now, Nurse,' said Andy, and went on in front, leading the horse from side to side up what seemed to be a very stiff and rough bit of a hill.

Marcella's feet were slipping every minute, the road was so rocky, and it seemed ages before the men halted. She then heard the sound of water rushing rapidly by, and the men talking together in Irish, and the next minute Andy turned to her and explained that the house was on the opposite side of the stream, and that the stepping stones were covered with water, and would she please take off her shoes and stockings and they would get her over safely between them.

Marcella did not relish the idea at all, but there is a true saying that 'needs must when a certain person drives.' Therefore she did as she was told, and, with two men in front of her, one gripping her hand firmly and the other holding the lantern, and with Andy behind her in case she should slip backwards, she began her perilous crossing. To the men of course it was nothing – they would have splashed across in a few moments – strong and rapid though the stream was. But to the city girl it was a perfect nightmare. The icy water reached at times almost to her knees, and she slipped at every step, and had hard work, even with help, to get across. She was shaking all over when at last she reached the other side.

The opposite bank seemed to be crowded with people, and exclamations and ejaculations in the Irish were poured upon her. She was then handed bodily over to two women, one of whom took her bag, and the other one of her hands, and they piloted her up a steep and muddy boreen to the door of the patient's house.

It was the usual abode of the small farmer in Donegal – a fair-sized, white-washed thatched cabin. The half door opened into a large kitchen, full now with a talking, gesticulating crowd of men and women – the latter, of course, in the majority. Two bedrooms – one on each side – opened off this. To the one on the left hand the women conducted Marcella, forcing a way for her through the staring crowd in the kitchen. The bedroom, which they now entered, was the usual type of room to which Marcella afterwards became so thoroughly accustomed, but which struck her now – seen for the first time – as the very essence of discomfort. The old-fashioned wooden bed was built into the wall, a table stood in the window, littered with dirty cups and saucers and crusts of bread; there were two rush-bottomed chairs and a large, very old, wooden press. That completed the furniture – nothing in the way of bedroom articles, no dressing table or washstand – not even a basin and jug.

Three very old women were sitting on the earthen floor, their backs against the wall; two were smoking short clay pipes of vile tobacco, and the third was taking snuff. There was a big turf fire on the hearth, and the wind was blowing the smoke out into the middle of the room, and the one window, which was so small as really to be of little use either for light or air, was hermetically sealed.

The patient was standing in the middle of the room, and greeted them in Irish as they entered. She was a tall, muscular woman, and Marcella saw at once that she was well over her first youth, being evidently many years her husband's senior.

To a nurse fresh from her training school, with the gospel of asepsis, fresh air, and hygienic surroundings still ringing in her ears, the picture before her now seemed simply terrible, and an overwhelming feeling of utter incapability to cope with the case took possession of Marcella. How was she to manage this case, according to her teaching, and how indeed manage it at all amid such surroundings?

She looked at the old cronies squatting on the floor and eyeing her with looks of distinct aversion and disapproval, and then she glanced at the two women who had guided her to the house. They, too, seemed to be watching her every movement, ready to criticise her smallest action, observing every detail with that remarkable quickness of observation which is found amongst them.

The patient was 'the one bright spot.' She could speak English perfectly, while the rest of the women 'had only a few words' of the foreign tongue. To her, then, Marcella addressed herself, and quietly asked her to get the others to leave the room. Mrs McNelis – Marcella discovered afterwards that her husband belonged to the same family as the pretty girl at Glenmore Post Office – looked surprised, but did as requested. The old women were plainly insulted; they poured forth a torrent of angry Irish, and then resumed their smoking and snuffing, without stirring from their seats. Marcella, however, remained firm, and Mrs McNelis, turning again to the others, spoke sharply to them. Marcella could not of course comprehend what she said, but it was evidently very much to the point, for the old cronies – any creatures more like the *Macbeth* witches Marcella thought she had never seen off the stage – rose to their feet and left the room, followed by the two other women, all talking together in the expressive Gaelic.

Marcella then turned her attention to her patient, and was surprised – and far from pleased – to find that this was her first baby. As a girl of eighteen she had left her native place and gone to America, where she remained until the death of her father, three years ago. She was then thirty-six, and returned home 'to look after the place' and her old mother, who, however, died a year later. Mary Gillespie, being then left alone with the house, a bit of land, and with two hundred pounds – her American savings – in the bank – had looked around for a suitable husband, and, with the assistance of the local matchmakers, matters had been arranged with one Pat McNelis, from a neighbouring townland. The woman had the house and land and a bit of money; the man was young and strong and a fine worker, and owned a couple of cows and a horse and cart – a most suitable match in every respect, according to local opinion – sentiment or anything approaching to it being simply never thought of amongst these people.

But there is one important person who detests these matches, and that is Dame Nature, and she was now determined that she would exact the penalty from this woman.

This Marcella soon realised, and to the inevitable question 'Will I be long, Nurse?' she thought it best to be fairly truthful and to reply, 'Yes, I'm afraid you will be rather a good while yet.' It was now after midnight, but the crowd in the kitchen showed no signs of going, and if Marcella had known her Donegal better, she would not have expected a move from any of them until the coming event was over.

One of the women came in presently to say that supper was ready. Marcella glanced through the doorway into the kitchen beyond, and saw a stout female turning out a huge creel of potatoes, boiled in their jackets, on to the table, while from a great pot swinging over the fire another helper was taking slices of salted fish.

'Bring me a bit in here, and I'll try and eat it,' announced Mrs McNelis, in the voice of the interesting invalid, while Marcella asked only for a cup of tea. The patient partook heartily of the fish supper, but Marcella could not touch the tea, which was brought to her in a large bowl.

She thought that she had never tasted such awful stuff in her life, and wondered what could be the matter with it; but later on, when she watched it being made, she marvelled no more. The tea is put into a pannikin or saucepan of boiling water – a small handful being thrown in and then stirred rapidly round and round, as if porridge was to be made out of it. It is then allowed to boil for about fifteen minutes, after which it is poured into bowls and handed round. It was the following morning, when Marcella, tired after her long night, went to look for a decent cup of tea, that she saw it being thus prepared.

'Oh, the tea is boiling!' she said.

One of the women nodded and smiled.

'Yes, yes!' she answered, proud to show off her English, 'but she not boiling long – not done yet.'

The night was over and the morning was passing, but the patient had made little progress since Marcella's arrival, save that she was cross and more nervous. Marcella knew by this time that the case would require a doctor, but if she sent for him now he could not do anything for some hours, and yet if she left it much later the night would be coming on again. She dreaded another long night in such uncongenial surroundings, and smiled now when she remembered her hurry of the previous evening. After all, the men might have sat all night in the kitchen and she would still have been in time enough for this case.

Two more long hours passed, and then she went into the kitchen to speak to a Mary McShane, who seemed more capable than the rest, and also could understand and speak English fairly well. The nurse's entrance interrupted the buzz of talk, of which her instinct told her that she had been the subject – and the subject, too, for both criticism and disapproval.

She was an innovation and foreigner, and only for the Yankee notions of Mary Gillespie – women seldom get their married title in the country parts of Ireland – she would never have been brought here at all. Dear God! Would she not think shame of herself – an unmarried girl like her! – to be attending such cases? And no call for her, like either with Nan Doherty and Kate McManus, two of the wisest of the 'wise women' ready to come any minute. Aye! and the poor creature above there wouldn't be all this time bearing her pains – they would have relieved her some way before this – and if the woman or the child should die – well, sure, that was the will of God and no one's fault!

But this one did nothing but wash her hands and ask for hot water and more hot water, and basins and basins! She hadn't even the man's coat thrown over the bed, as if the child could be born without that! And there was the window propped wide open, and the wind blowing in on the woman; sure that was enough of itself to put her pains back – God save us, whoever saw the like before!

Yes, Marcella could read their thoughts perfectly well as she beckoned Mrs McShane to her side. The minute she mentioned the word *doctor* there was a sudden stir all round the kitchen – looks of gratified satisfaction, especially amongst the old women; the 'I-told-you-so' expression appeared on all their faces.

'The doctor?' repeated Mary McShane, 'Yes, he lives a good way off. Three hours' drive anyway.'

Marcella glanced at her watch and saw it was 2 o'clock, so she explained that the doctor would be wanted, and said they were to send a messenger on a car. She would write a note and they must go at once. There were some objections and a good deal of delay, but at last the husband was off to Carragh, where the doctor lived.

'If he's at home, he ought to be here between eight and nine o'clock,' thought Marcella. 'He may be able to help by that time.'

It seemed to her that she had been there an eternity. Last night seemed ages away, and she was getting very tired; besides which the close atmosphere and want of eatable food, combined with the anxiety of the case, were bound to tell upon her. The patient was in greater pain now, and of course thought that it must be the nurse's fault that she was not over it all by this.

By eight o'clock that evening Marcella's one dominant wish and prayer was for the arrival of the doctor, and at half-past that hour he arrived. There was a sound of hustle outside as a car was led round to the farther side of the house – not the side by which Marcella had entered, as that was only a footpath – and then firm footsteps in the kitchen and a pleasant masculine voice exclaiming, 'Ye Gods! What an atmosphere! Now, then, clear out of my way the lot of you! I don't know what the devil brings you here at all! Where's the patient?'

There was a chorus of excited cries, and dozens of hands pointed to the bedroom door, but it was opened before he reached it, and the nurse stood on the threshold.

'Oh, doctor! I'm glad to see you,' she cried in relief. Thank goodness you have come!'

All the weight of responsibility, all the worry of the past twenty long hours seemed to slip from her shoulders as she met the keen glance of a pair of amused blue eyes.

Dr Adair, on his part, saw a tall girl in uniform, rather good-looking, but pale and tired now. She had soft brown hair and very honest, grey eyes – eyes which the doctor, who prided himself on his character reading, felt that he could trust absolutely.

'Hello! You're the new nurse, I suppose? Not accustomed yet to this sort of thing, eh? I'm a bit new at it myself, but I'm getting used to it by degrees! Well, where's the patient, and what's up?'

'Well, it will be a few hours more before we can do anything,' said Dr Adair, half an hour later. 'I'll go outside and have a cigarette.'

A few hours passed, and at last the doctor thought he could get to work. Marcella had been busy preparing everything that would be needed – his instruments were sterilised and all was ready.

'Is there a sensible woman amongst that lot outside that we could have in to give us a hand?' asked the doctor, 'I'll want your help with the chloroform, Nurse. Of course I'll put her under, but if you ...'

But the patient's ears were sharp. She stopped her groans to call out. 'No chloroform, doctor! I won't have any! Whatever I have to suffer I'll keep my senses about me.'

'Oh, Mrs McNelis, now don't be foolish,' cried Marcella, 'Why, I'm surprised at you that you haven't more sense.'

'My good woman! Of course you must have chloroform,' said the doctor briskly, 'and I can tell you that you should be jolly glad to get it.'

'No – I won't take it! – I won't take it! You'll murder me altogether if I let ye take my senses away! Oh, my God! Pat! Pat! They're killin' me! They're killin' me!'

Her screams brought the husband rushing into the room, and the next moment the doorway was filled with an excited crowd. The doctor swore audibly, but tried to explain quietly to the husband that the woman should be given chloroform. In vain. At the very mention of the word there was an outcry of anger and indignation, and after attempting to argue for a few moments, Dr Adair gave it up.

'It's no good, Nurse,' he said.

Marcella was aghast but, true to her training, she said nothing, and simply set about her duties.

'Now get out, all of you! Do you hear?' said the doctor. 'There's a bolt on the door, and I'm going to bolt it, and no one but myself and the nurse and Mrs McShane will be here. Now do you understand?' he added, turning to the husband. 'Your wife's life depends upon what I'm going to do now, and if I don't do it she or the child, or probably both, will die of exhaustion. She should be under chloroform; it is a barbarous thing not to allow me to give it to her; but, remember, it's your own wish and your wife will suffer more now, and more later on, from the shock through not having it. Once more, Mrs McNelis,' he said moving towards the bed, 'will you have it?'

'No! No doctor! I'll bear all, but let me keep my senses! Oh let me keep my senses!'

The doctor saw that it was useless to talk any more. The woman's eyes, with the pain drawn circles beneath them, held a look of terror at the thought, and, worn out with pain as she was, she still preferred to suffer even more rather than take the anaesthetic.

'Oh, but what queer people they are!' thought Marcella, as she lifted the kettle off the fire. A few minutes later, scream after scream rang through the room – screams that were answered in the kitchen by groans and sobs and prayers.

Then the cries quieted down, and above them could be heard a different sound – weak and gasping at first, but rapidly becoming stronger and more insistent, a cry that once heard is never mistaken – the cry of a newborn child.

The doctor was wiping the beads of perspiration off his forehead with a towel which Marcella held out to him, when he noticed how pale and wan she looked.

'This has been an awful case for you, Nurse,' he said, 'and you have been here so long! You must be worn out.'

'It's not that altogether, doctor,' she said, 'but I never saw such a case without chloroform before.'

'And of course this woman should have had it,' he replied, 'This sort of thing is sheer butchery, you know. I feel like – like a murderer of some sort when I have to inflict such pain on a conscious patient. But what could we do? You see the kind they are – and this extraordinary fear of an anaesthetic is very common hereabouts. Well, thank God it's over.'

And Marcella echoed the thanksgiving in her heart. Later on when the patient, who was rapidly becoming herself again and already 'remembered no more her anguish for joy that a man was born into the world' had been made comfortable, and the baby bathed and dressed, the doctor, who had been in the kitchen amusing himself talking to the old people there, looked in at Marcella and said, 'Hurry up, Nurse, and I'll drive you round by Glenmore on my car – it will save you waiting till word could be sent for your jarvey' for, needless to say, Young Andy had returned home long since.

'Oh Doctor! Thank you so much! But won't it take you a lot out of your way?'

'No, not much, and anyhow I'm going to drive you; so come along.'

And Marcella felt that she could never be thankful enough to him, for she was worn out. It was now nearly 4 o'clock on Monday morning, and she had left home at 10 o'clock on Saturday night. How anxious Ellen would be! But she could hardly think of Ellen or anyone else, she was so stupid for the want of sleep. She tried to keep her eyes open and to talk politely as they drove along, but in spite of all her efforts she felt herself nodding.

At last, towards 7 o'clock, the houses of Glenmore came in sight, and never did they seem so welcome! They are past 'Hell's Gates' and reach the crossroads, where Arabella rushes out at the sound of the car – all ears and eyes – and now there are the Coastguards' houses and the Post Office, and at last her own house, and Ellen coming down the garden path to meet her. The doctor helped her down from the car.

'Put her to bed, with a hot jar and a drink of hot milk,' he said to Ellen, adding with a smile as he saw the anxious look on the woman's face. 'Oh, she's all right: – just tired out. She'll probably sleep for a long while, keep her in bed till tomorrow morning. It will be time enough to visit that case then, Nurse. You'll find her all right! Goodbye, and thanks for your help' and he was off, driving down the road as fast as the horse could go.

'Miss Marcella, dear, what in the world happened you?' asked Ellen in consternation, 'you look half-dead!'

'Oh, don't ask me anything now,' said Marcella, 'all I want is my bed – just my bed! I'll be all right when I get a sleep.'

III

LOVE AND SURGERY IN DONEGAL

It had been daylight when she had gone to bed, and now it was quite dark. Half-awake and half-asleep, she stirred lazily and turned on her side, and as she did so, she gave a little cry for the movement hurt her, she was so stiff and cramped.

'What is the matter with me? And why do I feel so tired?' she thought, and then in a flash came remembrance, and she wondered what time it was and how long she had been asleep. Presently on her dawning consciousness came the sound of voices – one harsh and rasping, yet vaguely familiar, the other the well-known accents of Ellen.

'Och, aye,' the first voice was saying, 'I can tell ye Miss Doyle, that I know fine all about Mary Gillespie before iver Pat McNelis put a ring on her finger! She's a second cousin of my man's, and sullen soort of a girl she always was, too: and glad enough the ould man and woman were when she took the notion of gallivantin' off to Ameriky. It's likely she thought it's what she'd be makin' her fortune over there –

and, right enough, she brought a bit of money home with her – a matter of two hundred pounts I heard tell; it's in the bank at Kilbeg.'

She paused for a moment, and Marcella smiled to herself as she heard Ellen's frosty, 'Indeed, ma'am!' which was all the response she vouchsafed.

'Aye, indeed,' continued the other unabashed, 'and so Mick Doolan and Con Hegarty med up a match last Shrove twelve month between her and Pat McNelis. Very suitable, too, be all accounts, barring that she was getting a bit stale; but then she had the land and the place and needed a man to care it.'

There was no reply to this, only the sound of Ellen moving quickly round her kitchen. It was quite evident that she had no intention of sitting down for a gossip with Arabella Gillespie.

'When I heard tell on Sunday night,' continued that lady, 'that the nurse had got a call there, I just thought she'd be a bad case – she's over forty if she's a day! So when I saw the car this morning I ran out to ask what God had sent; but sure that new doctor was with her and he drivin' that fast that I hadn't a chance to speak to her. All the same if she'd seen me it's likely she would have med him stop.'

'Very likely indeed, ma'am,' from Ellen.

'Aye, that's what I was tellin' my man,' went on Arabella complacently, Ellen's mild sarcasm being completely lost on her, 'so I thought I would run up now and have a crack wid the nurse about Mary, seein' that she's a cousin of James.'

'Well, I'm sorry, ma'am, that you can't see her,' replied Ellen, 'but the nurse is sleeping, and, by the doctor's orders, she's not to be awakened.'

'Well, now, the crathur! It's gey tired she must be, and a great interest the doctor seems to take in her. Do you think now, Miss Doyle, that there might be any chance of them making a match of it?'

By Ellen's tone of voice when she replied, 'I'm sure I can't say, ma'am!' Marcella knew that she was what she would describe herself as being 'near the end of her tether!'

'Poor Ellen!' the girl thought. 'What a nuisance that woman is! I wish she would go – I *do* want a cup of tea!'

But it was nearly half an hour later when at last Arabella rose to take her leave, having given Ellen a full and lengthy history of Mrs McNelis – *nee* Gillespie. Her footsteps had no sooner died away down the garden path than Marcella called softly to Ellen, and the next minute the faithful soul was at her bedside.

Marcella then discovered that it was after 10 o'clock, and that she had slept soundly for thirteen hours.

'No wonder I feel a different person,' she said. 'And, oh Ellen! I'm dying for a cup of tea and something to eat!'

She slept all that night, too, and the next morning arose quite refreshed; took an early breakfast, and set off on Young Andy's car to see her patient. It was a lovely morning and the drive was a revelation to Marcella. Never had she imagined anything so wild and grand and yet so terrifyingly lonely and isolated as some of the country through which they passed. It was wilder even than the drive from Kilbeg to Glenmore, for that was at least a main road of sorts, and used frequently; but the road on which she now found herself seemed to be leading her right up to the bare mountain itself. How the horse and car ever travelled it on that night of storm and wind astonished her, but Young Andy and his mare seemed to take it all as a matter of course, and in reply to some remark of Marcella's only replied that 'there was many a road a sight worse than this wan!'

They did not go this time by the road which led to the stream and the stepping stones, but went round the other way – a slightly longer journey, but much more welcome to Marcella.

She found her patient sitting up in bed and partaking of a big bowl of well-boiled tea and some huge slices of toast.

She greeted Marcella cheerily, and it was quite obvious that she was intensely pleased with herself and very proud of her baby. And naturally so, from her point of view, for now no one could look down upon her and her husband would have reason to respect her. So she reasoned according to the traditions of her youth – traditions or, rather, beliefs which not all her years in America could ever obliterate.

Marcella spent nearly two hours in making mother and child comfortable, and then, just as she was shutting her bag and preparing to leave, she heard Dr Adair's voice outside, and the next moment he was shaking hands with her.

'Well, Nurse,' he said, 'and how are you? Got over your weekend pleasure trip, eh?'

'Oh yes, I'm quite all right,' replied Marcella. 'And just look at the patient! Isn't she wonderful, Doctor, after all she went through?'

'Just what I expected,' he said, adding in a lower voice, 'the recuperative power of these women is something marvellous, and they hardly ever suffer from shock, as a cultured woman would be certain to do.'

His visit over, they walked out through the half door into the bright sunshine beyond, and stood for a moment looking at the bare mountain road running like a silver thread far as the eye could see. It could only be called 'road' by courtesy, and as it wound its way higher up the mountain side it became just a rugged, narrow path. On either hand was a vista of wild bogland, dotted here and there with white-washed cabins.

'I had a case a few weeks ago,' said Dr Adair, 'higher up the mountain than this. I had to leave the car here and walk about three miles; it was pitch dark too, and only for the man with a lantern – of sorts – I would have never found my way at all.'

Marcella laughed, and told him of her voyage over the stepping-stones.

'Yes; midwifery is not much of a joke hereabouts,' he said, adding, 'I have to go round by Glenmore to see a burnt child. Send your jarvey home, Nurse, and I'll drive you on my car. I want you to see the case with me.'

Nothing loth, Marcella sent Young Andy, who was intercepted by Arabella at the crossroads and compelled to give a particular and faithful account of all that had passed as far as he had observed between the two – back to Glenmore, and accepted a seat on the doctor's more comfortable car.

The case to which they were going was about two miles from Glenmore.

'I was here on Saturday morning,' said Dr Adair, as they left the car and ascended a steep boreen which led to the small cabin. 'It's a little girl of about three, and she slipped on the floor and, in falling, knocked over a kettle of boiling water on herself. Only her right arm got scalded, but it's pretty deep. However, when they told me what was wrong – which they don't always do – and I brought picric acid with me and did up the arm in tip-top style. I told the parents that I would call in about three days' time to change the dressing, and I impressed upon them most carefully not to touch it until I came.'

'But surely they would never dream of doing so!' exclaimed Marcella.

'Oh! You little know them,' was the reply. 'However, I think these people will be all right, and as I got the picric acid on so soon I expect the case will do well.'

As he spoke they reached the house, and the doctor stooped his fair head to enter the half-door.

The interior was very dark after the sunshine outside, and at first Marcella could discern the room and its occupants very dimly, for the window was only a few inches in size.

But the flicker of the turf fire helped her, and presently she made out the wooden bed, roofed over and built into the wall; the table and rush-bottomed chairs; the old oak press and settle, and the kettle and big pot on the crook over the fire. A man and woman were standing on the earthen floor, and it seemed to Marcella that they were curiously sullen-looking and ill at ease. Seated on a 'wee creepy stool' by the hearth was a toothless old woman, looking any age up to a hundred; she had the child on her lap, and the little thing was moaning piteously every few minutes.

Then suddenly the doctor took two strides forward and stood before the old woman.

'What does this mean?' he asked angrily. 'Those are not my bandages! Who has been interfering with my dressing?' Swinging round on his heel he confronted the man.

'Didn't I tell you not to touch the arm until I came today?'

The man shifted uneasily as he responded with a sullen 'Aye.'

'Then what the devil do you mean by disobeying me?'

The woman, who seemed to have more courage than her husband, here interposed.

'Sure it was a long time, Doctor, not to be dressing the *leanbh,*' she said, 'and Nan Doherty was passing this way, and iverywan knows that it's the wise woman entirely she is.'

The doctor swore savagely as he beckoned to Marcella to take the child.

'As for you – you old wretch!' he said, 'I'll get you well punished if ever you dare to interfere with my work again!'

The old one only smiled at him, showing all her toothless gums in the process, but Marcella caught a rather malevolent gleam from her watery eyes.

'It's no good for you to be talkin' to her, Doctor,' said the man, 'sure she has no English – the crathur!'

'Oh, I know all about that,' returned Dr Adair, 'she has English enough to know what I'm saying, and – my God!' he broke off 'what have you been putting on the arm?'

Marcella had been deftly undoing a not over-clean rag which had replaced the gauze bandage so neatly arranged by the doctor, and, as she took it off, a dark-coloured and foully-smelling mess was revealed. She stopped her work and gazed, horror-struck, at Dr Adair.

'Sure it's cowdung, doctor,' said the woman complacently. 'It's what is always put on for a cure in these parts.'

'Aye, surely,' said the man sullenly, 'and many's the wan was cured with it before ever a doctor came near the place.'

Marcella never forgot the hour that followed; the cleaning of the stuff away from the arm, and then the placing of the poor little limb into a basin of boric lotion, keeping it there in a warm bath for half an hour. The child was a dear little mite, with big blue eyes and dark hair, and although she plainly knew no English she still seemed to realise that the nurse was doing her good, and clung to her pitifully. It was quite evident that Nan Doherty's treatment had caused her very great and unnecessary suffering.

The Doctor continued to read the Riot Act all the time until, at last, the arm was dressed and the child in bed and partaking of some hot milk.

The man and woman, looking rather ashamed of themselves, assured him that they would not let the arm be touched again until he came himself; and the old woman, still sitting serenely on the stool by the hearth, continued to smile with her toothless mouth and to glare wickedly with her watery eyes.

The doctor caught one of her glances as he was putting on his coat, and flung a last word at her:

'Now remember, Nan Doherty,' he said, 'if I ever catch you at any of your tricks again with my patients I'll have you put in jail, you old hag! Do you hear me now?'

The old lady smiled and nodded on the double, and looked as if he had paid her some special compliment, while the man again repeated, 'Sure she has no English, the crathur!'

'Oh, confound her!' cried the angry medico, 'she knows jolly well what I'm saying – and she had better mind it, too!' And he strode from the cabin, still in a white heat of rage. Marcella walked beside him in silence until they reached the road and the waiting horse and car. Dr Adair threw a few pennies to the bare-legged urchin who had been 'minding the horse' and, having settled Marcella comfortably, he took his own seat, and they started off to Glenmore.

'Well! What do you think of *that* for a case – eh?' he asked then. 'There's a lot of encouragement for a man who tries to do his duty in this God-forsaken hole – isn't there?'

'Oh, it's *awful!*' she replied. 'I never could have believed that any people could be so desperately stupid and ignorant.'

'They are not *stupid* by any means,' Dr Adair said, 'but the ignorance of ages is their heritage. That is not the *only* cure in which they believe – no nor the worst either, as you will discover after a while!'

When they reached Glenmore, Marcella asked him to come in and have a cup of tea, and he willingly consented. The hour that followed was a happy one for both of them, as they sat by the fire in the long, old-fashioned sitting room, enjoying Ellen's hot cakes and chatting about many things. Marcella found herself speaking quite freely to this keen young fellow with the blue eyes and friendly smile, and told him a good deal about herself and how good her Aunt Mary had been to her, and how she was trying now to be self-supporting and after a while to be able to repay a little of her aunt's kindness to her. 'My father and mother died when I was quite a tiny child,' she said, 'and they left hardly any money behind them. I am afraid they were young and thoughtless, and then Aunt Mary – my father's eldest sister – took me to live with her and has kept me ever since. She is unmarried and lives on a small annuity in a little house at Harold's Cross. She is such an old darling!' she added, smiling, 'and I am so glad that my training is over and that now I can earn my own living.'

Dr Adair listened, and, in return, told her about himself. Strange to say, he was also an orphan, and had hardly a relative in the world, with the exception of a rather crusty old uncle in Glasgow, who had helped to pay for his nephew when the latter was studying for the medical profession in Edinburgh. 'For I would not have been able to qualify without his help,' he said frankly. 'I have only a few pounds a year of my own.'

'If you are Scotch, I wonder you did not settle in Scotland?' said Marcella, with a shy smile.

He smiled in return as he replied, 'But Ireland was my mother's country, and I always had a wish to live there; and I wanted to live in a part that was really Irish and to study the people and their ways. I had ideals, too, of helping and uplifting them, of being someone upon whom they could depend.'

He paused and sighed rather wistfully.

'Yes!' murmured Marcella, who was keenly interested.

'Well,' he went on rather doubtfully, 'I am here nearly a year now, and although I am beginning to understand the people a little, still, someway, I seem to be making very little headway with them. They resent a stranger – or, as they say, a *foreigner* – coming amongst them, and also I think that they would rather have a Catholic doctor.'

'But there are a good many Protestants here, too,' interrupted Marcella.

'Ah! yes, but they are not Irish – not the really native Irish, I mean. Their very names will tell yon that. They are all of Scotch or English origin, and it is remarkable – and shows the real gulf there is between the races – how little they have changed in any characteristics since their ancestors helped in the plantation of Ulster.'

'But you are Scotch yourself,' said Marcella again, adding 'one would think you were Irish to hear you speak like that.'

He smiled.

'My mother was Irish, as I told you,' he said, 'really Irish; she was a McMahon from the Co. Clare, and should, of course, have been a Catholic, but her branch of the family, it appears, allowed themselves to become "perverted" – as the others call it – in the "bad times".'

'All the same you have both Catholic and real Irish blood in your veins,' said Marcella, laughing, 'and now I don't wonder a bit at your interest in the people here. You are far more Irish than I am,' she continued, 'for the larger half of me is Scotch – I am only a little bit Irish through my mother.'

'It seems to me that we two have quite a lot in common,' said the young doctor, as he leant back in his chair and sipped the tea, which was such a contrast to the extraordinary concoction which was brewed by his rough and ready housekeeper. He glanced around him meditatively and noted how homelike the queer old room had become, and noted also how pretty and womanly Nurse Campbell seemed as she sat opposite to him, teapot poised in hand, and said, 'More tea, Doctor? – just another cup?'

He sighed involuntarily as he held out his cup to be refilled, and Marcella, noting the sigh, looked at him. He laughed in a shame-faced way as he caught her glance. 'I beg your pardon,' he said, 'but I was just thinking how very cosy and homelike you were here. It's such a contrast to my digs at Carragh – and somehow it made me feel as if I was a homeless sort of chap that no one cared much about.'

Marcella was full of sympathy immediately – sympathy which showed itself very plainly in her big grey eyes.

'Oh Doctor Adair!' she said, 'don't talk that way. You will have a home of your own, and someone to love you, too, some day!' He lifted his eyes to her face and their glances met, and held for a moment, and then suddenly Marcella felt her face flush vividly and she turned her eyes away from him and began to talk quickly, incoherently, about anything she could call to mind.

But the friendship thus begun throve apace, and before very long the inevitable had happened and it had ceased to be friendship and had evolved into that indescribable something which is so much stronger, but, alas! seldom as lasting as the more platonic passion, and which, while it burns with a flame which is hotter and fiercer, is often more easily quenched – the something which men call Love.

And so when the New Year came to bleak Donegal, in cold and frost and snow, it seemed to Marcella Campbell and Allan Adair as though nothing mattered but the one supreme and wonderful fact that they cared for one another.

The coldest drives in rain and storm when they were together spelt happiness, the hardest work became light when shared between them.

And so, on the first day of February, when Marcella sent in her usual monthly report to her Superintendent in Dublin, she sent her resignation also, running down the road to post it herself, laughing softly as she dropped it into the box, and waving her hand gaily to pretty Mary McNelis.

Returning to her own house, she stood for a moment in the porch, enjoying the gleam of sunshine and the mild breeze. *This is a regular 'pet day'*, she thought. *It's a perfect Spring day – and what a contrast to last week!*

Happening to glance at the ground, she suddenly espied a snowdrop – peeping out in its white purity, as if surveying its surroundings and wondering was it too early in its appearance.

'Oh! You dear little thing!' cried Marcella, 'you shall be honoured by being worn in Allan's coat! Now, aren't you glad that you peeped out just then?'

But the Snowdrop made no answer; perhaps it hardly realised the honour in store for it.

IV

The Curtain Rises on Carmen

Hill Square, which is situated in one of the southern suburbs of Dublin, consists of large, old-fashioned houses, and although at one time it was considered quite a fashionable locality and its residents strictly composed of the very *elite* of mid-Victorian respectability, it had now fallen on evil days, and many of its houses were in a very old and dilapidated condition, while even the best of them 'took in' lodgers. No. 47 is one of the largest houses in the Square, and although not quite the shabbiest, it is still in a very ramshackle state and is badly in need of paper and paint.

The present tenant is Cornelius Vincent Bourke, from the Co. Galway. Beneath the same roof we will find his wife, who had been a widow when he married her, four years ago; her two daughters and one son by her first husband, Eileen and Letty and Philip Hewson; her twin sons of the present marriage, Vinny and Conny – both called after their illustrious parent according, needless to say, to his own request – and her cousin, Carmen Cavanagh. There was also

Miss Fallon, a lady boarder of uncertain age, and her cat, Billee; and last, but by no means least, was Sarah Devine, an ancient and trustworthy if not over-clean or tidy retainer. There were also three young men boarders. The dining room of No. 47 was to the right as one entered the wide, old-fashioned hall, and there we find Mrs Bourke on this cold night towards the end of February. She was small and slight and about forty-five, but looking much younger, and was still a pretty woman. In her girlhood, Cis Purefoy had been considered one of the prettiest girls in Dublin, and at eighteen she had married Jack Hewson, a solicitor with a good practice and house property which brought him about six hundred a year. But, unfortunately, drink was in his blood for generations past, and at the age of thirty-eight he died from alcoholic pneumonia, leaving his wife and three children to face the world without him. His affairs were very involved, 'hopelessly so!' said his brothers, George and Henry, who had been left trustees for the widow and orphans. Whether they spoke the truth when they affirmed that all they could manage to allow the widow, when everything was settled, was the princely sum of thirty shillings a week is known only to themselves, but Mrs Hewson, most un-businesslike and unsuspecting of women, implicitly believed them and even felt grateful beyond words when they got the two little girls, aged seven and five, into a cheap boarding-school at reduced fees. The boy, who was the eldest, and nine years of age when his father died, was allowed to remain with his mother and attend a day school. He had always been a delicate, dreamy child, and was the very apple of her eye.

So Mrs Hewson, after ten years of fairly luxurious living, had to give up her pleasant house in Rathgar, with her pony and trap, her cook, her housemaid and her children's nurse, and retire into genteel poverty at 47 Hill Square. Here she started housekeeping afresh, with only Sarah Devine, an old servant of her earlier days, who looked for little wages as long as she was with her beloved mistress.

Mrs Hewson arranged her furniture in the large old-fashioned rooms, and when all was ready, put up her 'Apartments' card in the window.

Two bank clerks and Miss Fallon were her first boarders, and shortly afterwards Mr Devereux, a middle-aged solicitor and an old friend of the family, called one day to suggest that she should take Carmen Cavanagh as boarder. Mrs Hewson had met Carmen several times – in fact, they were distant cousins – and although she did not know the girl herself very well, she knew the story of her birth and parentage, and it appealed irresistibly to the romantic side of the little widow.

Carmen was twelve years old when she went to live with Mrs Hewson, and at the time this story opens she was twenty-five, and had just finished her hospital and district training and was about to be appointed to a district of her own.

She had had a little money left her by her father, which, by Mr Devereux's careful management, had been sufficient to pay for her maintenance at Hill Square and to start her in the nursing profession afterwards. She was just now having a short holiday while waiting for her appointment and has gone out this evening 'to look at the shops' – a pastime of which Carmen is very fond.

Philip Hewson is now twenty-one, and while his days are spent at a desk in the city, his evenings and every moment of his spare time are devoted to music – his one passion – and on Sundays he plays the organ at a little church away near the Dublin mountains. The Hewsons are Protestants, unlike Carmen Cavanagh, who is a Catholic 'of sorts' as she would say herself. Eileen Hewson is now nineteen, and is with a fashionable milliner, where, for a minimum salary and long hours of work, she is allowed to learn the business, or 'art' as

Madame Lucie designates it – while Letty, the youngest, at the age of seventeen, is still working hard at her typing and shorthand; she is the only really practical and business-like person of the family and a complete contrast to the others in every way.

So that Jack Hewson's children are no longer much expense or trouble to their mother and would soon indeed be able to contribute well towards the family exchequer; and No. 47 would have been a very pleasant abode had it not been for a most extraordinary and utterly incomprehensible mistake which Mrs Hewson had made some six years previous to the opening of this story.

At that time she had had as boarder for over a year the same Cornelius Vincent Bourke of whom mention has already been made. He was a man of about fifty, small of stature and with a round, shining, clean-shaven face. His eyes were small – 'piggy' Carmen called them – and the top of his head was absolutely bald. He walked with a peculiar, mincing step, which he assured everyone was the 'Delaney walk' – his mother's family being Delaneys – and he also called his bald patch 'the Bourke spot' – as all the Bourkes from his part were supposed to boast of a similar mark of identity.

The amount of his wardrobe when he arrived at Hill Square would have been sufficient for six or seven men. Bandboxes lined the wall from floor to ceiling; suits of clothes of every description crammed wardrobe and press to bursting point; ties and socks of every conceivable shade filled his drawers to overflowing, and boots and shoes – on trees and out of them – were displayed all over the floor.

The first time Mrs Hewson and the young people caught a glimpse of this sartorial exhibition they laughed till they cried, while old Sarah stood in the midst of it all, blessing herself and muttering, 'the Lord save us!' in tones of part bewilderment and part admiration.

Mr Bourke informed Mrs Hewson that he was from the Co. Galway, the dust of which county he had shaken from his feet after a difference of opinion with his two sisters about the disposal of some land – land which was claimed by his sisters as lawfully theirs and which their brother, Cornelius, had wished to dispose of for his own advantage. Being foiled in this laudable desire by the sharpness of a lawyer employed by the priest of the parish in his sisters' interests, he had severed his connection with the Church of his Baptism and the County at one and the same time. His business in Dublin he vaguely alluded to as 'dealings in scrap iron' but, whatever it might be, it was certainly not business which took up much of his time, as he invariably kept to the privacy of his own room until after midday, when he would suddenly fling open his door and bawl through the house at the top of his voice for a *meal*. 'Here! Bring me a *meal*! Do you hear me now? A meal!' He would then dispose of a huge amount of food, sitting at the table in soiled dressing-gown and down-at-heel slippers, after which he would dress himself – the work of two hours – and, towards three o'clock, he would sally forth – dressed to kill – 'Faith, he'd beat Brannigan himself, so he would!' according to Sarah. Thus attired, he proceeded citywards and was invariably to be met with 'doing Grafton Street' at 4pm, and, according to Philip Hewson, 'making sheep's eyes at every girl he met.'

What time he spent at his business – if any – was unknown to the other denizens of No. 47, but they took it for granted that he did business of some sort, or else was possessed of good private means, for he certainly never seemed short of money. Everyone in the house became quite accustomed to him after a while; he was certainly regarded as very eccentric, but, as he paid well and punctually, this was passed over, and indeed poor Mrs Hewson would have passed over more than that for the sake of his money, for things just then were not going too well with her. The children were costing her a good deal; they were just at that age when they were too young to earn themselves, and yet required clothes and boots and the finishing of their education; and her brothers-in-law were not helping her as much as they had done in the first years of her widowhood; so that, after all, perhaps, it was not to be wondered at that when, after a while, Cornelius Vincent Bourke from the Co. Galway began making gallant speeches to his pretty little landlady – speeches which were soon followed by presents, substantial presents both for herself and the children – that she should begin to think that she might do worse than take this erratic but seemingly wealthy and good-natured person for a second husband.

Oh, if we could sometimes see into the future what sorrow and misery untold would be spared to us! How often do we hear the cry, 'If I had known! If I could live those years of my life over again how different they would be.' Or are these things written in our Book of Fate and must we go through with them to the bitter end? Ah, well, these questions must remain unanswered and unsolved for us to the end of time. Poor Cis Hewson, tired and weary, after years of that most sordid of all killjoys known as 'trying to make end meet!' and believing that in this second marriage she would at least have pecuniary ease, went out one morning with Mr Bourke and was married to him at the Registry Office.

Never was a woman more bitterly deceived, and never was a rash act more bitterly repented. Disillusion followed quickly, and before many months had gone by she realised clearly what a false step she had taken. There were no more gallant speeches, no more presents; on the contrary, she found herself much worse off from a pecuniary point of view than before her second marriage, for Mr C.V. Bourke now barely contributed enough to support himself, and, as for helping with his stepchildren, he was not backwards in telling her that he had no intention of keeping 'her beggar brats.' But although he did not maintain the household, he at once took the position of master of the home and everyone was expected to treat him as such. His harsh voice with the broad Galway accent could be heard at all hours of the day and night – for he had the most objectionable habit of prowling through the house and talking to himself during the small hours – whatever he ordered must be done at once. Old Sarah's daily existence became a perfect misery, for she never knew when she would hear his strident tones shouting over the bannisters for a *meal* – 'Bring me a *meal!* Do you hear me, ye old scarecrow? Where the blazes is that old hag?' – for his language was always strong and very often would not bear repeating. He would expect his 'meal' which meant a tray heavily laden with food, especially meat, at any hour he fancied, and seemed to imagine that the house should be an hotel, able to supply any sort of dishes at all hours and at a moment's notice. He was the cause of several of the boarders leaving, and Miss Fallon would have left also only that she had been so long with Mrs Bourke and had become really attached to her.

Altogether, instead of financial help from the second marriage a very opposite state of affairs was the immediate result. Mrs Bourke soon found that her present husband did not now pay the cost of his 'meals' much less anything over, and he now got his washing and mending and general attendance of every kind free of cost. He made no attempt either to pay the rent or even to help with it, and the poor woman was compelled to admit that she had made a very big mistake.

So for the first few years after her marriage things were very bad indeed, and to crown all, came the twins. During all this time Carmen Cavanagh was a help and comfort untold. Mrs Bourke could never forget how loyal the girl always was to her, and how bravely she faced the dreaded 'master' – the only being in the house who seemed absolutely undaunted and unafraid of him. They were at daggers drawn, of course, and could never meet – never pass on the stairs indeed – without an exchange of compliments. 'That brazen Papist hussy' was Mr Bourke's most frequent description of Carmen, while she generally alluded to him as the 'Galway bogtrotter.'

Religion, too, was another breach between them. Carmen, though by no means an exemplary Catholic herself, still could not help disliking him as a pervert, while on his part no name now was bad enough for all things Catholic. In reality he had no religious beliefs left to him; any little spirituality which he may have possessed while in the Catholic Church had now fled and left his soul swept and garnished and ready for those evil spirits which poor Mrs Bourke began to think were really in possession. And there is no doubt that very often his behaviour was that of one 'possessed.' Sleeping until midday, he would walk about the house half the night, and had a weird habit of entering every bedroom which he found unlocked and, coming to the bedside with a candle in his hand, would stand peering down into the face of the sleeper until he or she awoke – probably startled very much – when he would walk out again without a word, shutting the door after him in a quiet, ghostly manner most trying to the nerves. He nearly killed poor Miss Fallon with fright the first time he entered her little bed-sitting room, and Mrs Bourke had to provide keys for the boarders, who would otherwise have left in a body. Carmen alone refused to have a bolt on her door. She always slept in a small room off Mrs Bourke's, and since the arrival of the twins their loving father had migrated to his old room on the upper landing and left his peevish sons to interfere with his wife's repose, but not with his own; but he frequently visited them during the night in his usual weird style.

On a few nights he had strolled on into Carmen's room, but as she had promptly jumped out of bed on the third occasion and flung the contents of the water jug over him, he had not done it since.

All the house heard him that night as he flung, swearing, down the stairs, and Mrs Bourke lay shivering in her bed, almost afraid to go to sleep again for fear that he should return and wreak vengeance on someone. But Carmen left the door between the rooms open and laughed at her being so nervous. 'He'll not come back again, Cis, you may take my word for that,' she said. 'He is an arrant coward, like all bullies!' and she was right. The 'bogtrotter from Galway' had a wholesome dread of Carmen Cavanagh, for it was impossible to know what she would take it into her head to do or say next, and, above all, she was not afraid of him. Never had he had the exquisite joy of seeing *her* blanch or tremble under his angry glare or at the sound of his furious voice, and she was the only one during the first years of his marriage who always faced him without so much as the quiver of an eyelid. The result was inevitable with such a nature as that of Cornelius Bourke; he hated her with an unspeakable hatred, and nothing would have given him more satisfaction than to break her spirit. But he had to admit to himself that there seemed no immediate prospect of any such event.

As the years passed and the young Hewsons grew older, their first fear of their stepfather passed away, leaving however in its stead a sullen and bitter dislike. They never spoke to him when they could avoid it, and indeed they often showed great self-control in not replying to the taunts and sneers with which he indulged whenever he had the opportunity. Of course it was simply for their mother's sake that they endured him and stayed in the same house with him. They adored her and were only waiting until they were all earning better salaries to persuade her to leave their stepfather for good and all. In the meantime he did his best to destroy any little pleasure or happiness which might have been theirs and tried to make the life of each individual at No. 47 Hill Square – from his unfortunate wife down to Miss Fallon's cat, which fled with lightning rapidity at his approach – as uncomfortable as possible.

Quite recently he had joined one of those numerous sects which are always springing up from time to time, and had announced to the rest of the family that he was 'converted.' His 'conversion' however, made no difference in either his way of life or his conversation, but it showed itself in one very annoying phase. He would come home late at night, bringing with him other would-be 'converts' and would demand supper to be got ready for them immediately. They were composed, needless to say, of that scum of the city which would take a free meal from anyone and promise anything to get it; and poor Mrs Bourke only the night before this February evening when our chapter opens had been compelled to come down out of her bed and fry bacon and make coffee for two intoxicated soldiers whom her husband had waylaid and brought home with him to be 'converted.'

'I hope to goodness that he won't bring any of those dreadful people in tonight,' she was thinking, as she toasted slice after slice of bread in preparation for the family tea. 'Vinny, stop that screaming! What is the matter with you and why are you slapping Conny?'

The Bourke twins, now nearly four years old, were sprawling on the hearthrug and devouring – no other word could describe their manner of eating, for in this respect they were their father's children – slices of toast and fighting with each other at the same time. They were rather ugly and small and already, unfortunately, very like their male parent in appearance and manner. They would scream for their food when hungry and never stop till they got it, and they certainly had enormous appetites.

Mrs Bourke looked at them now in dismay.

'Good gracious!' she exclaimed, 'you greedy boys! Why you have already finished all the toast I made for you! No, you will not get any more! Oh, stop crying! Here is some bread and jam for you instead!' and having supplied them with huge slices, thickly smeared with jam, she returned to her toast-making and her rather weary thoughts. But in a few minutes she heard the click of the latchkey in the hall door, followed by a quick, light footstep coming down the hall; then the diningroom door opened and Carmen Cavanagh stood on the threshold, looking in at the pleasant, shabby, fire-lit room which had meant home to her for so long. She looked very pretty – almost beautiful indeed – as she stood there. She was not very tall, but slender and graceful, with soft, dusky hair peeping now from beneath her little fur cap, and big black eyes, her heritage from her Spanish mother. Lovely eyes, and yet they looked a bit wistful just now, or so Mrs Bourke thought as she turned, toasting-fork in hand, with the welcoming smile which she always had for Carmen.

'Why Carmen!' she said, as if noticing something strange about the girl, 'what is it? Have you had bad news? Do you know where you are to be sent?'

'Yes! Yes! To all your questions, Cis,' cried the other as she came across the room and knelt on the hearthrug while she drew off her gloves and held her cold hands to the fire, unceremoniously ousting the twins out of her way. 'Yes, I met Miss Bennett at the corner of Dawson Street; she told me that she was just going to write to me.'

'Well!' breathed Mrs Bourke anxiously. 'Oh, Carmen! Tell me quickly! *Where* are you going? Is it near Dublin at all?'

Carmen laughed suddenly. *'Near Dublin!'* she repeated, and then laughed again. 'I am going to Donegal, to Glenmore!' she said. Mrs Bourke could not speak.

'Yes,' went on the girl more quietly now. 'I am to take Marcella's place. You see her marriage is to be early in April, and she is getting a month's holiday first, so I am to go down there on the 5th of March and take up duty.'

Mrs Bourke made an effort then and spoke. 'Will Marcella be there when you go down?' she asked. 'That would be nice for you. It's such a lonely place and so far away!'

'No, Cella won't be there,' replied Carmen. 'She comes up to Dublin on the second of March to stay with her aunt at Harold's Cross. But of course I can have a talk with her and learn all I can about the place. I am to take a servant down with me, too, Cis, because, of course, Ellen is staying with Marcella – and is going back to live with her in Carragh after the wedding.' There was silence for a few minutes, and both gazed thoughtfully into the fire.

'How late all the others are this evening,' said Carmen, presently. 'Let us have our tea now, Cis – do – and send those *torments* down to the kitchen so that we can have a few minutes' peace! I want to talk to you.'

So the torments, much against their will, were despatched to the lower regions, and Mrs Bourke and Carmen sat down to their tea and toast. The girl was rather quiet, and her cousin glanced at her in a puzzled way. It was unlike Carmen to be so silent. She lifted her great eyes presently, and, meeting Mrs Bourke's glance, she smiled suddenly – Carmen's own vivid, radiant smile.

'You are wondering what I am thinking about,' she said. 'Well, I was just wishing that my mother had never made my father promise that I was not to go on the stage. Oh how I would love to be an actress. You know – *you know*, Cis that nature intended me for one! Why, acting comes as naturally to me as swimming to a duck! And here I am instead going to be a district nurse – *a district nurse* – dressing burnt babies, and septic fingers and legs, and looking after bedridden old dames, and having to be on duty day and night and all weathers! Ugh! How I hate it all!'

'Why, Carmen!' exclaimed Mrs Bourke, 'what is the matter with you? I never heard you speak so bitterly about your profession before. What has made you take such a vehement dislike to it – and especially now you have finished in the Home and got a district of your own?'

'That's just the reason why,' cried the other. 'I seem to realise now for the first time what my future will be, and ...'

'But, Carmen,' interrupted Mrs Bourke, 'you won't always be a nurse. You are sure to marry; and you – why, *you* could marry anyone! Think of the heaps of admirers you have and always have had since you were a little thing. Why –' with a smile at the remembrance, 'it is really amusing to see the way they fall before the glances of your big eyes!'

'Oh yes, that's all very well,' said Carmen, impatiently, 'but I don't care a pin about any of them – silly fools. And I don't know if ever I will care sufficiently for a man to risk marriage with him, although I know well that if I *did* fall in love it would be the real thing! I would go any lengths – I would go to the devil for a man I *loved!*'

Mrs Bourke looked at the girl uneasily.

'You certainly do say queer things, Carmen,' she said. 'And you are so tempestuous and passionate. I wish, for your own sake, that you were blessed with a more placid disposition.'

'Ah! well, I can't change,' said Carmen, 'and I don't know that I would really care to become one of your commonplace, commonsense, common or garden women, willing to make a sensible wife for a sensible husband, and to settle down to domestic bliss in Suburbia. No, thank you!'

Mrs Bourke sipped her tea slowly, surveying her cousin over the edge of her cup.

'Carmen,' she said suddenly, 'what life really would you have chosen if the choice had been yours to make?'

The girl laughed.

'Why, surely you know, Cis!' she said, 'the stage, of course! It is my vocation and the profession above all others for me. I am an actress by nature and by birth, and only for my mother's dying wish, and my father allowing himself to be so influenced by it, I would have trained for the boards years ago. And there's my voice, too!' she went on regretfully. 'My mother could leave me a voice nearly as good as her own and yet forbid me to ever even sing in public! Oh Cis, it does make me so mad sometimes even to think of what a different life I might have had!'

'Yes, there's no doubt you would have had a big success,' said Mrs Bourke wistfully. 'I often thought that it was a pity you could not follow in your mother's footsteps.'

'I wonder *why* she was so dead against it. *She* had a fine time and made a name for herself in a few years. What possessed her, then, to stipulate that I should never act in public? What do you remember about her, Cis? But you did not see much of her – did you?'

'No,' replied her cousin, gazing thoughtfully into the fire, as if she could see there a picture of the beautiful Spanish woman whom she remembered so faintly. 'No – I only saw her twice, once at the opera – she was "Carmen" that night, her favourite part – and, oh *such* a "Carmen" – and once when your father brought her to see me. She was very lovely, the real Spanish type, and she spoke English with the prettiest accent! I could do nothing but sit and look at her as if she was a picture. She was smaller than you, Carmen, very slight, and with tiny hands and feet, and a great mass of black hair. Her eyes were just like yours. Your poor father was simply infatuated with her – everyone could see that he adored her.'

'And he had her for such a short while,' said Carmen.

'Yes,' assented Mrs Bourke, 'she died, as you know, barely three years after their marriage. Your father had commenced to paint her in her favourite *role*, but the picture was never finished. I believe, too, that it would have been the best thing he ever did – for he just put all his heart into it. But he never painted another stroke after her death – if ever a man died of a broken heart, Carmen, he did.'

'Poor father,' said the girl, 'and he died in a year. No wonder, Cis, when he was so devoted to her, that he looked upon her dying wish as sacred.'

She sighed and ran her fingers through her dark hair with one of her expressive gestures.

'All the same,' she added, 'it's jolly hard lines on me!'

'Don't be always thinking about this,' said Mrs Bourke. 'I have noticed lately, Carmen, that you are more inclined to dwell upon these matters than you used to be.'

'Yes,' replied the girl, 'because lately I have been wishing so much that it was as an actress that I was about to start in life – not as a nurse.'

'Oh well, it can't be helped,' said Mrs Bourke, 'and you must just make the best of things as they are.'

'I suppose so,' said the other rather wearily. 'Of course, Cis,' she added, 'I *could* take matters into my own hands and do what I liked; but, someway, I can't help thinking that if I went against the wishes of my dead parents I would have no luck in anything I did – and someway I simply could not do it.'

'Oh! Don't dream of such a thing, Carmen,' cried Mrs Bourke, 'that would be a terrible thing to do.'

'Ah well, I suppose I must just go on with the nursing and see what Fortune will send me! Ah! here's Phil at last!'

Phil Hewson adored her, but Carmen always treated him as a young brother. His rather delicate face flushed with pleasure now as he saw her.

'Hallo! Carmen,' he cried, 'got back from town? I was kept a bit late this evening. Old Ready was in one of his tantrums and delayed us at the last minute.'

But Carmen was too full of her own news to listen to him.

'Oh, Phil,' she said, 'I'm going to Donegal – to Glenmore!'

'What!' he repeated incredulously.

'Yes, you needn't look so surprised! It's quite true, I'm off in a fortnight's time. Going to be buried alive down there to vegetate in that stagnation! Just *think* of it, Phil! Not a sinner even to talk to – for Marcella has gone and bagged the only eligible male within twenty miles or so! Now *can* you imagine me living – or rather existing – in such a place! *Can you?*'

'Why not?' was the rather morose reply. 'It might do you good in every way to lead the simple life for a bit.'

'Oh, indeed!' said Carmen, 'so that's your opinion, is it? Well, it's not mine. However, I have a fortnight still to the good, and you can bet your bottom dollar, old boy, that I'm going to enjoy that fortnight. I'm going to *live* every moment of the time! So prepare yourself to take me to the theatre or the pictures every night, except on three booked dates, when I'm going to dances.'

'What dances? And who are you going with?' asked Phil with angry disregard for grammar. He was standing by the fire warming himself, and looking down at Carmen, who had gone back to her seat on the hearthrug and seemed like some vivid picture, as the firelight gleamed on her dark hair and shining eyes.

'Oh never you mind – not with *you*, old glum face, that's certain!' was the provoking reply.

'Well, who is it that is going to take you?' asked Philip again. 'Surely, Mother,' turning to Mrs Bourke, 'you won't let Carmen go to these dances unless you know who she's going with? Is it that Standish fellow?'

'Wouldn't you – now *wouldn't* you – like to know?' was the only reply.

'Come to your tea, Phil, and don't mind Carmen's teasing!' said Mrs Bourke, who was one of the peace-makers of this world. She poured out his tea just as he liked it and as he sat down, placed the toast before him. 'Now make a good tea,' she said in her comforting voice, 'you must want it.'

Tea, like every meal at harum-scarum No. 47, was a movable, happy-go-lucky affair. Each member of the family as they came in sat down to table and took pot luck – the latest arrivals coming off rather badly, except Mrs Bourke was there, when she would make them fresh tea and toast and sympathise and comfort them as only she could.

The two girls, Eileen and Letty, came in together, having met on their way home, and their remarks on Carmen's news were characteristic.

'You won't have anyone to *dress* for down there!' said Eileen.

'It will do you all the good in the world,' said Letty, 'you will become quite staid and sensible after a few years there.'

'I will dress for my *looking glass* and I'm much more likely to become *absolutely dotty* than either staid or sensible!' retorted Carmen – which reply was also characteristic.

'Now, Phil, you can take me to the pictures,' she announced. 'I'll run up and get ready. We can go to the Princess – it's the nearest.'

And Philip Hewson felt that life was worth living again, as he hastily demolished the remains of his tea and left the room to make a quick toilette, for Carmen hated nothing so much as to be kept waiting.

'What a fool he is over Carmen!' said Eileen, 'and she is so absolutely indifferent to him.'

'A good job, too – it would be a most unsuitable match,' replied Letty, in her most sententious tones.

'Oh what a grandmother you are, Letty!' exclaimed Eileen, 'you might be seventy instead of seventeen!'

'*Someone* would need to have a little sense in this household,' replied Letty, as she composedly poured out her second cup of tea.

In the meanwhile, Philip has descended kitchenwards, where old Sarah was now alone, the twins having gone upstairs with their mother.

'I say, Sarah, where's the boot brush? I can't find it anywhere,' he said irately, 'and it was on that shelf there this morning.'

'Oh Master Phil, dear, is that yerself? The boot brush, is it? Sure the Master' – lowering her voice to a whisper and glancing fearfully over her shoulder, as if the personage in question might be lurking in some dark corner of the big kitchen, 'the Master flung it somewhere and lost it on me – I can't find it nowhere.'

'Oh C.V. flung it away, did he?' repeated Phil (for by those initials was their stepfather called by the Hewsons). 'And where did he fling it to?'

'Sure that's what I don't know; but wait there now for wan minit, like a darlint boy, and I'll go look!' The basement kitchen was very dark, its only light being a smoky oil lamp – any lamp for which Sarah was responsible was sure to smoke. She was stout and very untidy, always down-at-heel, and always looking as if she never washed her face or combed her hair. She stooped now and lit a bit of paper at the fire, and with this illumination she started to grope in all her various glory holes – behind the door, in the dresser, under the tables, behind the old wooden shutters. In the meantime her papers kept going out just as she reached the spot she was making for, and another bit would have to be lit while the first bit would be dropped and stamped upon.

Sarah never used any other light, no one ever saw her with either candle or match in her hand; and how it was she had not set fire to the house long ago was a mystery.

Philip watched her for a few minutes with what patience he could master and then exclaimed. 'Oh throw those bits of paper away, Sarah! Here's a match! Haven't you a candle?'

'Well now, I've ne'er a candle at all, Master Phil – but just hould the match for wan minit till I see did the ould fella throw it anyway hereabouts!'

'And who might ye be calling the auld fella? Eh! Ye auld hag! Ye auld witch! I'll auld fella ye! – I'll –'

Used as both Phil and Sarah were to the ghostly and sudden appearance of Mr Cornelius Bourke, they had both started at hearing his hated voice behind them. Phil recovered himself immediately, but poor Sarah gasped and promptly dropped the lighted match, which would have set her very grimy apron alight only for Phil stamping it quickly out.

This was pure joy to the master of the house, who chuckled with delight when he saw the poor woman bless herself, with shaking fingers.

'Ye ignorant auld Papist!' he said. 'Ye auld idolator!'

Phil was leaving the kitchen when his stepfather called harshly after him, 'And what might ye be wanting, me brave boy, eh? Is it the boot polish your lordship wanted to do up yer boots? I suppose ye are going out to some place of sin with that foreign Papist devil! Eh?'

'So you've been at your old game, listening at holes and corners, have you?' asked Phil, furiously, as he wheeled around and confronted his tormentor. 'Well, it's no business of yours where I go or what I do! So you may just hold your tongue!'

'Oh indeed! Is that so?' said the other, his foxy little eyes gleaming with malice. 'Take care of yerself, me young Lord

Tom Noddy! Take care I don't throw ye into the street – the whole beggar's lot of ye! I'll –'

But Phil was gone upstairs, and Sarah had made her escape into the coal cellar, where she knew from past she was fairly safe, as Cornelius Bourke did not like to soil his clothes; so after looking well round the kitchen, and finding nothing to purloin in the way of food, he turned out the lamp so as to give Sarah the trouble of finding a match and re-lighting it, and departed upstairs to see if his wife was to be run to earth and made to suffer for her son's insolence.

Phil rushed up to his room and changed his boots and presently came down to the hall, where Carmen joined him in a few minutes. He said nothing more about the dances, for he did not want her to turn 'crusty' again, and she was inclined to be rather nice to him.

She made such an adorable picture, too, in her smart sports coat and scarlet tam, and walked along so gaily beside him, with her little feet (of which she was exceedingly vain) neatly encased in brown brogues, that he felt it was enough to be able to be with her, and he wanted to forget for a while that she would soon be many miles away from him.

But she remembered it herself later.

'One day off my fortnight!' she said with a sigh, as Phil fitted the latchkey into the door on their return. 'Oh, no light, as usual! He's at home, then! No matter, Phil, I've a bit of candle in my pocket, for I know his tricks! Have you a match? That's right!'

All this was in the softest of whispers, and the candle lit, they peered around the hall and up the staircase, expecting to come suddenly upon the universal *bete noir*. Then, 'He must be gone upstairs,' said Phil, still in a whisper. 'Let us slip downstairs. Mother told me she would leave us some supper in the pantry – so that he wouldn't find it. She said she had some cold ham for us, and would leave it on the little table.'

'Oh! That's grand!' breathed Carmen, as they stole down the creaky stairs. 'I'm as hungry as – as a *Bourke!*'

But disappointment awaited them; the table was set for supper certainly, and a dish in the middle had evidently contained ham. It was now empty, and the bread and butter were also gone – likewise the jug of milk for making their cocoa. But lying on the empty dish was a dirty slip of paper with these words scrawled on it in pencil:

'Hope you will enjoy the supper I have left you.
'C.V.B.'

They gazed blankly before them for a moment. Then Phil said 'Damn!' and Carmen laughed – laughed loud and clear, so that their persecutor could hear her if, as was probable, he was listening and watching in his usual uncanny way.

'Never mind, Phil!' she said then. 'Come upstairs and I'll give you some biscuits. I have a tin hidden when *he* can't find it!'

So, in the true philosopher's spirit, which many years of C.V. Bourke had fostered, they departed to the upper regions.

V

ENTER PEG O' MY HEART

Carragh, Co. Donegal, on an April day – an April day of sun and soft winds, of a blue sky, which was mirrored in the big lough outside the village, and which seemed too to be reflected on the brown precipitous sides of Slieve-na-Carragh, that huge giant of a mountain which towered high over all the surrounding country.

In the little garden attached to the doctor's house, daffodils and primroses were 'a blowing and a growing' and to Marcella Adair, as she sat at the open window, engaged in the very prosaic task of darning her husband's socks, the world on that lovely day seemed a very good place in which to live and breathe and have one's being.

Four years of married life have passed over her head since we last saw her, but she is little changed. The same honest grey eyes look out on the world in the same frank fashion, and the same sunny smile hovers ever round her lips, and she still possesses 'a heart at leisure from itself' to help and sympathise with others. To her husband she was the perfect helpmeet; their union was ideal, and between them there existed that absolute trust and confidence, that perfect friendship, without which no marriage is complete.

Their life at Carragh was often dull and monotonous, and for the doctor difficult and laborious. He had forty miles of an area for his district, much of it rough mountain and bogland. A night call in the depths of winter often meant facing a herculean task. Many a time he would return home, drenched through and through, tired and spent in body and mind, and at such times he would thank God for the wife he had won. Never yet had he come home, no matter at what hour, without finding a warm fire in the bedroom and a singing kettle on the hob; while Marcella, wide awake in a moment, would slip into kimono and slippers and, drawing up the little table on which the tray was ready set, to the fire would make his cocoa and cut his bread and butter or sandwiches just the way he liked. Then, all his wants supplied, she would jump back into bed, and, sitting up and hugging her knees, would demand to hear all about the case, listening to every detail with the real interest of a colleague and fellow worker.

Often and often Allan Adair blessed his stars that he had married a nurse and many a time he would declare that no other woman was fit to be the wife of a country doctor. No one else could realise the trials and worries or understand the physical hardship of the work. The medical man in the next district had married a Dublin girl also, but one who had not been obliged to earn her own living and who had never been in such an isolated part of the world before. After the first few months their home life was a miserable failure from every point of view. The wife, a shallow, pretty little creature, became careless and untidy, both in the household management and in her own appearance. 'There's no one to notice what one wears here!' she would say, drearily and Dr Murray came home to cold comfort very often. Many a night had he been wet through, literally wet to the skin, and found no fire on his return home and no way of getting a hot drink; so he would pour out a stiff glass of whiskey and, throwing off his wet clothes, would slip into bed beside his sleeping wife, who never bothered to speak to him even if she awoke.

A greater contrast between his home life and that of Dr Adair could hardly be found. Marcella had often endeavoured, with rare tact, to get Mrs Murray to take more interest in her house and surroundings and in her husband's work, but she had soon to realise that it was useless. The disappointed woman was too full of her own grievances to think of anything else, and she expected unqualified sympathy from her neighbour, quite forgetting that Mrs Adair's circumstances were very similar to her own and that it was only the latter's loving nature and sunny disposition which helped her to get over many a difficulty and trial.

'I don't know why Mrs Murray takes such a black view of her life,' she said one day to Allan, 'it is such a pity! And now especially when the doctor needs her help so much. Poor fellow! I wonder will he be able to pull up!'

'It would be hard to say,' replied her husband. 'When a man once really takes to drink in these desolate regions, it is generally speaking sure to do for him!'

'It is just pitiful,' she sighed, 'and such a nice boy when he came first, just three years ago. Don't you remember, Allan, how we took to him at once? Who could ever imagine that the last two years could make such a difference in anyone!'

'Well, you know, sweetheart, that I blame that useless wife of his! If you had only seen the discomfort of that house last Thursday night when I went home with him from that case we attended together. No fire, not a cup of tea to be had, much less a good meal, of which he was surely in need. And it was only a little after eleven. Of course, he went straight to the ever-ready decanter, and on my honour I could hardly blame him! But I thanked Heaven, sweetheart, for the home and welcome waiting for me!'

Marcella thanked him with her eyes. 'I wonder if they had a child would things have been different?' she said then. 'Surely no man could want to drink if he had ...'

'A Peg o' My Heart to welcome him home!' finished the doctor, with a laugh, as he stooped and kissed his wife's soft hair.

Marcella was thinking of this conversation on the lovely April morning of which we write, for Dr Adair had been called out late on the preceding night to attend a 'mountain case' many miles away in Dr Murray's district, the latter being 'not well enough to attend' – a condition of affairs which was becoming pretty frequent of late, and very easy of diagnosis where Dr Murray was concerned.

Allan had not yet returned; it was drawing on to noon – and Marcella could not help feeling rather annoyed at the thought of the extra work which Dr Murray's 'indisposition' would be likely to cause her husband.

'As if he hadn't more than enough of his own as it is!' she thought rebelliously, as she folded one pair of socks and began upon another.

'Mummy! Mummy! Where is 'oo?'

'Here, sweetheart! At the window. Come along to Mummy.'

'I is tummin'.'

And Marcella Adair, lifting her eyes, suddenly aflame with mother love, saw her small daughter demurely trotting up the garden path. And so Peg enters the story.

Just three years old, dressed in a pink cotton frock, which shows liberally her fat, sturdy legs and dear little feet – such pretty feet and hands, Peg! With a sunbonnet half covering her silky brown curls, and a torn, not over-clean 'pinny' which she is holding out in front of her now full of flowers, such is Peg o' My Heart, as we see her first.

She smiled when she saw her mother, a serious, sedate little smile, as usual, and continued to walk carefully and slowly, clutching tightly to her pinafore, until she reached the low window ledge, to which she could nearly, but not quite, reach up. Marcella leant over and smiled at her, and the two made a delightful picture. Then, 'Peg has dot powers for 'oo!' announced Miss Adair. All her *f*s were *p*s; in fact, she had a most extraordinary way of speaking; her *s*'s were always put at the end of her words, even when they should be at the beginning. She would say, 'Pins my penny' or 'Pins my top' when she meant one to spin it for her, so that strangers when introduced to her for the first time were completely confounded and had to seek an interpreter's aid.

'Oh what lovely flowers for Mummy!' cried Marcella, reaching down for the few unfortunate daffodils and primroses whose heads had been ruthlessly pulled off and stuffed into the wee maiden's pinafore as an offering of love. 'How pretty they are!'

'Does 'oo yike dem?' in anxious tones, while the serious hazel eyes gaze earnestly at Marcella, as if searching for the truth.

'Like them!' exclaimed Marcella. 'I should just think I did! And won't you come in now, sweetheart, and have some milk and bread and butter?'

'Ess. Peg wants a gay,' was the reply, a 'gay' being her word for a drink – why, no one ever discovered.

Just as she was turning to go round to the side door of the house, which gave a view of the front gate and the road beyond, a sound of car wheels was heard, and, with a delightful scream of 'Daddy! Daddy!' the little fat legs went running down the path and reached the gate just as Dr Adair flung himself off the car and turned to see if Carmen

Cavanagh wanted assistance. But she was already on the ground and smothering Peg with kisses.

'Where is Mummy, darling?' they asked then, and, taking a hand of each, Peg triumphantly led them round to the side door and into the pleasant, homelike room, where Marcella, with a little exclamation of relief, came forward to meet them.

'What a long time you have been, Allan!' she cried. 'You must be dead beat! And you have Carmen with you. I'm so glad!'

'Yes, I had to send a car for her,' said the doctor, sinking rather wearily into a chair. 'I could not manage the case without help, and although it was not really in Carmen's district, I knew that she would stretch a point under the circumstances.'

'Well, I should think so!' replied Carmen. 'Oh Marcella, *such* a case!' And for the next few minutes only the case was discussed.

'But you must be worn out, there all night!' said Marcella then, 'and what about food? Could you get anything fit to eat?'

'Oh, the usual boiled tea and leathery soda bread in relays throughout the night,' said Carmen with a resigned laugh.

'Well, come upstairs and have a wash, and we will have lunch early. Don't let Peg worry you!' and Marcella shook a warning finger at the small lady, who was seated on Carmen's lap.

'As if *Peg* would ever worry me!' cried Carmen. 'Why, where would I be without her, I wonder?' Not in Donegal certainly; she knew that herself and so did the doctor and his wife. Nothing but Carmen's love for Peg, a love most intense and absorbing, had kept her so long in those dreary regions. When she had first come to Glenmore she had suffered terribly from the loneliness and isolation. She was worse off than Marcella had been, for she had had the companionship of the faithful Ellen, but poor Carmen had been left to the ministrations of a local girl, for no Dublin servant would stay; one who had not the very faintest notion of how a house should be kept, and whose ideas of cookery, according to her mistress, 'belonged to the Stone Age, for one certainly needed stone implements to cut any food she cooked!' When Marcella returned as Mrs Adair, and settled down in Carragh, about eight miles distant from Glenmore, life became a little brighter for Carmen, and, in spite of the terrible condition of the road between the two villages, a condition so bad, indeed, that only a fraction of it could be cycled, she often made it over to the homelike house where her old chum was always ready with a real welcome for her.

In the April of the following year Peg, or, to give the wee lady her right titles, Margaret Katherine, was born, and, from the very first moment in which she had felt the tiny baby fingers close on hers, Carmen had been devoted to the child, and would have completely spoilt her only for the wise, restraining influences of Marcella and the doctor.

For a young couple with their first baby, they were exceedingly wise and sensible, and from the very beginning Peg was brought up on what Carmen angrily declaimed as 'textbook rules.'

'Poor little darling,' she used to say, 'you are trying to turn her into a machine! Everything to be done by time and rote and iron regularity! It's all very well to lecture the mother in the district about these rules – but for a little angel like Peg o' My Heart! Why it's just *rot*!'

But Dr and Mrs Adair stuck to their guns, and, however galling their system of upbringing might appear to Carmen, it certainly turned out well as far as the object of it was concerned for now, at three years of age, a sweeter or more winsome little lass than Peg Adair could not have been found within the four walls of Ireland. She was totally unspoilt, perfectly obedient, and, as a result, a happy, healthy child, full of quaint mannerisms, ideas and thoughts of her very own. She had a very sweet disposition, absolutely unselfish, and her tiny heart held a wealth of love for all her world.

Devoted as she was to Carmen, and whom she had not seen now for some weeks, she at once slipped down from her knees when her mother told her to go to Ellen for her lunch, only waiting to give 'a hug all round' before leaving the room.

'Little duck!' said Carmen, gazing after her as her fat legs took her kitchen-wards.

Marcella laughed.

'How you *would* spoil that kiddie if you were let!' she said, adding, 'come on now and have a wash and brush up.'

Later in the day, sitting after lunch, round a cosy fire, the three found themselves discussing Dr Murray.

'I called in for a moment to see him when we were coming home this morning,' said Dr Adair, as he filled his pipe. 'I thought it best to let him know how that case went off, it being really his, you know, and I was anxious to know if there would be any chance of his getting back to duty soon.'

'Well?' interrogated Marcella, as he paused.

'Well, he has had an awful bout of it, and won't be fit for duty for another week, and only then if he keeps off the stuff during the interval. He is simply a mass of nerves at present. I never saw a man so gone to pieces in such a short time; it's pitiful, tragic!'

'Did you see him, Carmen? asked Marcella.

'No,' answered the doctor for her. 'I didn't bring her in with me, for I really didn't know in what condition I might find him. Poor devil! He was sober enough for the time being but terribly seedy and miserable. And no wonder in such surroundings! I wish you could have seen the absolute discomfort of the room in which I found him, a dying fire, with the chimney smoking, the dirty breakfast things still on the table, and dust and smuts thick over everything!'

'And where was the girl, and Mrs Murray?'

'Well, I found Mary Bridget in a filthy kitchen, and she informed me that Mrs Murray had gone to Kilbeg to stay for a few days with some friends of hers who are visiting at the hotel there.'

'Oh how *could* she – how *could* she leave him just now?' cried Marcella indignantly. 'Poor fellow! And he wants her help so badly! Do you remember, Allan, when he was here a few weeks ago, that awfully wet night when he was driving past and came in, how he told us that he was going to try and pull himself together again and make a fresh start?'

'Yes, I remember all right,' replied the doctor, as he contemplated the ceiling through a cloud of tobacco smoke, 'but I'm afraid, I'm terribly afraid, that he is too much of a nervous wreck now. I don't believe that he has the necessary moral stamina to enable him to make a fresh start. And everything is against him, his surroundings, the loneliness and isolation, no congenial friends near, and above all the want of a different kind of woman for a wife!'

Carmen Cavanagh was gazing into the fire with her big, black eyes. There was a very sombre look in their depths just then, and Marcella, happening to glance at her, was arrested by something strange in her appearance.

'What is it, Carmen?' she asked, with a quick intake of her breath. 'You look as if – as if you were *seeing* something!'

The girl addressed started, and, withdrawing her gaze from the fire, turned in a somewhat dazed fashion towards her friend.

'Oh how foolish I am!' she said then, 'but you know my horrid presentiments that I get sometimes! Well, just now I thought I saw someone hanging, *dead*! And his face, *the eyes!*'

She covered her face with her hands, as though to shut out the horrid sight, and shivered violently.

Marcella sat aghast for the moment, but Dr Adair, coming round to Carmen's side, laid a hand on her shaking shoulders.

'Come! Come! Carmen,' he said firmly. 'This won't do, you know! This is the result of the over-strain of last night, a case like that *does* take it out of one. I'll mix you a little draught, and then, after a cup of tea, I should advise bed. After a good sleep you will no longer be a seer of visions – good or bad!'

'Oh! But Allan!' she cried, pulling herself together with the self-control of the trained nurse. 'I must get back to Glenmore before dark. You know I am not supposed to stay a night away from my house.'

'Just you leave all that to me,' was the quiet reply. 'I'll be responsible for your absence.'

He left the room as he spoke, returning in a couple of moments with a medicine glass in his hand.

'Now then, drink this!' he said, 'and then off to bed with you. Marcella will bring you up a cup of tea presently, and after that I expect you will get to sleep; don't forget it's over thirty hours since you were in bed!'

But afterwards, when Marcella came downstairs from bringing up Carmen's tea and seeing her comfortably settled in the room that was always kept ready for her, she wore a worried, anxious look her husband was quick to notice.

'Hallo! little woman! What's up?' he asked, imprisoning in his own the hand which held out his tea cup.

'Oh, nothing much, dear,' his wife replied, 'only' and her anxious look deepened, 'I never like Carmen's presentiments – they *always* come true in the most weird manner!'

'Now, old girl, have sense!' said the doctor, 'and don't *you* begin to imagine things!'

But he did not continue the subject, for truth to tell, he did not care for Carmen's presentiments himself – as his wife had remarked, they had an uncanny way of coming true – but, needless to say, wild horses would not have dragged such a confession from him.

But in the morning, as he had foreseen, Carmen was a different person. She had been awakened very early by Peg scrambling, breathless and excited, into bed beside her.

'Peg tum to ee Tarmen,' she announced complacently, adding in a loud, tickling whisper in Carmen's ear. 'Mummy not know! Daddy not know!' And then she laughed in huge delight and, of course, the girl had to laugh with her at such a joke.

A delightful hour of play followed for the two of them, which was only too soon interrupted by Marcella's entrance to bear away Peg to be washed and dressed.

'Fancy! She slipped out of her cot and in to you and I never heard her,' said her mother to Carmen; and then to the culprit. 'You are a very naughty girl!'

'She's a little duck!' cried Carmen.

'Peg a 'ickle duck!' repeated the young lady complacently, looking back over her shoulder to blow a kiss to Carmen.

After breakfast the doctor's car came round, and he and Carmen started off. They were going first to visit the woman with whom they had been the previous night, and then he would drive her to her own house.

'Goodbye, Carmen! Come again as soon as you can!' called Marcella from the gate, as the car began to move.

'Doo-bye tum back aden to Peg!' echoed her small daughter, blowing kisses as quickly and as vigorously as she could.

'Goodbye, Ducksie! Goodbye, Cella!' and, with a wave of her hand, Carmen disappeared as the car rounded the corner of the road.

VI

THE KINGDOM OF PERPETUAL NIGHT

The morning was bright with sunshine as Dr Adair drove smartly along. Spring was all around, and even this bleak corner of Donegal was touched by its charm.

'Ripping morning, isn't it?' he said, with a side glance at his companion, who, now that she had left Carragh – and Peg! – behind, seemed to have become strangely silent.

'Yes,' she assented, but without much animation, 'yes – it's a lovely day.'

Dr Adair was rather puzzled. Carmen had appeared to be in her usual good spirits earlier in the morning, and he had imagined that she had quite recovered from her fit of the blues, or whatever it was that had troubled her. He had put it all down of course to over-fatigue and strain, but, all the same, as he looked at her now he had to admit that she was no longer tired-looking in a physical sense, but still within her wonderful black eyes hovered the same dark shadow – the brooding, sombre, *seeing* look – of the previous day.

'Feeling all right again, Carmen?' he hazarded tentatively.

'Oh yes, at least I suppose so! It's just this awful feeling of depression – of impending trouble – that is still over me! Don't laugh at me, Allan! I can't help it, and you know that I have reason to fear it!'

'Now try and not think about it,' he advised. 'You need a holiday – a change would do you all the good in the world. We must try and see if you can't manage a week in Dublin soon.' He was genuinely sorry for knowing how highly strung she was. 'Quite unfit for the profession' was his private opinion of her, and he knew that she really suffered when tormented by one of her strange 'presentiments.' But he frankly admitted that he did not understand her moods at such times, and was often thankful that Marcella was a sensible, matter-of-fact person who never indulged in temperamental emotions.

Arriving at the patient's house, they found everything going on satisfactorily, much to their relief, for the case had been a difficult and complicated one. Their drive had taken three hours, and it was now past noon.

'I am going to have a look in at Murray,' said the Doctor, as he turned the horse's head and drove in the direction of Dr Murray's house. 'To tell you the truth, Carmen,' he continued, idly flicking the horse's sides with his whip, 'I am very anxious about the poor chap – far more so than I confessed to Marcella. You see, she knows him so well, and has always been interested in him, and has tried so hard to help him and to improve his wife a bit, but it was all useless! He was to spend last night alone in the house. He told me that he had given Mary Bridget leave to go to a dance at Beggan crossroads, five miles away, and she was not to return until today, and of course Mrs Murray, I suppose, is still away with her friends.'

Carmen was listening with a white, strained face. 'And was he alone all night?' she asked.

'Yes, he was,' assented the Doctor, 'and he was in such a rotten, jumpy state yesterday, and above all so fearfully depressed – that terrible alcoholic depression – that I feel a bit upset about him. He was just in a condition to drink to excess, left alone like that, too, in that miserably uncomfortable place; and his house being so far on the outskirts of the village. I tried my best to persuade him to come home with me yesterday, but it was no good. He said that his wife had sent him a message to say that she *might* return last night. I think myself that the poor boy had written begging her to do so, and he was afraid that she might return and find no one there to welcome her.'

'And I wonder how many times *he* came home and found no one there to welcome him,' cried Carmen.

'Yes, that's true,' Allan replied, 'but you know how devoted the poor chap is to his wife. 'Dolly' is everything to him still, and I honestly believe that if only she were a different sort of woman – one who could be a real helpmate to a man, that he *would* be able to pull himself together again and conquer his wretched failing. But there you are; she's doll by name and doll by nature!'

They were driving along the sandy, uneven road, with the great expanse of bog on one side and the cliffs and the broad Atlantic on the other.

Carmen made a brave effort to throw off her depression. 'How lovely the sea looks this morning!' she said, 'one would hardly know what colour to call it; it seems to be a mixture of green and blue and grey, flecked with white. Oh, there's the Murray's house now! I don't see any smoke from the chimneys. The poor Doctor! I suppose he has got no breakfast yet, I know what Bridget is like after an all-night dance!'

Dr Adair said nothing but drove steadily on towards the house – a small, two-storied dwelling, badly in want of paint and repair. It stood back from the road, a gate leading up to the house by way of a very neglected front garden.

Just as they came within a hundred yards of the place a loud scream fell upon their ears, followed by another and another – screams of one in mortal agony or fear.

'Oh, who is it? Who is it?' whispered Carmen, with shaking lips.

The Doctor did not reply, but whipped up the horse and drove rapidly on. As they pulled up at the gate a woman rushed pell-mell out of the front door and down the path to the gate. There she paused, arrested by the sight of the car and its occupants; but she still continued to scream, and although it soon became evident that her senses were failing and her physical strength going, she screamed again and again, and when she felt her knees giving way under her she held on to the gate with her two hands, and the terrible screams, but fainter now, still came from her livid, trembling lips.

It was Mrs Murray, although at first the others had hardly recognised her, so changed was this distraught woman from the pretty, vapid little person of everyday life. The Doctor and Carmen went swiftly to her side, supporting her between them.

'Mrs Murray, what is it?' he asked, for Carmen was beyond speech. 'Try – try for God's sake and control yourself and tell us what has happened.'

She stopped then and looked at them with dull, unseeing eyes, but almost immediately the look of terror came again to her face, and she shook so violently that they could hardly hold her.

'What is it?' repeated Allan again, and his stern tone and firm touch seemed to have a slight effect upon her. She pointed over her shoulder towards the house with a shaking finger.

'I came – home – just now,' she said in a queer, strained whisper, 'and found – found ...'

And then she collapsed and would have fallen had not Dr Adair and Carmen lifted her between them and carried her into the house. They laid her on the sofa in the sitting room, and then stood and looked at one another – the unspoken question in their eyes. Then, 'you stay here and I'll go and investigate,' said Allan.

'No! No, let me come with you! I can't stay here alone! And – and it's best for us to know the worst together!' And they closed the door softly on Mrs Murray and went out into the dingy little hall.

The house was completely silent; not a sound came to them as they stood for a moment looking into each other's face with that question in their eyes. What was it that they were to find?

The room where Dr Murray was accustomed to see his patients, where he generally sat of an evening – his 'den' as it was called – was just across the hall, and Dr Adair stepped over and turned the handle with fingers that were not quite steady. But the room was absolutely empty; the ashes of a dead fire were in the grate, a dirty cup and saucer on the table – dust everywhere as usual – but nothing else.

They breathed an involuntary sigh of relief – a relief that they realised was only temporary – and went on to the small dining room. It was empty, as was also the dirty, untidy kitchen.

'Perhaps,' said the Doctor, speaking in the queer, nervous whisper which seemed to be the only way they *could* speak just then, 'perhaps after all nothing really happened. Perhaps Mrs Murray only thought ... My God! Don't look!'

There were three bedrooms on the landing above, and over them was a long loft, used as a box room. The entrance to this was at the end of the bedroom landing, and the only means of reaching up to it was by a ladder, which was generally placed against the wall for this purpose. It had now been thrown down and lay length wise on the floor, and from a loop of rope which was suspended from the loft above dangled the dead body of Dr Murray.

The gruesome sight came upon them so suddenly that Allan had not time to keep it from Carmen. Even before he spoke she had seen it. She gave one long look at the awful, livid face, the sightless, staring eyes, the dangling limbs, before she had the strength of mind to turn away. Then, after what seemed an eternity to her, she managed, by a supreme effort of willpower, to withdraw her eyes, and, covering her face with her hands, she tried to shut out the awful *thing* that was to come between her and her sleep for many a night. Dr Adair went over and examined the body and saw that death had occurred some hours ago; he came back then to Carmen.

'Oh Allan!' she whispered, as he put his arm round her and led her away. 'Oh Allan! The hanging man, and the *eyes!* The eyes that I saw in the fire yesterday. Oh! *I knew* I would see them again!'

'Carmen, try like a good girl and pull yourself together,' he said in rather shaky tones, as they descended the stairs. 'I wish to God that you had stayed downstairs, as I wanted you to – it was a shocking sight for you! But now we have to think of this poor creature.'

Mrs Murray's faintness had passed, and when they entered the room she was sitting up on the sofa, staring straight in front of her, with wide open, terror-stricken eyes – eyes which seemed as if they were still looking at the horror and would go on looking at it for always.

'We must get her out of this,' said the Doctor, in a low tone to Carmen; and then, going over to the sofa he said quietly and firmly. 'Now Mrs Murray, Nurse and I are going to take you over to Carragh to stay awhile with my wife.'

Her coat and hat were beside her. She had evidently run into the sitting room – they knew afterwards that she had found the back door unbolted – and hastily flung them off before going upstairs to look for her husband.

She made no response now, one way or another – indeed she might not have heard him at all, so little impression did he appear to make on her – but she allowed Carmen to put on her things, and between them they took her out to the car.

Dr Adair went back to the house and locked the door, bringing the key with him. Then he jumped on the car, and they started to drive down the hill which led to the little village of Knockbeggan, which had been the centre of poor Dr Murray's district.

'Are you comfortable, Mrs Murray? Do you feel cold?' Carmen asked, in a vain effort to obtain some sign from the silent figure seated so rigidly beside her, and realising the futility of her question even as she spoke. But there was no reply, and speech seeming someway impossible for the others too, they drove on in silence until Knockbeggan Police Barracks was reached. There were some curious glances thrown at Mrs Murray as they went through the village, but the Doctor did not delay a moment longer than was absolutely necessary. He gave the dumb-founded sergeant the facts in a few quick words, and, leaving him the key of the house, and saying he would return there himself when he had left Mrs Murray at Carragh, he flung himself out of the barracks and on to the car and drove quickly away.

Carmen shivered now and again, and several times a feeling of acute nausea overcame her as she beheld again in her mind's vision that awful sight dangling there in the house behind them. How long had he been there? How long was he dead, she wondered? She must ask Allan bye-and-bye. But no, she wouldn't, she would forget, forget all about it, shut it out from sight and memory. And all the time she knew that that would be impossible, knew that never again in all her life would she be able to forget it.

And after all that thing hanging there was only his body – only the shell for his immortal soul. And that soul – where was it? Carmen Cavanagh was not a good Catholic – she would have admitted so freely herself and especially since coming to Donegal, where she was far from a church and missed the many aids to devotion which had been all around her in Dublin – she had taken her religion very easily. But still the Faith had never left her. Dr Murray had been – nominally at least – a Catholic, and, with the doctrines of her Church clear before her, she sickened at the vision which seemed to rush upon her. Like the doomed Clarence of Shakespeare, she seemed to pass:

'the melancholy flood
With that grim ferryman which poets write of,
Unto the Kingdom of Perpetual Night.'

The soft April day was all around her, the sound and the tang of the sea, the blue sky and racing clouds, the sun shining on the little bog flowers, the well-known trot of the horse as they drove briskly along; but of all these familiar, everyday things Carmen saw and heard nothing. Coldness and darkness enveloped her, and she was as one who walked with shrinking and loathing beside a soul who was going on 'Unto the Kingdom of perpetual night.'

When at last, after a drive none of them would ever forget, they drew rein at Dr Adair's house, he leant across the well of the car and spoke to Carmen in a rapid undertone: 'Stay here with her for a moment. I must speak to Marcella first.'

He was only a short time gone – although it seemed very long to Carmen, sitting there beside that silent, inanimate woman – and then he returned, coming down the garden path with Marcella beside him.

Carmen, glancing half fearfully at her, saw that her face was absolutely colourless, but otherwise she seemed to be her accustomed gentle self. She came around the side of the car, and she and Allan between them lifted down Mrs

Murray; then Marcella put her arm round the poor woman and led her gently into house while the Doctor followed with Carmen.

How homely and soothing Marcella's pleasant room appeared! To Carmen it seemed like an awakening from a ghastly nightmare to find oneself safe amid familiar surroundings after a night of dreaming terror. But alas, her terror had been no dream, and gloom possessed her once more as she stood watching Marcella's tender care of the other woman – seating her in an armchair, drawing off her gloves and removing her hat – sending for hot tea.

Mrs Murray submitted to everything, but did not speak one word, sitting silent and rigid, like a woman carved in stone.

They left Ellen in the room with her then – for they hardly liked to leave her alone – and in the Doctor's study they presently discussed the matter together.

'She has had an awful shock,' he said, 'almost enough to affect her brain badly. She must have come home about noon today instead of last night, and the back door being evidently open, she went right in and probably ran upstairs without a thought of anything being wrong, to find – *that!*'

Carmen shivered violently, and Marcella, looking at her, was struck with the tragic sorrow of her face and her haggard, weary look.

'Oh Carmen, my *dear*,' she said, putting her arm round her, 'you must have felt this terribly!'

'Don't talk of it please!' whispered the girl. 'If I could forget! If I could *forget!*'

'Poor Carmen,' said Allan. 'I would have given anything not to have taken her into the house with me; but how was I to guess that? However, I must be off to Knockbeggan again almost immediately; the police will want me. Get me something to eat, Marcella, like a good girl, for I have a wretched time before me.'

They had a hasty lunch, but the eating was mostly pretence, and then the doctor went off again, and Mrs Adair and Carmen went down the passage towards the pleasant little room where they had left Mrs Murray. But before they reached it Ellen came out; the faithful creature had tears in her eyes, which she wiped hastily away on seeing her mistress.

'Miss Peg is within, Ma'am,' she whispered. 'She came in from her play in the garden just now, and the poor lady is taking notice of her. Oh thank God! Just peep in, Miss!' to Carmen. They both drew near on tiptoe, and, unobserved by the two in the room, they watched from the door.

Mrs Murray was still seated just as they had left her and in front of her, leaning on her lap and gazing up at her, was Peg. She had a very battered, not over-clean-looking rag doll in her arms, and this she suddenly held out to the quiet figure in the chair.

'Peg, div'oo her big baba – her *big, big* baba – to make oo better!'

The little voice was full of sympathy – the real, unfeigned sympathy of a child – and she thrust the doll, one of her most treasured possessions, into Mrs Murray's hands.

Mechanically it was received and held.

'Say 'Tank 'oo!' admonished Peg, and 'Thank you' came in a strained whisper from the stiff lips.

'Poor 'oo, poor 'oo,' went on the baby voice. 'What de matter? 'Oo *very* ick! Tell Peg! Peg make 'oo better wiv a kiss!'

And the little fat arms are stretched out and the soft little mouth held up. Ah! Peg! Peg o' My Heart! I think I can see you even now!

With a moan that turned to a sob, Mrs Murray stooped and caught the child to her, and over Peg's curly head she shed her first tears – tears that once they found vent came with great heart-breaking sobs of anguish.

Quietly, Marcella came to her side.

'Dear Mrs Murray,' she said softly, 'you will feel better soon – thanks to Peg. And will you let me take her now?'

And so the half-frightened little mortal was given over to Carmen. 'Peg not bold dirl – no?' she asked, with her queer little foreign-like intonation at the end of the sentence.

'No – no, Peg's a darling – a little duck!' cried Carmen, smothering her with kisses.

Meantime Marcella was endeavouring to comfort and console her distracted guest. But it was hard work; for it was not only *grief* that the unfortunate woman felt – the torments of remorse were hers too, and her one cry always was, 'Oh, if I had been a better wife to him – if I had been kinder! Oh, if I had him back again, how different I would be!'

God help those of us who have to remember our dead in such words!

VII

'DON'T FORGET PEG'

About three weeks after the tragic death of Dr Murray, Carmen Cavanagh sat at tea in her sitting room at Glenmore. It was a warm May day and the breeze wafting in through the open window was very soft and mild for Donegal.

Carmen, who had just come in off the district, was enjoying her tea and a home-made cake, which had been sent over from Carragh, and at the same time she was reading, with rather a puckered brow, a letter from Dublin, which had arrived while she was out. It was from her cousin Cis Bourke, and, while skimming the closely written pages Carmen seemed to be back again in spirit amidst the free-and-easy, comfortable untidiness of 47 Hill Square, Rathmines. Instead of the veronica-bordered path leading down to the little green gate – the same gate for which Marcella's tired fingers had groped on a certain September evening nearly five years ago – and the bare bog road beyond, she saw a strip of true suburban back garden, with Sarah hanging out the weekly wash; and instead of the boom of the Atlantic and the call of the curlews, she heard again the clang of the trams – ah the dear old Terenure line! – and the cries of the newsboys: 'Herald!' 'Late Buff!' 'Here y'are, Miss!' How her exiled heart ached for it all again!

'The Master is as usual,' wrote Mrs Bourke, 'indeed if anything he is *worse,* and never seems to stay in his bed at all these nights! His night wanderings would get on anyone's nerves, and I often wonder how the others stand it. Do you know what Letty's latest idea is? For us all to emigrate to Canada! She is quite determined about it, and I really fear she will work up the rest to go with her. Of course she wants me to go, taking the twins, but leaving *him* behind. I would hate to leave Ireland – and you – but really if you knew what a misery my life has been lately with that man you would not blame me. And certainly I do think that Phil and the girls will go, and how could I stay alone with C.V.? I honestly believe he would kill me. Phil seems at last to have given up all hope about you – and it is as well. You two would never have been happy, as I often told him, but the boy was always infatuated where you were concerned. I wish you could manage to come up to town for a few days and talk things over with us – could you? Let me know as soon as you can.'

'Poor Cis!' sighed Carmen, as she finished the letter. 'I think I'll go over to Carragh tomorrow and see Allan about getting a week's leave. It might cheer me up a bit – and dear knows I need it!'

She spoke truly, for she had sustained a very great shock, and, try as she might, she could not shake off its effects. The suicide of Dr Murray seemed to haunt her waking and dreaming – an ugly, leering spectre for ever at her side.

The fact that this man had been, at least nominally, a Catholic had made it appear all the more terrible to Carmen. That he who *knew* – who surely believed! – the teachings of the Church, could do this thing! And in some queer, inexplicable way it seemed to react upon her own spiritual condition, and to make her shudder with fear and apprehension for her soul's welfare. She was not a good Catholic – and she knew that she was not – and it often seemed to her that she never would be, as if her soul was so entangled, so encumbered, with this world and its troubles and joys that it would never be able to throw off its earthly toils and develop its true spirituality. And yet it was generally a matter of indifference to Carmen Cavanagh, or had been until this sordid, drink-soiled tragedy had touched her. All the horrid details remained seared on her brain. The inquest – Mrs Murray's hysteria – the verdict – as merciful as it could be made – 'suicide while of unsound mind'; Dr Adair of course, certifying that owing to the excessive amount of alcohol taken, the man had not been responsible for his actions.

The funeral too – it had seemed a thing of horror unspeakable – and then there had been talk of Masses – the priest had been doubtful, and had spoken more sternly to poor Mrs Murray than he need have done. Such at least was Carmen's opinion, but she and Fr McGinley had never got on well together. The priest was essentially a man of the people – the son of a Donegal peasant – a clever, gifted boy, who had worked his way on to the priesthood, but who still retained the narrowmindedness and many of the prejudices of his class. But he was a splendid priest for those amongst whom his lot was thrown, and was really a very saintly, if somewhat scrupulous, man.

He and Carmen Cavanagh, however, were poles apart. To her, accustomed to her suave, polished Jesuit confessor, Fr McGinley appeared narrow beyond words – almost ignorant – and not all her Catholic reverence for his office could reconcile her to the man himself, while to him she appeared to be everything that in his opinion a woman should not be. Her independent way of speaking; her manner of expressing herself – 'Dublin slang' he designated most of her gay, expressive talk; her very clothes – silk stockings and high-heeled shoes in summer, and blouses with 'glad necks' – an abomination in his sight. And in winter she had a foreign way of wearing a fur or a hat so that it was bound to attract attention – why even her very uniform seemed to be less demure than that of other nurses! Then her intimate friendship with the Adairs – estimable people of course, but still Protestants – did not please him. On the whole his opinion of Carmen was very poor, and he was not surprised that such a frivolous person should be so seldom at confession and Holy Communion.

Perhaps had Fr McGinley been less rigid in his views, and had had more of the milk of mere human kindness within him, Carmen Cavanagh might have been found kneeling more often within his confessional; or even if she had had a choice of confessors. But the parish priest was a very old man – a priest of the old school, educated on the Continent, and gentlemanly and courteous to the last degree, but now really past his duty, and he seldom left his study and his beloved books. His curate lived with him and did practically the entire work of the parish, and, with the one exception of Carmen, he was idolised by all around.

The next morning Carmen, who was not busy on the district just then, got her few cases over early, and by noon was cycling along the road to Carragh. It was a delightful day, and as she rode along by the lough side and saw the blue sky mirrored in its depths and felt the soft breeze which was gently swaying the white bog cotton, scattered all through the great bog on her left, she found herself wondering whether this could be indeed the same road down which she had often struggled during the past winter, blown literally off her feet by the hurricanes which tore down upon her in terrific force from Slieve-na-Carragh. How calm and stately the giant mountain seemed now, like a great sentinel guarding the bend of the road, which brought one suddenly within view of Carragh village. Very lovely all the country was today; the tiny harbour of Carragh, with its queer fishing boats, the white cabins by the wayside and the ivy-covered church. The next moment she is descending her last hill and is in sight of the village, the Post Office and hotel, combined being the first buildings which she will pass.

'Wilson's, as the hotel was generally called, after its proprietor, was a good-sized house, directly across the road from Dr Adair's gate. It was a very popular place for tourists during the summer months, for Mr Wilson, a Belfast man with all the commercial instincts of one hailing from that town, knew how to cater for the moneyed folk – mostly English or Scotch, or better still, American – who liked to 'do the Donegal highlands' with a maximum of ease and a minimum of discomfort.

May was rather early in the year for these visitors, and Carmel felt rather surprised to see two cars from Kilbeg at the hotel, the first containing passengers and the second their luggage, and they were in the very act of depositing their fares on the ground when Carmen caught sight of them. Out of mere idle curiosity – and because they or anyone fresh was a god-send to her – she dismounted and wheeled her bicycle slowly down the steep hill which led to Carragh village, taking a good survey of the strangers as she did so.

They were four in number – an elderly lady and gentleman, a young girl, and a man of about thirty-five to forty. All were got up in the inevitable tourist style – tweed knickers, with Norfolk coats and cap for the men, and severely tailored coats and skirts for the feminine portion.

As Carmen came near, the elderly lady, with an agonised face, was starting her ordeal of getting off the car – an ordeal indeed, as it always is to the uninitiated Englishwoman of uncertain age. With one hand she clasped firmly to the car rail, loth to let it go, and with the other she tightly clutched the younger man's arm.

'Come on, Aunt Alice,' Carmen heard him say in a clear English accent, 'don't be afraid. Just jump and you will be all right.'

There was a gasp and a scuffle, and the lady, very ungracefully, landed on Mother Earth.

Try as she would, Carmen could not keep the amusement from her expressive face, and the man, as he steered his stout relative across the pebbly road, glanced at the girl and caught the look of the big black eyes, dancing with fun. He gave a quick start of surprise at the unexpected vision and turned involuntarily to look after her as she opened the gate of the pretty white house opposite and wheeled her cycle up the garden path.

'Good heavens, what a face!' he thought, 'a perfect beauty! Not a native, I'll swear – must be a visitor here, too!'

For Carmen had changed out of uniform, and looked exceedingly well in her smart coat and skirt and white blouse, not forgetting the silk stockings and buckled shoes detested by Fr McGinley, who even now was gazing after her in cold disapproval from the Presbytery window.

A delighted shriek from Peg announced Carmen's arrival to the Doctor and Marcella as they were sitting down to lunch.

'Hallo Carmen! Just in time!' they cried cordially, as the girl entered with Peg clinging to her. After lunch the Dublin visit was discussed, Dr Adair approving whole-heartedly, for he knew that the girl wanted a complete change of environment, and wanted it badly.

'Take a fortnight,' he urged. 'I'll give you a letter for your committee saying that I consider it necessary that you should have a short holiday.'

'Yes, a week would be no good,' said Marcella, 'and enjoy yourself, Carmen. Live the dear old Dublin life again, and forget that there is such a place as County Donegal on the face of the globe.'

'Don't *porget* Peg!' said a small voice from the shelter of Carmen's arms, and there was a general laugh, as Carmen, hugging the little one tightly, promised that she certainly would not 'porget Peg!'

'You watch for the postman, Peg!' she said, 'and you'll see that I haven't forgotten you!'

The evening came all too soon and presently Carmen was cycling home again, riding rather thoughtfully along, idly watching the sun setting over the lough. When about three miles beyond Carragh she descried a man's figure in front of her, and as she came nearer she saw it was the younger of the two men whom she had seen arriving at Wilson's Hotel earlier in the day. She rode past him slowly, some imp of mischief causing her to send him a smile and a lightning flash from her wonderful eyes. Surprised, he raised his cap mechanically and stared, in spite of himself, almost rudely – admiration clearly written in his glance. Carmen flushed and rode on more quickly.

'I wonder who he is?' she thought. 'Someway or other he looks like a medico. Some London swank, probably,' and she had soon forgotten all about him in the bustle of preparation for her journey.

Back again in Rathmines, she threw herself heart and soul into all her old enjoyments and pleasures. Phil, as usual, was her willing slave – not to mention numerous other poor moths – medical students, bank clerks, and various minor officials connected with the Local Government and Congested Districts Boards – to whom Carmen had only to lift her little finger to bring them running to her side. Hardly an evening passed that she was not at the theatre or the pictures or, now that the weather was becoming more summery, down at Dalkey or Bray, or strolling along the Kingstown Pier by the side of some infatuated specimen of the other sex.

'Well, really, Carmen,' said Mrs Bourke one day – she was just the same placid, gentle little woman, only a trifle more worried and tired-looking – 'really I don't know how you can exist up in Donegal if it is as bad as you say. Who or what takes the place of all your admirers? How do you live without them?'

Carmen laughed.

'They never cost me a thought!' she said – which was absolutely true. 'When they are here and always running after me I let them do it, and I amuse myself with them. Why not? What else are they for?' She shrugged her shoulders, with one of her foreign gestures. 'But I don't care a continental cent for any single one of the lot of them! And they know it, too – poor fools!' she snapped her fingers contemptuously.

'Dear me! Carmen, you are very like your mother!' was Mrs Bourke's reply, as she spread jam on the twin's slices of bread. It was their early tea hour, and they were seated at the diningroom table, demolishing huge 'door steps', big boys of eight now, and more like their father than ever in appearance, but with a certain amount of their mother's good disposition to counteract the paternal element. They had, however, most certainly inherited their father's appetite.

'Yes, you are very like your mother,' continued Mrs Bourke, 'and with all her charms and fascinations, and I often *do* wonder how in the world you stay up there.' She always spoke of Donegal as of some inaccessible spot perched on the top of huge mountains, or even in the very clouds, so far away did it seem to her Dublin mind – 'with no one except the Adairs to speak to. No, Vinny, I really will *not* give you a fourth cup. Hurry now and get to your lessons!'

'*Up there!*' repeated Carmen, with a laugh. 'One would think I was inhabiting the mountains of the moon! Not indeed that I could be any further away from civilisation if I was in that planet! For all I know, I might be a lot better off there than I am in Donegal.'

'Well, as I said before,' replied her cousin, 'I don't know what keeps you there – except it is that child – you must be perfectly devoted to her.'

'Yes, it's Peg,' said Carmen. 'And I *am* devoted to her, Cis – I don't know what I would do without her!'

'I never thought you would get so fond of a child,' said Mrs Bourke, 'and it's rather a mistake, you know, Carmen. Suppose Dr Adair left Carragh for another district, which he may do any day, for I'm sure he is too good a doctor to stay there all his life – or the child might die; with children one never knows –'

But Carmen interrupted her fiercely.

'Don't! Don't say it!' she cried. 'Oh Cis! I often dread that myself. *Dread* it and wonder what I would do if anything did happen to her! I simply can't bear to think of it!'

'Oh well, don't!' said the other cheerfully. 'You have had more than enough of tragedy lately – and here's Phil! Aren't you going down to Bray this evening?'

Carmen was consulted by all the members of the family about Letty's idea of going to Canada. Of course she was dead against it, but she frankly acknowledged that it was from reasons of pure selfishness on her part.

'For it might be good for the rest of you,' she admitted, 'but I would be left so lonely then without a home in dear old Dublin where I could come! What would I do at all?'

'Come with us, Carmen, of course!' cried Eileen.

'The very place for your profession,' said Letty, 'you would be sure to do well.'

'*Marry me* and come out as Mrs Hewson!' whispered Phil, as he leant over her chair.

But Carmen saw a childish face, with serious, hazel eyes, and heard a little voice saying, *'Don't porget Peg!'* and she shook her head resolutely.

Of Cornelius Vincent Bourke she saw little, but his dulcet voice was often heard in corridor or passage, or haranguing poor old Sarah down in the basement. Sometimes they passed on the stairs or in the hall, when Carmen with eyes flashing and head erect, would sail by as though she saw him not, and he glancing at her out of his foxy little eyes, would mutter, 'Brazen Papist hussy!'

Marcella wrote very often, and there was always a long detailed message from Peg – quaint, serious little messages assuring Carmen that she (Peg) would 'write in the morning!'

The girl sent her parcels with lavish generosity. Of course, Carmen never had a penny to put by out of her salary at any time – money always melted in her hands and left her often wondering *where* it could have gone to! Dolls, boxes of chocolate, and tea sets, all found their way to Donegal just now; indeed, hardly a day passed that she did not remember the child in some way – if only by a picture postcard. And Marcella told how the wee lady would be at the garden gate every day, watching anxiously and in growing excitement for the advent of 'Johnny the Post.'

'For Miss Peggy Adair,' he would read carefully as he handed the parcel or postcard, and 'Por Miss Peggy 'Dair!' she would repeat complacently in her quaint tones, as her fat legs carried her back to the house – her treasure hugged tightly in her arms.

Carmen had been ten days in Dublin when she got a letter from Marcella which filled her with vague fears.

'You will be sorry to hear,' it said, 'that Peg does not seem to be as well as usual these last few days. She is tired and languid, not a bit like herself, and last night she had a slight temperature. I hope it won't signify – and don't suppose it will really. Allan seems more anxious than I am – but he is worried in every way now and very hard worked on account of an outbreak of diphtheria in some of the houses in Dr Murray's district – you know what terrible hovels they are! The poor boy's successor is not here yet, although he has been appointed, and so Allan has still to do *locum*. But the other is expected in a few days, and Allan says you are not to worry about the work, as he is well able for it – indeed he did not want me to mention anything about it, but somehow I felt I must tell you about Peg. Of course we are taking every care about disinfection – Allan is doing all he can that way, both for himself and in the infected houses. But *you* know how hard that is here! They simply do not or *cannot* understand the necessity for such steps. Still we are hoping to be able to stamp it under before it spreads. Now, don't worry, but just enjoy your last few days of holidays. I will write daily and let you know about Peg; she sends her dearest love of kisses to "dear Tarmen" and told me twice to tell you *not to porget Peg!'*

But Carmen's face was white and strained before she came to the end of the letter.

'Diphtheria – and *Peg!'* she thought. 'What if it should be that – with Allan going into the infection daily! Oh! How careless they are! And Marcella drives me mad with her easy-going optimism!'

She flew to Mrs Bourke with the letter, and of course that lady promptly pooh-poohed all her fears and dread.

'You are always in one extreme or the other, Carmen,' she said, 'either up in the seventh heaven or down in the lowest depths! And here you are meeting trouble halfway. The child will be all right – it's probably the hot weather coming on – that always upsets children. If you worry you will take all the good out of your holiday.'

'Oh, but Cis,' said the girl miserably. 'I have a feeling, a presentiment ...'

'Oh, for Heaven's sake!' cried the other, 'don't – *don't* start your presentiments and visions again! They – they always bring bad luck!'

'Well, but I can't help having them!' said Carmen, staring white-faced and haggard in front of her and seeing nothing of the objects around her, 'and now I *know* that I'm going to have bad news, and that soon!'

'Anyway you certainly are enough to bring it upon yourself, going on in that fashion!' replied Mrs Bourke in tones which for her were very curt. But, like some others, she knew and dreaded Carmen's 'presentiments!'

And Carmen was not to be cheered; indeed her anxiety only increased as the day passed, and that night she hardly slept at all – always before her was the beloved little face, and always in her ears rang the sweet treble – 'Don't porget Peg!'

The next morning about 10 o'clock she was sitting in the dining-room with Mrs Bourke; the remains of her late breakfast were still on the table, but she had really eaten nothing, only drank her tea feverishly, and now she was idly staring at the tea leaves in the bottom of her cup – tossing and turning them from time to time.

Mrs Bourke looked at her and smiled, trying to veil her real anxiety for the girl, who was looking so haggard and wan after her sleepless night.

'Well, Carmen,' she said, 'What do you see? Something good I hope.'

There was no answer immediately. Carmen was still gazing fixedly into her cup. Then she said in a queer voice, 'No – nothing good, Cis. I see a sick bed – and Peg – and danger!'

'What nonsense!' cried the other. 'I wonder you can be so foolish, Carmen – and so superstitious! You are worrying yourself ill over the child – you have got her on your brain! And probably by now she is all right – in fact, she's sure to be, because if she had been worse you would certainly have had a letter this morning, and the post has gone long ago. So cheer up now and –'

She stopped suddenly as she heard the click of the front gate, and, looking through the window, saw a telegraph boy coming up the steps.

VIII

THE FIGHT FOR A LIFE

'Peg want Tarmen! – Peg want Tarmen! – Peg want gay!'

Over and over, all through the long, interminable night, had the little restless being, tossing ceaselessly in her cot, called for these two things. The drink was held to her lips whenever she asked it – and often when she did not – but the pain of swallowing was so great that it would be pushed away with a look of frightened surprise. Why was it that she could not enjoy a drink when she was thirsty? Oh so thirsty! – wondered the child mind in perplexity. But the other – Carmen – never came, although she had called and called. In some vague way it seemed to her that surely Carmen – her dear Carmen – would make her better. No one else seemed able to do it – not Mammy or even Daddy – Daddy who made everyone else better! And so the husky, cracked little voice, hardly above a whisper now, still cried for 'Tarmen! Tarmen!' and once Marcella, bending over the cot in an agony of anxiety, heard the baby lips whisper, as if in reproach, the words that they had spoken to Carmen when she was going to Dublin – *'Don't porget Peg.'*

She straightened herself suddenly, and looked across the cot at Allan, standing haggard and weary, after the night's vigil.

'We must send for Carmen,' she said.

'I'll wire as soon as the office opens,' he assented, and his gaze went back to the little being they loved so well.

'I wish we had sent for her yesterday,' said Marcella, 'before the change for the worse came. Even if she can do no more than has been done – and we know she can't – still – still when Peg wants her.'

Her voice broke and she turned away. Allan put his arms round her and she buried her face in his rough tweed to hide its working even from him. She must keep up ... oh she must keep up, for his sake. Poor Allan who had been working like a brick ever since this awful epidemic had started – working singlehanded and doing both his own district and that which had been Dr Murray's. The diphtheria had spread, in spite of all he could do, with fearful rapidity, and his own district was now infected as well as the one further away. The new Medical Officer for the latter place was expected daily, but in the meantime Dr Adair had been working day and night – literally so – for he had had hardly any sleep for the last few days, and all the time he was at work amidst the cases outside he was torn with anxiety about the precious little patient in his own house. Marcella was his right hand at this time. Their common trouble seemed, if possible, to bind them even more closely together, and the Doctor's one consolation when away from home was the remembrance of his wife. It was only the day before that Peg had developed really serious symptoms, but since then she had become worse very rapidly, with a high temperature and swollen throat, which, on examination, revealed the dreaded patches of false membrane on the tonsils. Allan Adair's hands shook slightly as he put down the spatula and turned to meet Marcella's frightened look – but he came of a fighting race, and although he felt that the odds were heavy against him, he still fought on and would so fight to the end. The epidemic had spread so quickly through the villages of Knockbeggan and Carragh that now there was scarcely a cabin without one or two sufferers. Some had the disease slightly – others were as bad as they possibly could be. Sanitation, except in some of the better houses in Carragh, was absolutely *nil* and it was a simple impossibility to get the inhabitants to understand the merest elements of hygiene or disinfection. As for isolation – it just could not be done.

Dr Adair had wired for a generous supply of antitoxin and for another medical man to help him, and also wired to Dr Hegarty, who had been appointed to Kilbeggan to come as soon as he could.

Only the night before the antitoxin had arrived, and he had been so thankful to get it. Peg had been given an injection, but no improvement had followed as yet – it only seemed to cause her more suffering – but he was hoping for better results later. All night he and Marcella had worked for the little one they loved so well – swabbing and spraying the throat, keeping the steam kettle going, coaxing her to take nourishment and necessary stimulants, and watching the heart's action so anxiously and carefully for the dreaded cardiac failure – and all the time they saw her becoming steadily worse.

And now it was morning, the cocks were crowing, the birds singing – it was six o'clock on a May morning, and all without seemed beautiful, all nature alive and happy. But within the room – and within many another near – hovered the dark shadow of the Reaper, who reaps where he will, not only amongst the bearded grain, but who mows down also 'the flowers that grow between' – little tender flowers that are twined so tightly around the hearts that love them.

The bedroom door opened and Ellen came in – tired, haggard, but loving and faithful Ellen.

'The tea is wet, Miss Marcella, darlint,' she said, reverting in her distress and sympathy to her old way of speaking. 'Will yourself and the Doctor go down and try and take a bit of breakfast – and let me stay here for a while?'

'Yes, Allan, you must eat. You have a hard day before you,' said Marcella; and then to Ellen. 'We won't be long, try and get her to take a little drink now and then, that's all.'

By eight o'clock Allan had got his wire off to Carmen, and had wired again for another medical man to help him. Then, with a plentiful supply of antitoxin, he set out on his rounds. For six hours he worked like a galley slave, going from cabin to cabin, opening windows, swabbing throats, pouring in nourishment and talking, talking, explaining over and over again to these people what they were to do and what they were not to do. And in all cases, where he was allowed, giving the anti-toxin, but in very many cases it was refused. Oh, the difficulty, the sickening uselessness, of trying to cope with and to fight against the ingrained ignorance and prejudices of a primitive people. It is a gigantic and wearing task, and Allan Adair, dead tired physically and torn with anxiety about Peg, was pretty well fagged out when at last, just about three o'clock, he once more turned in at his own gate.

The front door was open, and he went straight upstairs. Marcella had heard his footsteps and met him at the threshold; he had only to look into her eyes to know that there was no improvement – he could read the verdict there even before he stood at the cot and bent down over the precious little body within it. Ah! Is there anything one feels more than to stand by the bedside of a loved one and not to be able to relieve their pain – to *know* that we can do no more than we have done. This fact can only be truly realised by nurses and doctors – the laity never realise it, for how often we hear distracted relatives crying again and again, 'Can you do *nothing* more, Doctor? Is there *nothing* else you can try?' But we of the profession know when we are at the end of our resources, and although we never give up the fight, although we still keep on doing all we can, we know well that the issue now is not in our hands. Poor Peg o' My Heart! Is this restless, moaning little being, with the dusky face and pain-encircled eyes, with the poor swollen throat, the tossed damp curls – is this the gay, sweet toddler of a few short days ago, the little ray of sunshine who was always so sorry for other people's troubles, always so anxious to lavish sympathy and to offer all the love of her tiny heart if it would do any good? How often when Marcella had had a headache had the sweet little lips been pressed to hers and the quaint tones whispered, 'Peg make 'oo better wiv a kiss!'

And now Peg herself is sick – so sick – and perhaps she is wondering vaguely in her poor little fevered brain why no one can make *her* better. But she is not speaking at all now – no sound comes from the parched lips. It takes her all her time to breathe.

'A wire came from Carmen,' said Marcella, 'she will arrive at Kilbeg about ten tonight. I have arranged for Dan Sweeney's car to meet her there. I suppose it will be midnight by the time she gets here.'

'No news of another medico?' asked Allan, dropping wearily into a chair.

'No, none. It does seem a shame!' she replied. 'You will never be able to keep it up, Allan. You must be worn out even now! Go down and get your dinner. Ellen has it all ready.'

'And you, sweetheart?'

'I? Oh, I had mine long ago!'

'Are you sure? Keep up your strength if you can, old girl, for the sake of Peg – and of your poor hubby too!'

'Don't worry, dear boy,' she said, speaking as bravely as she could. 'I'll look after myself! Go now and get something to eat, and then lie down for a few hours – you simply *must* or you will collapse.'

He did as she wished, for he knew that he could not afford to drop out of the ranks just then – too much depended on him. But he wished intensely that another medical man might arrive soon, and so set him at liberty to devote himself more closely to Peg, and also to rest a little, for he began to feel that the strain was too much for him.

But rest was not to be had yet. Dr Adair was only lying down half an hour when two urgent messages came for him – and both cases were in the same direction – some miles, too, outside the village. Both messengers affirmed that the patients were very bad – 'very bad entirely, and would the doctor come quickly, for the love of God!'

There was no choice in the matter, and Marcella went to waken him; but when she stood for a moment at his bedside, looking down at his tired, haggard face while he slept the sleep of exhaustion, she felt it bitterly hard that she should have to do so.

He started up when she touched him.

'Peg?' he asked at once – showing where his thoughts were.

'No,' she answered, 'it's a call – two indeed – and, oh Allan, poor old boy – they are both away over in Glen-na-Sheena.'

'Good Lord!' he groaned. 'Nine miles beyond the village, and such a road! And if Peg should get worse, I'll be hours away.'

'Don't, dear,' she replied, 'don't imagine the worst. I'll do my best with her, and you *must* go! There is no one else.'

No, there was no one else, and although he knew himself, and his wife knew too, that he was really physically unfit, still it was his duty. And so he went, grumbling and swearing a bit while he pulled himself together; slipping in to take a last look at Peg while his man brought round the car.

There was no change in her. He was not sure whether she knew him or not – she gave no sign. Marcella was by the car, seeing to his rugs and big overcoats, for the nights were still chilly.

'There's a packet of sandwiches in your pocket,' she said, 'and coffee in the thermos. Do use them, dear, and – and don't be longer than you can help!'

He forced a smile to his tired lips.

'I'll be as quick as I possibly can, sweetheart,' he said.

She flung her arms round him and kissed him passionately; how gladly she would have gone in his stead and saved him if she could!

Her heart was bitter within her as she watched him start off on his long drive, knowing how unfit he was to cope with more work just then. But Allan squared his shoulders and drove steadily off – it was his duty, and he must do it.

There is many another country dispensary doctor doing the same kind of thing day and night all over Ireland and getting little in the way of either thanks or pay in return. As far as they are concerned the world seems to think that virtue is its own reward.

The train in which Carmen Cavanagh travelled reached Strabane at eight o'clock that evening. Here she had to change into the miserable, slow 'local' which would probably reach Kilbeg between nine and ten; and from there she would have a drive of ten miles to Carragh.

It had turned out a wet night, misty and cold, and Carmen shivered as she walked up and down the platform waiting for the Kilbeg train. It came at last, however, and the guard, who was a Carragh man and knew Carmen – she having attended his wife – came up to her and put her into a first class carriage. She thanked him listlessly, caring little how she travelled, for her mental suffering was so acute that it dimmed all physical discomfort. One idea, one thought alone, filled her mind to the exclusion of all else and she remained immovable after the guard had left, staring straight in front of her, with her big eyes full of brooding misery and doubt.

How was it with Peg? If she only knew. If she only knew! There was one other passenger in the carriage with her, but she did not even see him – a tall, well-groomed man, with all the impedimenta of a first-class; rugs and wraps and heaps of magazines were strewn on the seat beside him. His gaze had been attracted to Carmen the moment she had entered his carriage, for he had recognised her at once as 'the girl with the black eyes' as he had mentally dubbed her, on the day when she had sprung so suddenly upon his tired vision in the little Donegal village where he had come for pure air and rest and peace – none of which had been attributes of his London existence lately.

But what had changed the girl? Some big trouble evidently. His trained eye saw at once that she was suffering from a mental strain – an anxiety of mind which obsessed her to the exclusion of all else.

For a few moments he observed her in silence, while she still remained totally oblivious of his presence.

'Excuse me, won't you,' he said then, in his most winning voice – and those who knew Victor Walpole always affirmed that his voice was one of his greatest charms – and he had many others – 'won't you take one of these rugs? The night is chilly and I think you would find it comfortable.'

Even as he spoke he was deftly wrapping it round her. Carmen raised her eyes to thank him, rather wearily, and then she looked again, roused for the moment out of her misery.

'Thank you,' she said. 'I – I think I have seen you before?'

He smiled delightedly, glad to see that she remembered. 'Why, yes!' he replied. 'I had the pleasure of seeing you twice at Carragh. I suppose you are returning there now?'

The shadow came back to her face.

'I don't live at Carragh,' she said dully, 'but I'm going there now.'

The man hesitated for a moment, and then boldly took the bull by the horns.

'Forgive me, won't you?' he said, 'but I'm a medical man and I can see that you are suffering in some way. Could I be of any use? If so ...'

'Oh, *I'm* all right!' cried the girl. 'It's Peg – Peg!'

Her lips trembled and he turned away, feigning to arrange his rug, while she fought for composure.

Presently he spoke again.

'And Peg?' he asked. 'She is a friend of yours, I suppose?'

'A *friend!*' repeated Carmen. 'Why, she's just *Peg!* Peg o' My Heart – and all the world to me!'

'Well now! Just tell me all about her, won't you? While this express walks along the rails – and you will find that you will bear your anxiety better by sharing with someone else.'

And so Carmen told him all, and was surprised in a vague sort of way to find herself talking so freely to this handsome, well-groomed stranger, with the keen grey eyes. She described her work at Glenmore, her friendship with the Adairs – all about Peg, of course! – Dr Murray's suicide, and the shock it had been to her, her holiday in Dublin, and the fateful wire of the early morning which was bringing her back as fast as possible to her child friend.

Mr Walpole – he was an F.R.C.S. – listened with intense interest, and when she had finished speaking, he said, 'I'm awfully glad that you have told me all this, for I'm rather a dab at throats, you know – in fact, that's my special line and I'm very keen on it. So if you've no objection – and I think in a case of this kind that we may certainly waive all ceremony! – I will come with you tonight and have a talk with Dr Adair, who perhaps will allow me to see the little one.'

'Oh, thank you so much!' cried Carmen. 'Of course Allan will be delighted! He must be nearly done up with this terrible epidemic, and then the anxiety about Peg as well!'

They arrived at Kilbeg about 9.30, and Victor Walpole insisted on Carmen going into the hotel and having a cup of tea before they both mounted the waiting car and started on their ten miles' drive to Carragh.

That same night, about an hour later, Allan Adair reached his home again, physically fagged – every muscle in his body aching. He had seen his two cases and found them both rather bad, and had been called in *en route* to several others, and had found a 'wake' in progress in one house where the patient – a very bad case – had died on the previous day! The cabin was crammed to the door – the only means of ventilation – and the atmosphere was indescribable. He stormed into the midst of them and said all that he could to try and get them to understand the criminal risk they were running: but even as he talked he knew that he might as well preach to the Atlantic below. Yes, it was a very weary man who stumbled up his garden path later in the night, with one desire and wish left to him – that he could sleep.

There is probably nothing harder to fight against than the want of sleep when we have gone without it for a certain time. Some of us can go longer than others, but there comes a limit to everyone's endurance, and then nothing seems to matter in heaven above or earth beneath but just to lie down anyway – anywhere – and *sleep.*

And so to Allan just then even the thought of Peg seemed, through sheer physical weariness, to have become fainter, and even to climb the stairs appeared a tremendous task. So he went straight into Marcella's pretty sitting room at the back of the house and flung himself wearily into an armchair; he knew that she would hear him and come to him at once – as she did. But the moment he caught sight of her face he sprang from his seat – weariness and self forgotten, vividly alive again in mind and body – at the something he read there.

'Peg?' he breathed rather than spoke.

She nodded her head; it almost seemed that she could not speak. Then she was beside him twisting the lapels of his coat in her two hands – almost shaking him in frantic anguish.

'Allan! – Allan!' she said, in a strained, unnatural voice. 'She's dying – she's dying. Oh come – come!'

In two strides he was up the stairs, bending over the cot, and the picture he saw there told him all.

The pitiful drawn little face, so dusky now in hue; the difficult, difficult little breaths – each one costing the poor wee body such an infinity of labour – the restless hands – Peg's pretty little hands – beating the coverlet as though searching for air – air.

Such was Peg – Peg o' His Heart – as he stooped and looked at her.

Raising his eyes they met those of his wife.

'*Well!*' she breathed.

He straightened himself slowly.

'There's only one chance,' he said then.

'You mean?' but even as she questioned he saw that she knew.

'Yes,' he said. 'I mean tracheotomy. There's nothing else can help her – now.'

She came to his side and he put his arms around her, and together they looked silently at the little daughter who had made the sunshine of their lives ever since she had come, like 'a smile of God' to their home.

Allan spoke then, his tones curt to keep his voice steady. 'There's not a moment to spare, sweetheart – we must hurry if it is to be done – in time!'

'And you – you will do it, Allan?'

He seemed to stand suddenly very firm and erect as he answered his wife.

'Yes,' he said. 'I will, with God's help – and your help too, sweetheart! You won't fail me now. I know. Oh darling, don't think that I don't know what it is that I have to ask you to face! But we must do it together for Peg's sake!'

Perhaps into the minds of both of them may have flashed memories of their hospital life, when a 'trachey' was a joy to see – so exciting, so quick, such a delightful bit of surgery to witness! And Marcella suddenly recollected a pretty fair-haired child, a 'trachey' in her ward, and how casually and rather abruptly she had spoken to the anxious-eyed mother, seated in dumb anguish on a bench in the ward corridor. 'Oh, she'll be all right, Missis! Don't you worry – why it's nothing!'

Nothing! Ah! dear God! but it was *something* now when she was in the mother's place. But she must face it – she *must.* She and Allan: there were only the two of them – and God.

'I'll get the instruments ready, Allan,' she said, trying to keep the tremor from her voice. 'There is hot coffee in the kitchen; Ellen has it ready; drink some and I will see to the rest.'

She left the room, walking as in a dream down the passage to the surgery, and over and over again she was repeating to herself. 'It's a patient, an ordinary patient, and Allan has asked me to help him. That's all! I don't *know* the patient – it's a stranger and I'm to help Allan.'

She opened the instrument case and with steady fingers selected the necessary instruments. Tracheotomy tubes and dilators, hooks and forceps, scissors, needles, sutures, ligatures.

'Anything else?' she muttered. 'Ah, yes, of course! Spencer Wells' forceps and some retractors.'

Often in happy days – how far away they seemed now, far, far out of reach, she had laughed at her husband for keeping such a complete set of instruments in a little country dispensary, and he had answered in his characteristic style. 'One never knows what might turn up even here, sweetheart, and I should never forgive myself then if I had not everything that was needed for saving life.'

How thankful she would have been now if this operation had been on anyone she knew – on – on Peg, for instance! But it was a stranger – only a patient of Allan's, and she was to help. Oh, she must remember that.

Calmly she filled the steriliser and put it on to boil and got swabs and lotions ready, thinking of everything as though the trained brain of her nursing years was acting subconsciously, and always trying to get that brain to think of 'the patient' – never for one moment allowing herself to realise that it was Peg – *her* Peg! Then she slipped on a big linen overall and was ready for Allan.

He had swallowed some coffee hastily, and was now scrubbing up his hands. Not a sign of lassitude or worriness was to be seen; except for a certain tense look on his face. He was the keen surgeon to his very finger tips – those typically surgical fingers which Marcella so admired.

Quietly, but quickly, all was made ready by the cot side, and they stood ready to begin – always avoiding one another's eyes and never speaking about Peg; she was the 'patient' and they were back in hospital again.

Ah, well! It was a gallant make-believe!

'I'll just give her a whiff,' said Allan. 'Give me the mask. A few drops will do, and you will have to swab and hold the retractors.'

Tracheotomy is a very quick operation, and in a very short space of time it was all over. Allan's skilful fingers had never faltered for an instant, and Marcella had stood quietly holding the retractors, and swabbing when necessary, as coolly as she had ever done in her hospital days.

And their reward? Surely it was worth it all to see the sudden change of colour in the little face, the dusky purple hue giving place to a more natural look, and the laboured breathing becoming easier every moment. Almost before the tube was fixed in position the child was a different being.

Neither Allan nor Marcella spoke a word until they had deftly cleared away the instruments and dirty lotions and arranged on a convenient table all that would be necessary for the night; then they turned towards the cot again.

Peg was quietly sleeping.

Almost at the same moment they heard the sound of a car stopping at the gate.

'That will be Carmen,' said Marcella. 'I'll go and meet her.'

But, turning to leave the room, she suddenly found that she was going down – down into darkness and space, and Allan was just in time to catch her before she fell.

IX

PARTED

In the early dawn, Peg o' My Heart opened her eyes and looked about her – very tired and weak, poor wee mortal, but much better in every way. Her cot was still surrounded by curtains, and the steam kettle was singing away. Her throat felt very funny, and she was just wondering if she could call for Mammy when her curtains parted and someone who must have been sitting near rose and bent over her. It was her beloved Carmen – a white-faced but shining-eyed Carmen – who held a feeding cup to Peg's lips and talked so softly and tenderly while coaxing her to have a drink.

'No, ducksie, you mustn't talk! Your poor throat is sore still. Drink this now for Carmen, won't you? Poor Mammy is asleep, she was so tired minding Peg, and Daddy, too, is gone to bed. But they will soon be back again, and Carmen will be here all the time, and never leave her little ducksie any more.'

So the girl spoke – all the love of her heart in her eyes, anticipating every detail about which the little one would want to know, as only one who understood children could have done. A ghost of a smile hovered round the little lips, and a whisper of 'Tarmen' was just faintly breathed, and then Peg was sleeping again.

'Oh she's better! She's better!' said the girl softly and looked across at the man who was standing at the window watching her.

'Oh decidedly so!' he assented smilingly. 'I should think she has a very good chance now. What a splendid type of man Adair seems to be! Not one in a hundred would have faced such a job with his own child. The mother, too! She's quite wonderful!'

'Oh yes, they are splendid in every way,' replied Carmen, as she left the sleeping child and came over to the window, where she stood gazing absently down on the village street – so grey and desolate in the light of early dawn. 'And Allan has had such a time this last week!' she continued. 'I can never really forgive him for not sending for me sooner! And no other doctor to give him a hand – no wonder he looks so completely worn out!'

'Well! I'm rather glad that I took the notion to return here for another week or so, and to leave my relatives in Derry,' said Victor Walpole. 'I can at least give him some assistance until the epidemic blows over.'

'Oh, that is kind of you!' cried Carmen, 'but it does not seem right to make you work when you are here for a holiday!'

'Ah! well,' replied the other, 'I really think, you know, that complete change of scene and manner of life is a holiday in itself; and then I have been idle for two weeks as it is. But I am surprised that Adair does not pack all these cases off to hospital! The idea of trying to treat them in their own homes seems absurd.'

'It's more absurd to talk of sending them to hospital!' flashed back Carmen. 'Now just think of the journey! Some of them live twenty to forty miles from the railway, and, once in the train, they have several hours still. Why, they would not be able for it even if there was no risk of infection to other people! You forget where you are, Mr Walpole, and imagine that you are still in London and have only to telephone for the ambulance.'

He smiled in a rather shame-faced manner.

'That's perfectly true,' he admitted. 'For the moment I had really forgotten the conditions of life here.'

'Well,' said Carmen, 'just try if you can and imagine what poor Allan has gone through since this thing began! And the people are so ignorant about such matters; they haven't the faintest notion of how to treat such a case – and worse still, they won't do as we tell them, but will put more faith in some silly charm from a wise woman than in anything we do for them.'

'Yes,' replied the London surgeon, 'they seem to be terribly ignorant; it's really marvellous that in a country which is so near England – within such a short distance of the very centre of civilisation – there should be such a deplorable amount of ignorance and superstition.'

For a moment Carmen stood silent, gazing at him as though she could not believe that she had heard him right. That she should criticise the people around appeared to her quite justifiable, but that this stranger, this Englishman, should dare to disparage her country and its people – that he should speak of their ignorance and superstition in his would-be superior manner – *that* was more than Carmen's Irish-Spanish blood could bear. So, to Victor Walpole's infinite surprise and dismay, he found himself confronting her flashing eyes and flushed cheeks and being compelled to listen to some home truths to which he was quite unaccustomed.

'And you can talk like this!' she cried. 'You! You!' with furious emphasis. 'An Englishman like you! One of that race who has kept our unfortunate people in ignorance and slavery for hundreds of years! Whose fault is it that our people are ignorant? Who forbade them to learn – but forbade them in vain! Why had we to have hedge schools and schoolmasters so that our people might learn in secret? Who kept all the means of learning as much as possible from us? Who destroyed our trades and industries? Who persecuted us to the death under the Penal Laws? Who overtaxes and oppresses us to the present day? Who ...'

'Carmen!' Marcella was standing in the room, having entered unperceived. 'Carmen! What is the matter?'

But Carmen had eyes only for the unfortunate Saxon, who was regarding her in stupefied amazement.

'Do you want to hear more?' she demanded. 'You, with your English hypocrisy and would-be friendliness! We know too well in Ireland what the smile of an Englishman means! Oh!' with a sudden contemptuous gesture, 'for pity's sake go! Before I wake Peg!'

And Victor Walpole, with a half-vexed, half-amused glance at Mrs Adair, departed downstairs.

'Oh Carmen! How could you speak like that to him?' exclaimed Marcella in real distress, 'he has been so kind, sitting up all night with Peg, and then he is a stranger and a guest!'

Carmen looked a little ashamed of herself, as she met her friend's accusing glance.

'I shouldn't have spoken like that, I know, Marcella,' she admitted, 'and in your house, too. But he ... oh he annoyed me, and you know what a temper I have! But it was wrong of me, especially now – when I should be so thankful about Peg and not be thinking of anything else!' For she would not admit to Marcella – or even to her own heart – that she was already thinking too much about the English surgeon, and had in some queer way felt almost glad of an excuse to try and dislike him,

Peg got better every day; it was a joy unspeakable to those who loved her to watch the little one becoming more and more like her own self, and Marcella's heart would have been overflowing with thankfulness but for a terrible anxiety and fear which oppressed her just now about Allan. Dr Hegarty had arrived the day after Carmen – to whom, by the way, he immediately fell a victim! – and had volunteered to work both his own district and Dr Adair's until the latter should feel in good form again after a rest; and Victor Walpole had offered his services also as helper – he really wished to help Allan, for whom he felt a very real regard, and also he knew that such work in Donegal would prove an interesting and unique experience.

So Dr Adair had had a complete rest since the night of Peg's operation, and yet he had not recovered his old energy – but, on the contrary, seemed to become weaker and more languid every day, and in a week's time he was a patient himself. From the very first those who watched him felt very anxious; he had no acute throat symptoms like Peg, but the infection seemed to poison his whole system, and he was totally unable to rally from the terrible weakness.

It seemed to Marcella that she was living in some strange dream from which there appeared to be no awakening, and yet she did not realise that Allan would not recover – even when he was actually sinking she still thought that he would rally. And those who knew better hesitated to tell her.

Those were strange, sad days in the pretty house in Carragh village. Peg was not able to be up yet, although getting stronger every day, and she still remained in her cot in the pleasant front bedroom, which had also been her parents. But she never saw Daddy now. Carmen told her that he was sleeping in the spare room – and poor Mammy very seldom came to bed! So Peg sometimes felt a bit lonely, in spite of Carmen being so attentive; and then one day Mammy's Aunt Mary from Dublin arrived, and installed herself as Peg's chief attendant, and from that day she saw less of Carmen. But by now the child understood that her Daddy was sick, and, like the good wee mortal that she was, gave little trouble.

And so the long days passed, and there came an evening when Carmen and the two doctors stood together in the sitting room – Marcella being upstairs in the sickroom.

'And you are sure – you really think that there is no hope?' asked Carmen.

Both nodded silently, their faces showing their real regret for the man whose life was ebbing so surely and quickly away.

'Marcella doesn't understand,' said Carmen. 'She thinks he will get better. Oh what will we do? Who will tell her?'

'Perhaps the minister?' suggested Dr Hegarty.

'Mr Harris?' said Carmen. 'Allan never cared for him – he's a cold, rather pompous man. But of course if you think I should send for him,' she turned inquiringly to the Englishman. 'Dr Hegarty and I are Catholics,' she said, 'and we are not very certain whether Protestants always wish to have their minister at such a time. But you will know, of course. What would you advise?'

Victor Walpole shrugged his shoulders.

'I'm afraid that I am hardly a competent judge,' he said. 'I don't profess to hold any definite religious opinions – Protestant or otherwise. I am not in the least what is called orthodox. You see,' noting the surprised faces of the other two, 'with us in London religion really hardly counts – but here, I must say, it appears to be a very definite factor. However, as I don't know anything about poor Adair's opinions, I can't very well advise in this case.'

Before the others could answer him, Marcella entered the room, coming in as quietly and composedly as usual, and they looked at her in silence, wondering how much she knew or realised about her husband's condition.

She went over to the window and stood looking out for a moment: then she turned to the two men.

'You think him worse?' she asked.

There was a momentary pause, and then Victor Walpole answered her very gently.

'Yes, I'm sorry, Mrs Adair, but we certainly consider that your husband is very – is dangerously ill.'

Marcella said nothing; her face hardly changed in expression, and those watching her instantly knew that she did not realise what it meant – that she was, in fact, incapable of doing so.

Carmen moved rather timidly to her side.

'We were wondering, Cella,' she said, 'whether you would care to have Mr Harris come and see Allan?'

'Mr Harris?' repeated Marcella dully. 'Oh – the minister? No, I don't think so, Carmen. What good would it be? What could he do?'

'Still at a time like this,' hazarded Dr Hegarty, and Carmen added. 'Perhaps Allan would like to see him, Cella – wouldn't you ask him?'

'Oh very well, if you wish it – if you think I should,' replied Marcella in the same dull, weary tones, and she left the room even as she spoke. Carmen and Dr Hegarty looked at one another, the bond of their common Catholicity drawing them together, for neither of them could help thinking of the contrast between Marcella's attitude and that of a Catholic woman in the same circumstances.

But it was the stranger who voiced their thoughts.

'She takes it rather differently from the Catholic way,' he said, as he gazed meditatively at his cigarette. 'Good Lord, but I have got a few surprises about religion since I have been working here! Right or wrong, good or bad, they *believe* in their religion – absolutely! And as for their priest – that Fr McGinley – if ever a man was a hero he is one! There's not a house in his parish – and just think of what that word means here, miles and miles of bog and mountain – that he has not visited. Why, he must live on his bicycle! I meet him at all hours, day and night – he never seems to tire or grow wearied – a most extraordinary man! I ventured to suggest to him yesterday that he should take a rest, he looked so fagged, but he turned on me quite curtly and as good as told me to mind my own business. He doesn't seem to care for me, but I simply have to admire him, and you people must be jolly proud of him!'

Dr Hegarty raised his eyebrows in some bewilderment, and Carmen shrugged her shoulders impatiently.

'But he's the priest,' said the former, 'and of course he must visit the people.'

'Why, yes, of course,' echoed Carmen, 'there's nothing special in what he's doing – it's his work, and any priest would do the same.'

There was a knock at the door, and Ellen entered.

'The mistress says will you go upstairs – the master is awake,' she said.

Allan Adair was lying very quietly – the fatal quietness of weakness – in the bed in the spare room, which had been his sick room now for nearly a fortnight. Marcella, who was seated in a low chair beside him, holding his hands, looked up as they entered.

'He has just awakened,' she said, 'would you' – glancing at Walpole – 'speak to him about what you mentioned to me?'

The English surgeon came over to the bed and placed his fingers on the poor, thready pulse.

'Well, old man,' he said, 'and how do you feel now?'

'Oh, not too bad, only rather weak,' was the husky answer.

'Yes, you, you are not getting very strong, are you?' went on the other, clearing his throat and wishing that he had any other task to face except this one. 'We were wondering if – if you would care to see a – minister?'

There was a moment's silence. Marcella listened absently to a bee which had found its way into the room and was noisily buzzing and beating against the window, and from the room across the landing she heard Peg's gay little voice talking to her Aunt Mary.

'When Peg's better she will pull powers for poor Daddy!'

The thin, hot hand within her own suddenly became rigid and tense, and then it relaxed again, and he spoke.

'So I am going to peg out?' he said quietly. 'Well, I've been partly thinking as much myself – you've only confirmed my diagnosis!' and the ghost of his old gay smile hovered round the blue lips.

He turned to his wife and met her quiet, calm eyes, with the same look of constant love within their depths.

'Not now! Not now!' was the prayer of her poor heart – 'Not now! Must he see my agony – my sorrow!'

'I must talk to you, sweetheart,' he said, and looked at the others.

'But about the minister?' asked Dr Hegarty, hating to worry the sick man, but honestly believing that he was doing his duty in reminding him, so to speak, of his spiritual state.

Carmen was beyond words of any kind – standing at the door, her big eyes full of misery, she seemed the very picture of grief.

'Ah yes, the minister,' repeated Allan, wearily. 'I don't think we will trouble him. Don't send for him – what good could he do for me? If I am to face my God soon, well, He knows that I always tried to do my duty, and I am content for Him to judge me.'

His eyes turned to Marcella again.

'We have only a short time now, sweetheart,' he said, 'and there is a lot to talk about.'

The others slipped from the room and left them alone together.

Allan died the next morning, just as the June sun was rising over Slieve-na-Carragh.

The sick room was very quiet; the two medical men were standing at the window; Carmen was on her knees beside a chair at the foot of the bed, her rosary beads in her hand trying to pray, while Marcella was still beside the bed clasping the beloved hands in hers, as though she would fain give to him some of her own health and life. A stray sunbeam found its way to the dying man's pillow and roused him from the stupor in which he had lain for some hours now.

He stirred a little and tried to raise his head. 'Why! – it's morning,' he said faintly. 'Are you awake, sweetheart?'

She bowed her head on his hands, but could not answer.

'Morning,' he said again, 'And all those red ticket cases waiting! I must be off to my work. Goodbye, sweetheart.'

One hand strayed to her bent head and rested on her hair, but he never spoke again. Before the sun had risen much higher Allan Adair had gone to tell his Master that he had done his duty.

X

DRIFTING

On a very warm evening in early July, Marcella Adair stood in her dismantled and almost empty sitting room, helping Ellen to finish the packing of two large wooden cases which contained most of her books and some other of her household treasures. She was leaving Donegal in a few days, and having arranged for some of her heavier luggage to be sent on to Dublin in advance, these boxes, amongst others, had to be ready for Dan Sweeney early on the following morning. There are few experiences so harrowing as the breaking up of a home where one has been very happy – especially the home of a young couple starting life together and probably making many a sacrifice in order that the little house may be well and prettily furnished – the home where the first years of married love were spent, and where the first child was welcomed with such joy and hope. To Marcella, going about her work, dry-eyed and haggard-looking, every article around her had a definite meaning of its own – some tender associations known only to herself.

There was the big easy chair where Allan would sit of a winter's evening while she knelt on the hearth-rug beside him and listened to his day's experiences. She was not going to part with that chair – she could not.

Some of the furniture had been taken over with the house by Dr Adair's successor, but Marcella was keeping a good deal of it, her aunt having promised to store it for her until she was settled. She was going back to district work again to make a home for herself and Peg, for she had resolved not to touch the five hundred pounds for which poor Allan had been insured. That was to be set aside for Peg – on this point the child's mother was determined – and she had already written to her previous Superintendent asking to be given a district. Where she would be sent she did not as yet know – and cared little, but she was feverishly anxious to get away from Donegal, where everything, and every person, and every landmark spelt Allan – Allan – Allan.

Yes, there was the new carpet which Ellen had just taken from the drawing room and was beginning to roll up. Marcella followed it with her sad eyes, remembering how she and Allan had saved up for months to buy it at the carpet factory in Kilbeg. She would keep it, too; and the dinner service, for which she had saved out of the housekeeping money, and which had graced the dinner table as a surprise for Allan's last birthday. There were other more intimate reminders, too; the little bedroom table, on which she had been wont to have his supper things ready, when he was out late; the fender, where she would put his slippers to warm – she can almost see them there now; the pipe-rack hanging over the fireplace, with his favourite pipes.

All these inanimate objects were like separate knives piercing her to the heart, staring her so cruelly in the face, while he – *he* for whose sake she had loved them – was gone from her sight for ever. How her heart ached for him – ached with a constant, intolerable pain – with a hopeless agony of longing from which there was no relief – her days and nights being just one long misery for her widowed heart.

There are many types of widows, and the majority of them take their loss so lightly and as a rule console themselves so quickly that it almost makes one sceptical of married love. But now and then we meet such a woman as Marcella – one who is a widow indeed – and then there is borne in upon us the terrible suffering which is endured when two have really loved and have become one in thought and deed, when 'two have been one flesh' – and when one is taken and the other left. Tennyson's words have become very hackneyed through frequent repetition, but they still possess the power of expressing above all others the constant cry of the bereaved heart; and as Marcella Adair had gone about her lonely house during those last miserable days, the one longing of her soul had been just –

'For the touch of a vanished hand
And the sound of a voice that is still.'

It is a longing the poignancy of which we all know one time or another during our life – or if we don't know it, then we have only partly lived.

But Marcella's wound was too deep for outward expression – so deep was it that it had drained the life blood from her cheeks and the fountains from her eyes; and so while Ellen went about the sad work of packing and removing, with the tears streaming down her rugged cheeks, her young mistress was stony-faced and calm, staring at each beloved object with her tearless grey eyes – eyes which held such an infinity of misery within their depths.

Carmen Cavanagh was staying at Carragh for those last few days before Mrs Adair's departure, and she was standing now at the sitting room door, looking long and sadly at her beloved friend – unperceived by Marcella, who still continued her weary task of sorting and packing.

'I think we will find room for these cushions in that box, Ellen,' she was saying, as Carmen came across the room. The girl tried to assume a cheerful demeanour as she called out: 'Come along and have tea, Cella! Peg and I have carried it out to the garden – it's cooler there, and all is ready.'

'Very well, in a moment,' replied the other, and very shortly afterwards she followed Carmen into the garden behind the house where, under an old apple tree, the table was set.

Into the minds of both women flashed the remembrance of other summer evenings when tea had been spread in the same place – happy, gay times which seemed such centuries away now. Why, one evening only a few weeks ago – Marcella remembered it with sudden painful vividness – when she had been busy with her household work and Allan was out on a call, Carmen had come over from Glenmore and, with Peg's invaluable help, had arranged the tea like this under the old apple tree. Marcella had just been going to pour out when her quick ears caught the well-known sound of the doctor's horse and car coming down the road. She had paused, teapot in hand, to cry out, 'Oh now we can wait for Allan!' – and 'Wait for Daddy!' Peg had echoed, as she flew to meet him.

Only a few weeks ago, and now? Never again – never, never again – would she wait tea for Allan. It is just such little homely pinpricks that cause us the most pain. 'Pour out for me, Carmen,' she said, 'I'm – tired' and her lips tightened as she spoke.

'She might have said heart-sick and weary and been nearer the truth,' thought Carmen, adding aloud, 'Peg has had her tea – she was hungry, she said – and now she has gone for a walk with Jennie Gillespie. I thought it as well to let her go.'

'Yes, she's better out of the house these times,' assented Marcella, 'and she – Oh Carmen! – she makes it harder for me to bear I think!'

Carmen stared at her in astonishment.

'*Peg* makes it harder for you?' she repeated. 'Why Cella, what *do* you mean? Surely she is your comfort now – what would you do without her? Just picture it!'

'I know,' said the other, 'and yet, Carmen, I can hardly bear her near me now.'

She paused for a moment, staring in front of her, while Carmen gazed at her in bewilderment. There was silence between them for a few minutes, and then Carmen spoke. 'Well! I can't understand you, Cella,' she said. 'What *do* you mean? And when you so nearly lost her too!'

'Yes – that's just it,' was the unexpected reply. 'I never meant to tell you, Carmen, but I must speak about it – it may do me good. When Peg was so bad that night that Allan operated on her, I prayed to God as I never prayed before in all my life; I begged and implored Him to spare her to us, and I told Him that He might take anything else from me, or send me any other trouble or sorrow – if only He would leave me Peg.'

'Well?' said Carmen, as the other paused.

'Well!' replied Marcella, with bitterness in her voice. 'He has taken me at my word, indeed – for He has left me without Allan. And oh Carmen! Peg is very dear to me, but – but she is not Allan!' Her voice broke suddenly, and she covered her face with her hands.

Carmen put her arms round her very tenderly.

'Ah, don't grieve so, Cella – don't dear!' she said, 'you know we must believe that God knows best, and that He always does the right thing.'

'I only know that He is very hard and cruel!' said Marcella. 'He took Allan from me. Oh, how could He do it?'

'Don't – don't talk like that, Cella!' cried Carmen, in real distress. 'It's not like you to be so hard and bitter – you are not like yourself since all this trouble has come upon you. But it will pass, Cella – dear, dear old girl – it will pass!'

But Marcella Adair shook her head, and a hard, sullen look crept into the grey eyes that had once been so frank and sunny.

'I am done with religion, anyway,' she said, 'not that I ever troubled about it much, but I used to believe that God was a merciful and just God. I know better now!'

Carmen said nothing more on the subject; her own faith at this time seemed to be slipping almost intangibly from her grasp, and she had nothing spiritual to offer to a desolate soul.

And she was herself facing a very big ordeal and a bitter grief – nothing less than the parting from Peg o' Her Heart. Carmen fully intended to leave Donegal and to ask for a district elsewhere – if possible near where Marcella would be settled – but that she knew would take time, and it was impossible to know if they would get districts near each other. So it was inevitable that she must be parted from her friends for some months at least, and the thought of losing Peg was hard to bear. And yet – she had to confess it to herself – she could better bear the parting from her now than if she had gone some months ago. Another and a more potent influence had come into Carmen's life, and although she had tried to resist it – to put it away from her – she knew in her heart that she was powerless to do so.

Years ago she had told Mrs Bourke that if ever she loved a man she would do so with all her strength, and that there was nothing she would not do or suffer for him. And now the great passion had come to her, and Carmen Cavanagh knew that she loved Victor Walpole with all her heart – better than her life – aye, better than her very soul itself. And, with love's perfect instinct, she knew that her love was returned, and the knowledge filled her with a joy that was terrible – an intoxication, an obsession, which dwarfed all else in her eyes. She had fought against her passion for him when she had first realised it, for he was a non-Catholic and an Englishman – a combination which she had always detested in her hot-headed, impulsive fashion. Beyond these two details and that he was well known in the London world of surgery, and apparently well off, she knew nothing of him. And now she had come to that pass in which she cared nothing for any of these facts. She loved him – the *man* himself – let him be what he might, good, bad or indifferent, it mattered now not one jot to Carmen. Her Spanish-Irish temperament was aflame, and it seemed to her that she had never lived till now. The other Carmen had been only a milk and water personality who had walked through life with shut eyes and unawakened heart. Now all was changed. For her the sun shone and the birds sang and life at last was *Life!* And so even her affection for Peg became slightly faint and blurred, like a lesser light before the sun, and she had been able to comprehend better than Marcella knew that bitter cry of the widowed heart – 'Peg is very dear to me – but oh, she is not *Allan!*'

Yes, she was very dear to Carmen too, but she was not Victor and the girl was obliged to realise that it was the man now who held absolute sway over the heart in which Peg had once reigned supreme. He completely dominated her every thought; it seemed to her that never was he absent from her mind for a minute, and yet, when she turned her head now at the sound of a footstep on the gravel and saw him in the flesh, the blood rushed to her face and her heart raced so quickly that she could hardly speak. And she had already met him earlier on the same day.

Marcella noticed nothing, because her own sorrow blinded her to all that was passing even before her very eyes; but Victor Walpole saw and read aright the signs of

Carmen's confusion. He was, however, too absolutely a man of the world to let his feelings be seen; so he greeted both women with his customary ease and fell into desultory talk, while Marcella poured him out some tea.

But when the latter rose presently and with a brief word of apology returned to her interrupted packing, he leant across the tiny tea table and his eyes held Carmen's – held them for a fraction of time and then the girl's eyes wavered, and she looked away.

He reached out a hand – the thin, flexible hand of the born surgeon – and it closed over her little brown one – Carmen would never wear gloves in the country during the summer, and so her hands were always as tanned as a gypsy's.

'Carmen!' he breathed softly, 'come for a stroll round the field.'

At the end of the rather sloping garden there was a hedge of sorts, through which an opening led into a large field – a most fascinating Donegal field, with great grey boulders scattered about it on which one could sit and talk, and a fairy ring, situated in a hollow surrounded by stunted hawthorn bushes, where the 'little people' came out and danced on moonlight nights!

This field had always been a favourite spot with Allan and Marcella, and Peggy indeed regarded it as her own special property, always speaking of it as 'Peggy's *pield*'.

Carmen had introduced Victor to its charms and so together they strolled towards it now, the beauty and peace of the summer evening surrounding them on every side. But a strange silence had fallen upon them, and even when they were seated on a rocky hillock, gazing down into the fairy hollow, neither of them spoke for some minutes.

Victor Walpole was quite determined to make Carmen Cavanagh his wife. He had never loved a woman – and there had been others in his life – with the passion and abandon which he felt for her. In his more sober moments he was compelled to realise that her religion and, in a certain sense, her nationality might prove objections to their union; but he was so hotly in love that he felt he was strong enough to sweep away these and any other barrier that might arise. Where Carmen was in question he was a mere primitive man, ready to fight to obtain the woman he wanted, and he would have been perfectly ready and willing to carry her off by physical force, if such a course had been feasible in these prosaic days. Even as it was, he had almost determined to take such a step rather than lose her.

He turned and looked at her, and all the passion and love of his heart suddenly broke from his lips in one quick cry of '*Carmen!*'

But it was enough and the same wonderful story – old as the giant mountain looking down upon them, and yet always so new to the listening woman – was told to Carmen Cavanagh by the man who loved her, and whom she loved with all the strength of her woman's heart.

How long they sat there they did not know – hours and minutes count the same at such periods in our lives – but after a while, the first unspeakable rapture over, they found themselves becoming more or less reasonable beings once more and discussing their future – Carmen listening with shy delight while Victor mapped out their coming life together.

'I suppose, darling,' he said, 'the fact of your being a Catholic will not put any difficulties in the way? I don't understand quite how your Church regards marriage with a non-Catholic; but as you know, I really have no definite creed, and would be perfectly willing to agree to all you wished in the matter.'

Carmen gave a smothered exclamation as she realised that she had actually forgotten all about this fact, but the unspeakable joy of knowing that he loved her had blotted every other consideration completely out of her mind.

' *Oh!*' she cried now, in a shamefaced manner, 'I – I had forgotten all about that!'

Victor laughed contentedly as he kissed the radiant face upturned to his.

'Well, that shows that you are not a very strict or narrow Catholic!' he said. 'And I'm jolly glad of it! But what about your priest? Fr McGinley, for instance?'

Carmen had stiffened momentarily at his first words. Although she knew herself that she could not honestly be designated as a strict Catholic, still she had felt her lover's frank comment almost as the lash of a whip. But she shook off this feeling immediately, and replied to his question in a quiet, matter-of-fact manner.

'A priest will marry us, of course,' she said, 'if you agree to – to certain conditions. It won't be quite the same as if you were a Catholic – they don't like mixed marriages, you know – and the Church doesn't really give us her blessing – but they will marry us all the same.'

'And that's all we want!' cried the man.

'As to Fr McGinley,' went on Carmen, 'of course I should not *dream* of consulting *him* about the matter. He is so narrow-minded, and he – he would not understand. It will be best to go to a priest in Dublin.'

'Very well dearest,' he assented, 'whatever you wish, of course. This part of the business can be left to you entirely and I am willing to agree to everything, so you can settle it as you like. But now that we are talking seriously, I think that it is only fair that I should tell you that I was – married before.'

Involuntarily Carmen withdrew from his arms – it seemed to her dreadful – and a thing that hurt, to think that he had loved another woman and had called her wife – that he should have been a widower, and she not to know it!

'Why, Carmen!' he said tenderly, 'are you vexed, dearest?'

She pulled herself together then and tried to smile. After all perhaps it had all been long ago!

'No, no, Victor, of course I'm not vexed! It seemed strange to me to think of you being married before – that's all. How long – you don't mind speaking about it, do you? How long is your – your wife dead?'

The man gave a short laugh.

'As a matter of fact, she does not happen to be dead,' he said, 'by all accounts, she is very much alive!'

The girl beside him looked at him in blank amazement for a moment. Then she knew that she must be mistaken – she could not have heard aright, of course.

She moistened her lips and spoke again.

'I – I don't understand,' she said. 'I asked you how long it was since your wife died?'

'Yes darling – I know,' he replied, 'and I answered you. She is not dead – we were divorced two years ago, but she has married again since. Why Carmen – my dearest – what is wrong? Surely you don't mind now when all this is ancient history?'

But there was no answer from the girl at his side; she simply sat quite rigid, looking at him with wide open eyes – her great black eyes, which seemed now to hold a fearful dread – a misery beyond words.

'Carmen!' he said again, trying to put his arms around her. 'What is it? Why do you take it like this?'

She repulsed his caressing arms and, removing as if by an effort her eyes from his, stared in front of her down into the fairy hollow, and if any of the 'little people' were watching, surely they must have felt sorry for the tragedy which was written on one poor mortal's face; or would they only return to their elfin tricks and pastimes with the unsympathetic cry of 'Lord, what fools these mortals be!'

Carmen spoke then and she rather wondered at the sound of her own voice – it seemed strained – cracked almost. 'If you are divorced,' she said, 'I cannot marry you.'

The man stared at her incredulously. 'Cannot marry me! But why not? I am perfectly free, just as if I had never been married, and the marriage will be absolutely legal. Surely you know the English law about the matter?'

'Yes,' said the girl, still staring straight in front of her, 'yes. And I know the law of the Catholic Church, too.'

There was silence for the space of a moment before Victor Walpole spoke. 'Good Lord!' he said then softly, 'I had forgotten that!'

Carmen made him no answer, and after waiting for a short while, half expecting that she would say something, he burst out hotly. 'Oh, but I say, darling! Surely you are not going to let this come between us? When the ceremony will be perfectly legal and binding by law, you would not be so foolish as to allow the antiquated rules of any Church to interfere in the matter?'

'No priest would marry us,' she said.

'Well, what matter? We can be married at the Registry Office.'

She turned her head then and looked at him – smiling half pitifully at his anxiety as she said. 'It would be no marriage in the eye of the Church.'

'What matter?' he cried again. 'It would be a legal marriage all the same. What more do we want?'

'You don't understand,' she said then, very sadly, very quietly. 'If I went through this – this ceremony with you, I would in the eyes of my Church not be your wife at all, we would simply be living together openly in sin. And I could not even remain a practical Catholic myself – I could not go to the Sacraments. Oh, Victor! It is impossible. I could not do it, even for you – even for you – whom I love. Oh *how* I love you.' And she broke down suddenly and completely, sobbing unrestrainedly within his arms, allowing herself the shelter of them – as she told herself – for the last time.

In vain he talked, bringing forward every specious argument and plea of which he could think. Then at last. 'At least you will think it over?' he pleaded. 'Don't make such a decision without taking time! It will mean so much to both of us! And after all, you know, Carmen, dearest, things are changing every day – and especially in the matter of marriage and divorce, rapid progress has been made lately. The modern man and woman refuse absolutely to be shackled and fettered by ecclesiastical opinion in these cases, and no doubt you will see your Church, too, giving way in this matter before long.'

She smiled in spite of her pain – a wan, little smile that went to Victor's heart.

'Oh my dear,' she said, 'you don't know what you are talking about! The Catholic Church doesn't change,' and the absolute finality of her voice made him partly realise the great barrier which now stood in the path of his desire.

'Well, anyway, dear, you *will* take time and think about it – won't you? I will have to go back to London immediately – tomorrow; my practice has been left too long to my *locum* as it is. So let us arrange to correspond as friends for a while, and after some months – say at Xmas – I will come again to see you.'

'Perhaps I won't be here,' said Carmen dully. 'I have asked to be transferred. The loneliness here will be awful now that Peg and Cella won't be near me. Oh! I hope Miss Davison will send me somewhere else!'

Victor Walpole said nothing. In his own mind he was thinking that this very loneliness of which she spoke might prove a powerful ally for him.

'Wherever you may be, dearest, I'll come to you,' he said then, 'and I have good hopes that you will see things in a more reasonable light after a time.'

'I will never see things in any other light than that in which I see them now,' said Carmen, 'but whether I will yield to temptation and give up my Faith for your sake – that is another matter which only time can prove.'

She turned a very haggard face towards him, and he kissed her with a tender passion which brought the tears again to her eyes.

'I should not let you kiss me,' she said. 'You are a married man in my eyes, you know.'

He gave a laugh of genuine amusement, as he replied. 'I can assure you my darling, that I don't look upon myself as one! I wish you didn't take these matters with such – such medieval seriousness! But, after all, I suppose it constitutes some of your charm for a pagan like myself.'

'Tarmen! – Tarmen! Where is 'oo? Here's Peg!'

'I'm here, sweetheart! Come along.'

The next minute Peg appeared coming across the uneven field, her fat legs swerving perilously under her as she climbed and slipped over boulders and hillocks to Carmen's side. The girl stooped and kissed her, and, having hugged her fiercely in return, fixed her questioning young eyes upon Victor in a long, severe glance.

'Hallo Kid!' he said – he was very fond of her in his own fashion – 'aren't you going to give me a kiss too?'

Peg shook her head violently, and then tilted it disdainfully. 'No! Peg don't kiss *mans!*' she asserted virtuously.

Both her hearers laughed delightedly, for this was a well-known fiction of Peg's.

Carmen rose from her rocky seat, and she and Victor strolled toward the house with Peg trotting between them.

As they came to the side door the child ran on in front, and Victor detained the girl for a moment to speak a last word to her.

'You *will* think of what I have been saying – won't you, Carmen,' he said, 'and try – do try to see things from my point of view?'

She looked at him sadly.

'Yes; I will give you no decided answer before Xmas,' she replied, speaking in a dull, monotonous voice, very unlike her usual gay tones. 'And anyway at present I am not capable of making up my mind one way or another. I feel just like a bit of miserable drift wood, floating downstream, and blown along by every wind and breeze and not knowing to where, in the end, I will drift finally. But indeed I suppose only God – or the Devil – knows that.'

So on the following morning Victor Walpole set out for London Town, and on the day after Marcella and Peg returned to the dear old city by the Liffey's banks.

And Carmen was left alone at Glenmore, in bleak, lonely Donegal.

XI

A Pleasant Evening

Mrs Bourke was sitting at the window of No. 47 Hill Square. She was patching the twins' school knickers and wondering how on earth they managed to tear such terrible holes in them. The window was open for the evening was oppressively warm, and from the dusty square opposite the voices of the children playing and nursemaids scolding, could be plainly heard, while in the distance sounded the clang of the trams and the quarterly chimes from the clock of the Town Hall.

It was only five o'clock, and Mrs Bourke was congratulating herself on the fact that she had a clear hour before the family tea. The twins were playing in the Square, 'Himself' was out – presumably 'doing' Grafton Street as usual – and only Sarah could be heard below in the basement kitchen, as her elephantine tread went slowly backwards and forwards.

'I'll just have time to finish these knickers before the others come in,' thought the weary mistress of the house as she rethreaded her needle, but before another stitch was placed in the nether garments of the lusty scions of the House of Bourke, the front gate gave the usual creak which always heralded someone's approach, and looking out, Mrs Bourke saw a tall lady in mourning accompanied by a little girl in a plain white frock, coming towards the hall door.

Mrs Bourke jumped to her feet, flinging her work on the floor.

'Why! it's Marcella Adair and Peg!' she cried, and flew to open the door with all her old impetuosity.

'Marcella, my dear!' she said. 'I'm so glad to see you,' and she flung her arms round the tall, slight woman in black, and then stooped to kiss the sweetly grave little face of Peg.

'Come in! Come in!' she went on, leading them into the diningroom. 'Sit down, Marcella – but wait, let me help you off with your hat and coat. It's so hot and black things are so heavy! Now, Peg, give me your hat and sit down and rest, dearie, till Conny and Vinny come in – they are only in the Square – and you can all have a fine play together after tea. Won't that be nice?'

Peg did not make any verbal reply but gazed long and seriously at this lady, whom she did not know very well, as she had only met her once before, a few weeks previously, when she and her mother had come to Hill Square one day soon after their arrival in Dublin. However, Peg was rather inclined to like Mrs Bourke; she had the child's true instinct for reading faces and character, but she had not been very favourably impressed by the twins. So, being a very truthful young person, except on certain comparatively rare occasions, she did not express any great joy at once again meeting the young Bourkes.

'Well! Have you any news?' went on Mrs Bourke, turning to Marcella, who had seated herself on a chair near the open window.

Allan's widow, after her five years in the bracing, rarefied air of Donegal, felt as if she could hardly breathe in the city these hot August days. It was only a temporary feeling, and she knew that her lungs would soon become acclimatised again to their native surroundings, but in the meantime even this discomfort seemed to accentuate in some way her bitter loss and desolation, her changed and empty life.

'Yes,' she answered now, in reply to Mrs Bourke's eager query. 'I have been appointed to Rathbrook.'

'Rathbrook!' interrupted the other. 'Oh Marcella, isn't that splendid! Why, it's quite close to town – only about half an hour's walk from the tram! When did you hear? Tell me all about it.'

Marcella Adair smiled rather wearily. It seemed strange to her that Cis Bourke should take such a vivid interest in where she was going and care so much to hear about it, while she herself felt so utterly indifferent.

'I was in the office yesterday,' she said, 'and the Superintendent told me. Nurse Taylor is leaving next week and I am to take up duty. There is no cottage with that district unfortunately – Nurse Taylor had rooms over the Post Office – so I will have to look for one – and pay the rent myself too. I think the work is rather heavy, as there is Child Welfare work to be done as well as the general nursing, and they have a Baby Club and a Dental Clinic for School Children, and so on. The area, too, is very large.'

'Well, don't overdo it, Marcella,' said Mrs Bourke. 'I don't suppose that you will feel so inclined or be so fit for the work as you were before ... before your marriage. It will be a bit hard for you now to go back to certain hours and rules and regulations again – and to be out in all weathers, too. So take it a bit easy at first if you can until you get in on it again.'

'I will have to do the work while I'm on duty,' said the other, adding, 'it's not the work, Cis, that I mind so much as the committee. I believe that they are not – very kind, and are rather difficult to get on with.'

'Do you know any of them? What kind are they – socially, I mean?'

'I know a few by repute, and they are mostly of the new rich genus,' said Marcella.

'Anyhow they can't make it unpleasant for you if you do your work – can they?' said the other, adding with a laugh, 'they can't *eat* you anyway! And here's Eileen and Letty, and I see the twins coming across the Square.'

Even as she spoke the Hewson girls entered and greeted Marcella cordially, both looking very white and tired after their hot day in the city. They were followed almost immediately by the twins, who pulled up shyly at the door when they saw the visitors, and stood awkwardly looking in until their mother called them.

'Come in, boys! Don't you see Mrs Adair and Peggy? Come and shake hands.'

They advanced clumsily, very like their father in appearance, with straight, lanky hair, and small, foxy eyes, set in nondescript freckled features; but they possessed a fund of good nature and honesty which was never in his disposition.

The contrast between their demeanour and that of Peg was irresistibly amusing. Miss Adair sat on a high chair, with her pretty feet dangling and her hands crossed sedately in her lap, and surveyed these two members of the opposite sex with a calm serene gaze which was intensely disconcerting to them. On being told to shake hands she daintily extended the tips of her fingers, very like a young queen to her courtiers. Conny and Vinny shook them awkwardly and spasmodically and then, with a muttered remark about 'getting tidy for tea' fled precipitately.

Peg gazed after their vanishing forms in meditative silence for a brief space and then remarked, as it might be to the ceiling above her head, 'Peg don't yike boys!'

It was not until Philip Hewson had come in, and the family were seated round the tea table, that Carmen's name was mentioned.

'I have not had a letter for over a fortnight,' said Mrs Bourke, 'and she generally writes so regularly. When did you hear last, Marcella?'

'About a week ago,' was the reply, 'but not a very satisfactory letter. She seems terribly downhearted. I suppose it's the loneliness.'

It may be stated that Mrs Adair was absolutely ignorant of Carmen's love affair, as was also Cis Bourke. Marcella had been too stupid and dazed with her own grief to notice how things were moving during those last days at Carragh, and Carmen, for reasons of her own, had taken no one into her confidence.

'Oh, of course she must miss you dreadfully,' said Letty. 'I wish she could get a district near town, I'm sure Carmen is about the last type of individual to live alone!'

Philip said nothing, but his face wore what his sisters were wont to designate as 'Phil's haggard, sentimental look!' However, everybody's attention was just then attracted to the open front window, at which had suddenly appeared the smartly attired figure of the master of the house, just returned from his Grafton Street constitutional. The click of the gate had passed unnoticed, and, hearing talk and gay chatter, Mr Bourke, instead of entering the house at once, had slipped across the tiny suburban flowerbed and now stood gazing in at his family and the visitors with his mean, foxy eyes. They were all taken completely unawares, and each individual member immediately felt uncomfortable and ill at ease –almost as if they had been guilty of some wrongdoing. Such was the usual result of his sudden appearance in the bosom of his family, and nothing gave him greater pleasure than to exercise his strange power of making all around him as unhappy and uncomfortable as possible. The present moment was, therefore, a situation after his own heart. So paralysed were they all that no one spoke a word, and the silence held until he broke it himself.

'So! so!' smiling ironically. 'My dear wife has visitors! Ah yes, to be sure, the charming Mrs Adair and her young daughter! Delightful! Delightful!'

Here he raised his hat and bowed low, the immortal bald patch coming into full view as he did so and causing his stepson to long, with a murderous longing, to fling his teacup – or the bread knife – at it.

'Welcome! Welcome, dear lady, to my humble abode! This is an unexpected but delightful visit. One moment and I will join your happy throng,' and before his unfortunate hearers could realise their ill-luck he was in the room. Marcella replied to his effusive welcome – she knew, of course, that he cordially detested her – the mere fact of her great friendship with Carmen Cavanagh was enough – with chilly politeness. She was really vexed, as were all the others, at his unexpectedly early return from town, and they all knew that the evening – as far as any pleasure for them went – was practically over; Cornelius Vincent Bourke was out to enjoy himself.

He now came towards Peg and held out his fat, white hand with a would-be ingratiating smile.

'And this is Miss Peggy! What a charming little maiden! Ah, if only my clumsy, ill-mannered sots' – his voice changed suddenly as if by magic into a perfect snarl, and he threw a venomous glance at the wretched twins, who were literally trembling in their seats, their terror of their father being very real – the one dread of their young lives. 'Yes, if those good-for-nothing louts could take an example from this young lady!' – here he attempted to take Peg's hand adding, as she drew it back quickly. 'Surely you are not shy, little one? Well, well, perhaps a kiss?' stooping over her.

But Peg sat back determinedly as she cried. 'Go way! Peg don't yike 'oo! Nasty man!'

Brave Peg o' My Heart! Probably no other of all those assembled round the tea table would have dared so much, and several of those present felt like cheering her. But C.V. Bourke was not one to let even a child pass unpunished.

'So now, ha ha!' he chuckled. 'So we are shy, we coquet! And so young! Fie! fie!' and he *playfully* pinched the little fat arm.

Peg smothered the sudden cry of pain as if she knew instinctively that it would please him to know that he had hurt her and, although the sweet face changed colour and the lips quivered for a moment, she sat quietly and said nothing. But her expression was that of a child who is hurt or punished unjustly – a wistful look of hurt surprise.

Nonplussed, the persecutor looked around as if for a fresh victim and, seating himself beside his wife, demanded a cup of tea.

'Such a pleasure to be served by your charming hands, my dear, although really, my love, I wish you would take a little more care of them – some manicuring, for instance. One hardly likes to remark, but really your hands ...!'

Cis Bourke's hands had been noted for their beauty at one time, but she had little chance to care for their appearance now and much hard work to do with them. She was however, very sensitive – as her fond husband knew, and she now flushed painfully and slid the offending numbers beneath the tablecloth.

'Nay – do not hide their lily whiteness!' continued the tormentor, delighted at the wretched faces around him. 'I assure you ... Yes, Sarah, what is it?' – his voice becoming a furious shout. 'Don't stand there gaping like an idiot! What the devil do you want? I'll throw the teapot at you – you old hag. You useless bag of bones!'

Shaking and trembling, as she always did when reduced to the abject terror inspired in her by the dreadful 'Master', poor Sarah was heard to mutter something about 'the new minister having called to see the mistress.'

Mr Bourke's voice and face changed at once into pleasant lines. Here was more fish for his net – he was having the time of his life this hot August evening!

'The minister?' he repeated. 'My good woman, where is he? Where is the minister of the Gospel that I may go and clasp his hand?'

'In the sitting room above, sir,' gasped Sarah. 'I put him up there till I told the mistress,' she explained, very much as though the clerical visitor was some kind of parcel.

'I'll see to him,' cried C.V. Bourke, rising from his seat. 'I'll welcome this good man to my poor abode,' and he left the room.

'Oh, this is dreadful!' whispered poor Mrs Bourke, as she heard his footsteps overhead. 'What will he do next? What will he say?'

'This must be the new curate of the Chapel of Ease,' said Letty. 'He'll think he is in a lunatic asylum.'

'He won't be far out as far as his chief entertainer goes!' said Philip grimly.

'I think *we* had better go home,' said Marcella, half rising from her seat.

'Oh no! Wait, do wait!' cried the girls, and even as they spoke their stepfather's returning footsteps were heard descending the stairs, and he entered the room accompanied by the Rev. John Melvin, a very young, very shy curate.

Mr Bourke paused dramatically in the doorway, and the clergyman of course had to do likewise.

'Behold, my dear Mr Melvin!' said the former, striking one of his favourite attitudes. 'Behold, my little family! My dear wife – the joy and blessing of my life, my beloved twin boys – the comfort of their poor Dad's heart – and my dear stepdaughters and stepson, to whom I hope and trust I have ever been as a devoted father since the day on which I took upon myself the responsibility of providing for their wants and comforts! And this is a guest of ours – Mrs Adair – upon whom, alas the Hand of the Lord has lately been heavy – and her charming little girl. And now, my dear Mr Melvin, you will surely join us in a humble cup of tea?'

Mrs Bourke had risen to shake hands, the others following suit, and Philip now brought forward a chair for the curate, while Mrs Bourke offered him the cup of tea.

'Thank you – no!' he protested shyly. 'I have had tea very recently. What a warm evening, is it not? Real August weather!'

The conversation meandered on along the usual lines, while Mr Bourke, having seated himself, called the twins to him and, putting an arm around each, he *playfully* pinched and nipped them on various parts of their anatomy. His unfortunate victims knew better than to offer any sign of protest, and although at times the water came to their eyes in spite of themselves, they bore their pain manfully and well. Their mother and the rest saw perfectly what they were suffering but had to pretend that they noticed nothing.

Mr Melvin, not being a very quick-witted or observant individual, was quite unconscious of what was passing before his eyes and after a little more conversation, during which he expressed a hope of seeing all the family regularly at church, he rose to his feet to make his adieux.

'Oh my dear Mr Melvin!' here interposed the saintly master of the household, 'you will surely offer up a prayer before you go?'

And the unfortunate curate, very shy and nervous, knelt down – the others of course having to follow his example, and poor Conny, only barely managing to suppress a cry at an extra cruel pinch from his fond parent – and stumbled through a few prayers.

'Thank you – thank you so much!' said Mr Bourke, shaking hands fervently. 'This has been great privilege! I am sadly afraid that my dear family regard me as being rather strict – too pious, so to speak! But that is my nature – I cannot help it. And they are young. Ah yes, they are young! Time and my poor efforts' – fixing his wife and stepdaughters out of the corner of his eyes – 'may change them! I have hopes, Mr Melvin, I have great hopes,' and so speaking he accompanied the curate to the door and saw him off the premises with much politeness.

'A very charming man – evidently sincerely religious too,' thought that worthy as he walked away. 'A pity his family are not more like him! Those stepchildren seem quite sullen and morose – I expect he has often trouble with them.'

On re-entering the dining room, Mr Bourke found Marcella and Peg preparing to depart.

'What, going?' he cried in affected dismay. 'Surely not yet! It's quite early still and we have not had half our chat.'

'Thank you, but I must be getting home,' said Marcella coldly and C.V. Bourke had presently the pleasure of watching her walking away from the house, Peg holding tightly to her hand, and Philip accompanying them. As he stood at the window gazing after them he felt that he had really had quite a pleasant evening. Yes, certainly the evening had been delightful, and he glanced with satisfaction at his wife who, looking tired out, weary and depressed, was taking the twins to the kitchen to look at their poor arms and legs, and then he smiled softly as his two stepdaughters slipped upstairs to the refuge of their own room.

Sarah, however, was left to him; she was clearing away the tea things and he turned his attention to her for a while, making her break a cup through sheer fright.

'You will pay for that. It's a most valuable article too. Yes, you will pay for that out of your next month's wages – you old hag. You blind old bat.'

Sarah fled with the tray, and nothing living remained but the cat. Having sent her flying through the open window, he seated himself in the most comfortable armchair he could find, and proceeded to smoke the pipe of peace after a strenuous but successful evening.

XII

Our Philanthropists

'Religion clean and undefiled before God and the Father is –!'

By the beginning of September Marcella Adair was at Rathbrook – a district nurse once more. She had managed to secure a four-roomed cottage, and she and Peg were soon settled in it with the faithful Ellen to look after them. Many a time Marcella thanked the bit of good fortune which gave her Ellen; she was indeed the one comfort left to her, and she often wondered what she would have done without her. She could depend so absolutely upon her, and the fact of being able to leave Peg in her charge with complete confidence was a great ease to her mind. And then Ellen always managed to have such appetising meals ready – and at such a small cost, which was consideration now that shillings were not too plentiful with Marcella Adair – and she knew well that if she had had to put up with the vagaries of an ordinary 'slavey' things would have been very different. She knew, too, that the wages she was now able to pay Ellen were quite inadequate for her services, but having hinted as much to her one day, the faithful creature was so distressed and upset at the idea of ever having to leave her beloved mistress and 'Miss Peg, the darlint!' that Marcella never broached the subject again.

The work at Rathbrook, as Marcella had expected, was very heavy and she was on duty practically all day, and had been for so long now unaccustomed to the drudgery of district work that she was generally tired out by evening. As a matter of fact, this was just the best kind of life for her at present, for it left her neither time nor inclination to fret or brood over the past.

She had two dispensary doctors to please – one a very pleasant man to work with, the other an abnormal individual, with all kinds of strange vagaries and mannerisms, an extraordinary voice and accent and a professed hatred of all womankind.

She saw nothing of the Ladies' Committee for the first few weeks, as many of the members were still at the seaside and the Baby Club was closed. But in the middle of September it re-opened and Marcella, feeling rather nervous and strange, prepared for her first afternoon there. It was a large-sized building, with a corrugated zinc roof – one of those portable affairs which are used for various purposes. Benches were arranged down each side and a raised platform – called 'the stage' – was at the far end, while at the other end near the door were two gas stoves and a dresser with crockery, two large kitchen tables, and some big presses.

The caretaker of the club, a neat little woman with a scared look in her timid grey eyes, was busily setting out the cups and saucers on one of the tables, in preparation for the Mothers' tea, as Marcella entered the building on the afternoon of the re-opening.

'Good evening, Mrs Mulligan,' she said, 'there are a good many mothers and babies waiting outside – I suppose I had better let them come in and sit down.'

The caretaker looked quite horrified.

'Oh no, Nurse!' she said, 'no one is allowed until *the ladies* come.' She pronounced the magic words *the ladies* as if they had been Royal Personages at the very least.

'Oh very well,' replied Marcella, 'I thought the poor women would be tired, some of them are carrying babies in their arms.'

'Oh well, Nurse, they know the time we generally open the door. Certainly Mrs Weston is a little later than usual today,' glancing at the clock on the dresser. 'She must have motored into town first.'

She was arranging some small cups and saucers by themselves at one end of the table as she spoke.

'What pretty cups!' said Marcella. 'Arn't you afraid that the women might break them?'

Mrs Mulligan stared at her in pitying contempt.

'These are for *the ladies*,' she said primly, 'they do be wanting a cup of tea before the Club opens.'

Even as she spoke the whirr of a motor car was heard outside, and she ran to fling open the door to the important arrivals.

Mrs Weston was a tall, grey-haired woman with a thin, squeaky voice and jarring laugh. She walked very badly, turning her feet outwards in some extraordinary way, and swaying her body from side to side. She wore the inevitable fur coat and came in carrying a cashbox and bunch of keys, and followed by a plain, stout young woman – a Miss Dover who was a poor relation, and was always brought to the Baby Club to make herself useful and to carry parcels, of which she had an armful just now. The chauffeur brought up the rear, carrying a large basket containing halfpenny buns – the period was pre-war – for the Mothers' Tea.

'Oh here we are, Mrs Mulligan! Has the milk come?' said Mrs Weston, as she rustled forward, her keys jangling.

Then as she caught sight of Marcella. 'Oh, you are the new Nurse, I suppose? You might just take the buns out of the basket and put one on each saucer for the mothers; we don't give them plates.'

'Yes, Ma'am – the milk is here,' interposed Mrs Mulligan, 'but it's a little short today, Ma'am! Mrs O'Brien couldn't give me the full quantity.'

'Oh well, perhaps Mrs Hardy will bring some – she is not here yet! And in any case there are some tins of "condensed" in the press – they will do for the Mothers' second cup of tea.'

Marcella, feeling very small and snubbed, was arranging the halfpenny buns on the saucers as directed, and before she had finished three other members of the Ladies' Committee had arrived. These were a Mrs Hardy, a small, plain woman very dowdily dressed in mid-Victorian fashion, and clasping in her arms the expected bottle of milk; Mrs Barker, a very large person, with a red face and the feet and voice of a ploughman, and lastly Miss Anita Browne, the highly-educated and exceedingly stylish daughter of a wealthy shopkeeper.

There was a perfect chorus of gushing, greeting and inquiries after mutual friends, but no notice was taken of Marcella by anyone except Miss Dover, who good-naturedly tried to put her at her ease by telling her what her duties would be.

'When Mrs Weston and the others have had their tea,' she explained, 'they will go up to the top of the hall, where they have the Dorcas table – cheap clothes, you know, and then we will open the door and you and I will stand at it. You will enter each woman's name in this book and the number of children she brings with her; be sure and mark the infants under a year in that special division to themselves as they are counted separately – and I'll take the pennies.'

And so it followed. There was a general rustle of *the ladies* towards the stage end, and simultaneously Mrs Mulligan opened the door, and there was a rush of mothers and children to enter the hall. Marcella duly entered their names – wondering greatly how she would ever get to know all these individual mothers and babies! – and Miss Dover held out the large delph mug into which each woman dropped her penny. Young and old – aged more by grinding poverty and constant worry than by years – clean and dirty, tidy and slovenly, ugly and pretty – in passed the mothers, carrying in their arms fat babies, thin babies, babies like angel cherubs, babies like ugly old men, babies clean and babies dirty, babies sleeping and babies crying. And they came too in 'prams' and go-carts, which blocked up passage and entrance and caused many an acrimonious scrimmage amongst their owners. And round their mothers' feet, and holding to their skirts, came the 'children under five' – numberless as the sands of the sea to Marcella's tired gaze.

By degrees they were all seated, and presently the tea was carried round by Miss Dover and Miss Browne – the latter holding her head so high in the air, and handing out the teacups so disdainfully, that it hurt Marcella to think that the poor women should be served in such a manner.

The building soon became very close – permeated with the atmosphere of 'the great unwashed'; the babies appeared to be all crying at once, the children yelled and fought, and it seemed to Marcella that pandemonium reigned.

But 'the Ladies' looked on complacently – they were evidently used to it – and while poor Marcella weighed baby after baby, feeling more hot and tired after each one, they sat on chairs behind the Dorcas table and smiled serenely. The mothers, for their part, were chatting volubly one to another, and many domestic stories and recitals of grievances were exchanged to the accompaniment of 'Sez I' and 'Sez she' and 'It's the truth I'm tellin' yer, woman, dear!'

And the children went on screaming and fighting around the floor, and certainly succeeded in making a fearful row.

Mrs Mulligan glanced reproachfully at Nurse Adair, as she passed by, carrying a tray.

'They're very noisy today,' she remarked in her prim way. 'You should tell them to be quiet, Nurse. If Mrs Boston was here she would soon make them behave.'

Even as Marcella was wondering who Mrs Boston might be, a strident but good-tempered voice was heard near the entrance door calling loudly. 'Now, now. What does all this noise mean? Who owns this child? Oh it's yours, Mrs Molloy! Well take him off the floor!'

Talking as she came, she approached the centre table where Marcella was still engaged with the weighing machine.

'You are Nurse Adair, I suppose?' she said brusquely but not unkindly, and, to Marcella's surprise she held out her hand – a courtesy to which none of the other ladies had condescended. 'I'm Mrs Boston, I see you are getting into the way of things – that's right. You will soon understand the working of this place. Of course, you are supposed to deliver a lecture every week to the mothers after you have weighed the babies – on various subjects, you know, connected with Infant Welfare. Make them bright and interesting, and you will have to shout well, too!' – with a laugh – 'or you won't be able to drown the babies' voices! However, I don't suppose you are prepared with one today, so we will excuse you – this being your first Club day. Now, they are far too noisy, and I'm going to make them behave better.'

Mounting the stage, she clapped her hands vigorously and, having spoken a few sharp words, succeeded in restoring some kind of order.

But it was only for a short time; the noise and chatter, the crying and screaming, was soon as bad as ever and the atmosphere became worse and worse, so that when at last 'the Ladies' rose, and the Club dispersed, Marcella heaved a sigh of genuine relief. The mothers with babies in arms, and children toddling after them, drifted away in groups of twos and threes, and the others packed their progeny into prams and go-carts – some at the feet – strapping and tucking them in and sailed off to their various destinations, criticising 'the Ladies' and the 'new nurse' as they went.

Then 'the Ladies' put away in the press all the unbought or partially paid for garments. Mrs Weston and the faithful Miss Dover counted the mothers' pennies, which went towards the tea expenses, and the others made up the accounts of the various Coal and Boot Clubs attached to the organisation. They departed at last with many effusive goodbyes, Mrs Weston, as usual taking little Mrs Hardy in her motor, and Miss Brown sailing away on her bike, while poor Miss Dover departed on her long walk into the suburb, where she helped her sister to keep a second-rate boarding school.

Marcella and Mrs Mulligan, standing by the table as 'the Ladies' sailed out, received a nod from one or two, but no notice from most of them with the exception of Mrs Boston, who called out a loud and genial goodbye.

Oh, how glad Marcella was that it was over for another week. How she wished the Club was monthly instead of weekly; but she had it every Monday to face, and during the week she had to visit mothers and try to get to know them all as well as doing all the general nursing of the district and to attend the Dental Clinic for the school children every Tuesday morning.

As the weeks passed she became more used to the work, but still found it very trying and hard – she never seemed to be able to overtake all she had to do.

'I am never able to feel that I am really finished,' she said one evening to Mrs Bourke who, wonderful to relate, had found time to run out and see her. 'I seem to be always trying to get through the work and the visits and it all seems to keep mounting up – up, in spite of all my efforts! And then, Cis, the salary is very small – only £96 – and I have to pay rent and coal and everything out of that! And Peg is still a bit delicate, and I must give her plenty of milk and so on.'

'Yes, and you will neglect yourself,' said Mrs Bourke, 'and with the winter coming on, you ought to try and take care of yourself as much as possible and mind your health and strength. Wouldn't the Committee raise your pay if you asked them? Surely the fact of you being a widow with a child to provide for, should melt the hearts of such great philanthropists?'

Marcella smiled rather grimly. 'My dear Cis, you don't know them!' she said, 'they won't give a penny to anything, except it would get their names in the papers or be well talked about! Why, they don't really care an atom about any of those poor women and children that attend the Club. I have asked again and again for a little help for really deserving cases – poor women struggling to live decently on mere pittances, and others overwhelmed by sickness or other trouble – and they would not give me a halfpenny to help them! I have quite given up expecting it now.'

'But why do they bother with the Club then?'

'Because it is well advertised and the President, Lady Milton, is a fashionable dame and attends all the Castle functions! And then their names appear in the *Annual Report* and they are praised and flattered at the annual meeting for their "untiring efforts and self-sacrificing work for the good of humanity and the future of the race!" Oh Cis, it sickens me sometimes when I know what their *work* and *self-sacrifice* really amounts to!'

Marcella spoke bitterly, and she could not help it. She knew her salary was less than it should be, and she worked hard and conscientiously. She often thought of the wealth of those on the Committee, of their fine houses and gardens, their servants and motors – they had everything they could wish for in this world. And then she would think of the hard, sordid lives of the poor women who came to the Club, and of her own struggling existence, always struggling and trying to make ends meet, and at times an angry bitterness – a sullen hardness – filled her heart and soul.

'Are they kind to you at all?' asked Cis Bourke. 'I mean do they ever send you any fruit or vegetables or eggs? It would mean so little to them – nothing, in fact! – and be such a help to you.'

'Oh no, never!' replied Marcella, 'not that I want to be under a compliment to them, Cis! I'd rather not. But still I often think that if I was in their place – our position reversed, so to speak – how differently I would act towards the nurse! But then, of course, I *know* what a nurse's life is like, and I know, too, what it means to live on such a small salary – and they *don't!*'

'Oh but they must have some idea of the life you live,' said Mrs Bourke, 'and they can see for themselves how hard you work. I think it is perfectly horrid of them to be so *mean!* A lot of old *cats* as Carmen would say!' she concluded laughingly.

Marcella smiled too, but her face clouded involuntarily at the mention of Carmen's name – for she had been strangely anxious about her beloved chum of late.

'I had a letter from her last week,' she said, 'and although she was *trying* to be cheerful, it was a poor attempt. She seems desperately lonely.'

'Yes – she must be,' replied the other, adding. 'Has she applied to be transferred yet?'

'No,' said Marcella, 'and that's just what I can't understand. She says she is going to wait until after Xmas before she writes to the Superintendent.'

'But *why?*' asked Mrs Bourke in surprised tones. 'Why is she waiting so long? It is only the beginning of October now and she might have got away from that dreadful place before the winter set in, if only she had asked sooner.'

'Yes, I know,' said Marcella, with a puzzled look in her grey eyes. 'I simply can't understand it, Cis, and I'm sure there is some reason for it that we don't know.'

'But she is such a chum of yours,' interposed the other, 'even if she didn't confide in me, I'm sure, Marcella, that she would tell you everything.'

'I don't know, Cis,' speaking in a slow and hesitating voice. 'I have been thinking lately that perhaps I was a bit blind to outside things during those last awful days at Carragh. There was a man staying there – you may have heard me speak of him, that London surgeon, Mr Walpole – and I begin to think now that perhaps – perhaps there was something between them.'

'But – but,' Mrs Bourke sat open-eyed in amazement.

'Yes – I know it must seem strange to you that I didn't notice it before; but I was dazed and stupid then and cared for nothing outside my own misery and desolation.'

She paused for a moment as her voice broke, but almost immediately she went on again.

'But now I am *sure* – my instinct tells me – that there *is* something between them.'

'What was he like?' asked Mrs Bourke curiously, as she remembered all and sundry who had fallen victim to Carmen's wonderful charm in the past and had been treated with scant ceremony by their goddess.

'Oh, the usual style of the big London specialist – he's a throat man, you know – Harley Street type,' said Marcella, 'rather good-looking and always perfectly groomed; older than Carmen by several years, I should think, and he had rather a good face for character – clean-shaven, with a firm, *nice* mouth – and with keen blue eyes that saw everything.

He was awfully kind to Peg and to – Allan. I hardly realised his kindness then, but I know now how good he was to us.'

'And do you think that Carmen ...?' hazarded the other.

'Yes,' replied Marcella, 'I think her feelings are involved, and very deeply too. But whether she will marry him or not – if he has asked her – is another thing.'

'Why wouldn't she – if she is fond of him? Although indeed I don't think that I would advise anyone to marry,' said poor Cis Bourke with a rueful smile.

'Well, he is an Englishman and a Protestant – at least I suppose so – and Carmen always hated both in some unreasoning way,' said Marcella.

'Oh, she will overlook his nationality if she really cares for him,' said Mrs Bourke, and then as the remembrance of a certain conversation she had once had with her cousin a few years ago on this very subject recurred to her mind, she added half fearfully, 'Carmen will fall very deeply and terribly in love when she does love at all. I imagine she would let nothing stand between her and the man she cared for! But of course, the religion is another matter. You know how strict the Church of Rome is about mixed marriages.'

'Yes, that is what I am thinking about,' said Marcella, 'still I suppose they could get a dispensation of something of that sort. Couldn't they? I don't know much about the laws of the Catholic Church on such matters. Do you, Cis?'

'No – nothing,' replied Mrs Bourke, 'and I don't want to know either! I am always so sorry that Carmen belongs to it, although certainly I must admit that she is not at all bigoted.'

'Do you know, Cis,' said Marcella slowly, 'I have often thought that it must be – well – a very *comforting* sort of religion! Just fancy if I could only believe that I might pray for Allan – and that my prayers could do him good – could help him in some way! Oh Cis, I wish I could believe it! Half of my loneliness would be gone then.'

'Good gracious!' exclaimed Mrs, Bourke, 'I do hope, Marcella, that you will never think of such a thing. Their religion is absurd – quite idolatrous! What on earth has been putting such ideas into your head?'

'I don't know,' was the reply, 'except perhaps it is seeing Ellen so happy in her religion. Really, Cis, her faith seems to buoy her up in the most wonderful way. She can always say "Welcome be the Will of God!" or "God is good." Something like that always – even when everything seems to go wrong, and I – I get no good, no comfort at all from *my* religion – such as it is! It may be my own fault, I suppose indeed that it is! But, oh Cis, I am so lonely – so lonely, without *him!*'

The tears welled up into the grey eyes of which Allan Adair had been so fond, and fell on the dress for Peg which she was making.

'Oh, I know, Marcella dear. I know!' cried tender-hearted Mrs Bourke. 'It must be simply terrible for you! But it will pass in time – or, at least, you will not feel it so badly, and, anyway, I'm sure that the Church of Rome could do nothing for you! If you only heard the stories that C.V. tells ...'

'Oh don't cite *him,* please!' said Marcella, with a shudder. 'Any Church was well rid of him! And anyway Protestantism doesn't seem to have improved him much. Is he behaving any better these days?'

The wife of the gentleman in question shook her still pretty head.

'No,' she said gloomily. 'No – it's worse he seems to get! When Sarah had the dinner cooked last Sunday, he went down to the kitchen and took the whole joint out of the oven just when she was going to bring it to table. He put it on a dish – keeping Sarah at bay with the carving knife, not indeed that she was likely to make much of a protest – and helped himself to a pile of vegetables. He then carried the lot off to his bedroom and evidently feasted alone there. And we have not seen the joint since, but this is Tuesday so likely the bare bones will be brought down on his tray tomorrow!'

'Oh Cis!' cried Marcella, unable to help laughing.

'Oh yes, you can laugh.' said the other, secretly glad however that she had managed to turn Marcella's mind from her own troubles. 'You can laugh, but if you had live with him you would feel more like weeping! But it can't last, and I see Canada coming nearer on the horizon every day!'

'Oh Cis, don't go!' pleaded the other.

'My dear, I'll *have* to go! I'll be borne off with the rest of my family. Letty is determined,' replied her visitor. 'And now my dear, I must really depart; I have stayed too long as it is.'

'Oh, but it was delightful to have you! Come again soon!' cried Marcella.

'Well, I'll try,' was the reply, 'but you know, Marcella, how hard it is for me to snatch an evening off. I haven't even a slavey's privileges!' and she laughed and sighed as she drew on her shabby gloves.

A few weeks later Marcella took Peg into the city to buy her a few articles that she needed – boots for the winter amongst other things. It was very seldom now that the child had her mother to accompany her anywhere – she generally went out with Ellen – and so she was in a great state of excitement when they set out.

It was quite a fine autumn afternoon when they started and they got halfway through their shopping before it began to rain, but then it came down so heavily that Marcella looked around her for shelter. They were passing a well-known Catholic Church at the time, and to her surprise Peg seemed to know the building. Pulling Marcella excitedly by the hand she cried, 'oh Mummy! Tum in and see Peg's yovely yady. She lives in dere!'

In surprise, Marcella allowed herself to be led inside and Peg, still clasping her hand tightly, guided her straight to the Virgin's Altar.

'Yook now, Mummy!' she said in an intensely excited whisper. 'Dat's Peg's yovely yady! Peg yoves her, and she yoves Peg!' and, rather to Marcella's consternation, her small daughter knelt down and, folding her hands, gazed fondly up at the Blessed Mother.

'She has been here with Ellen, I suppose,' thought Marcella. 'I'll have to speak about it when I go home – although I don't see that it matters much if it pleases the child! After all, nothing really matters now as far as I am concerned – I'm just sick of it all!' and she sank wearily on to the seat, allowing her gaze to travel curiously around the Church, looking at the beautiful High Altar, at the stained windows, the side altars and various statues, and noticing the groups of silent worshippers kneeling here and there. And then her gaze came back to the altar and the sanctuary lamp swinging before, and she wondered still more about this strange religion and what it all meant.

'It's a queer religion,' she thought, but added almost in spite of herself, 'and there must be something in it – these people all believe it so firmly and get such comfort from it! Oh how I wish that I was like them.'

Then she bent down and whispered to Peg, 'were you here before, dearie? Did Ellen bring you?' and Peg nodded her head vigorously.

'Div Peg a penny!' she then demanded, and Marcella, curious to see what she would do with it, produced the required coin. 'Peg yight a candle por 'oo!' was the next remark, and before her mother grasped her meaning, her little legs were carrying her fast to the candle box in front of Our Lady's Shrine, and the little arms were trying to reach up to put in the penny.

'Wait now for a minute, honey, jewel' said a fat woman, rising from her orisons beside her. 'Wait now and I'll lift ye! God bless the little darlint!'

'Tank 'oo' said Miss Adair politely, as she dropped in her penny and then shaking with excitement, selected her candle and, with her new friend's assistance, lit it and stuck it triumphantly in its place.

'God love ye!' said the woman, as she put Peg safely down again. 'And may Our Blessed Lady send ye all graces and blessings this day! 'Tis the likes of ye that is dear to her heart.'

The rain was still coming down but not quite so heavily, when they emerged again into the street, but Marcella had only a few more purchases to make and then, having treated herself to tea and Peg to milk and cakes, she managed to board a crowded tram, homeward bound.

It was a good half-hour's quick walking from the tram terminus to Rathbrook and, with Peg and the numerous parcels, Marcella knew that it would take nearer three-quarters this evening. So it was with dismay that she saw that it was heavily raining again as they left the tram, and between everything it was a hard task to hold up her umbrella – so much so that she gave up the attempt, after a few moments. The child, too, looked pale and tired although when Marcella questioned her, she said bravely, 'Peg all yight – soon be home now! Peg has big legs and can walk!' looking up at her mother, with her own dear little laugh.

Halfway to Rathbrook a motor overtook them, and, as it slowed down, Marcella recognised it as Mrs Weston's.

'Why, she is going to give us a lift!' thought Marcella, thankfully. 'Oh I *am* glad for Peg's sake and it is really kind of her. Peg, we will have a nice ride now!' she said quickly to the child as, in obedience to Mrs Weston's beckoning hand, she went to the side of the motor – a delighted Peg following. But Marcella was not asked to enter and no notice whatever was taken of Peg. Instead, two large cumbersome parcels were handed through the window.

'Ah! I thought it was you, Nurse! These are some garments for the Club; you might just take them will you now, and it will save me stopping as I pass. Get the key from Mrs Mulligan and put them in the Dorcas press. What a disagreeable evening! You can drive on, Kenny!'

And Marcella and Peg were left in the muddy road with the rain pouring down, and two more heavy parcels to add to their load.

There was just a little sob from Peg. The child was woefully tired, and the disappointment had been great. Marcella stooped and kissed her.

'Don't mind, darling!' she cried. 'I'm so sorry you are disappointed, and I was sure Mrs Weston was going to drive us home! Oh, if only she had – why she must be nearly there now! Are you *very* tired, dearie?' but she knew when she saw the child's white face that she was. 'I would carry you, but I have too many parcels!'

'Peg can walk!' was the sturdy answer, as the small damsel started off without her mother's hand. 'Teep 'oor hands por the parcels. Peg walk all yight!'

And Marcella's heart went out to the little one who, for the rest of the way, walked so bravely along the muddy, weary road. They reached their own house at last, and both were glad to see Ellen's honest face and to find the cheery tea table ready. Peg indeed was almost too tired to eat and, after a very small supper, went off to bed.

Later on when Marcella stole softly to the side of her cot and stood looking down at her, she thought she looked very white and tired still, and suddenly bent and kissed her with more real love than she had felt since Allan's death. She had thought that the wellspring of all love – that for her little daughter – had dried up for ever within her. But tonight, as she remembered the brave little soul who had trotted so sturdily – and yet she knew how wearily – by her side, she realised that in leaving her Peg God had left her a treasure indeed, and her heart melted to the child. And as she stood there, the mother-love strong once more within her, she found herself thinking with a strange persistency of the church where 'Peg's pretty yady' stood looking down on the tired and weary ones of earth, with the love and sympathy of motherhood divine.

XIII

LONELINESS

The winter was coming to Donegal; coming with rain and storm; coming with bleak, grey days and long, dark nights; when the storm fiend would whistle from the heights of Slieve-na-Carragh and tear down the glen and by the lough road scattering all before him; and when the Atlantic would be churned madly into huge, seething billows and giant waves, which dashed like fiends incarnate against the rocky shore. Then would the lightkeepers on the island be prisoners for many weary weeks, and perhaps months; then would 'Paddy the Post' and his faithful pony often have a hard task to get over the distance between Ardglen and Glenmore, and 'Maggie the Post' a harder one still on those days when she would happen to have a letter for 'the mountains'; and then would Carmen, lying awake often through the dark nights listening to the noise of the storm and sullen boom of the Atlantic, hear with dismay the loud knock which would call her to a maternity case – probably many miles away, over bog and hills.

She had gone through four previous winters at Glenmore, and they had been hard, and very hard; but this one she dreaded more than any of the others, for she had a great loneliness now to add to every other discomfort. Formerly the thought of the Adairs always sustained her and kept up her spirits, even though the weather had often confined her more or less to her own district – still the reassuring thought always remained that they were *there* comparatively near – and that she had Allan to fall back upon in any emergency. And, of course, too, there had been Peg, a ray of sunshine for the darkest day.

But now all was changed. Her three dear ones were gone – one to his well-earned rest, and the other two far away to dear County Dublin – that lovely county the very name of which caused Carmen to hate more than ever the bleak spot in which she was left. And instead of the doctor's house at Carragh being the ideal home towards which her loving thoughts had so often turned in the past, it was now a rather dreary and decidedly untidy residence, where poor Dr Hegarty spent as few hours as possible. He had fallen in love with Carmen almost the first day he saw her, and had already twice begged her to marry him. He seemed incapable of taking no for an answer and so she felt rather awkward when they met, which they had to do fairly often. It must be admitted, however, that the doctor himself made it more often than was absolutely necessary, thinking nothing of going several miles out of his way for the pleasure of calling at the nurse's queer old house in Glenmore – when the least poor Carmen could do was to offer him a cup of tea!

'Well, there is one thing for which I may bless the winter here,' she thought, one evening in early November as she watched him drive away in the gathering darkness after a protracted afternoon call, 'he won't be able to come here so often during the coming months – and won't want to either,

I'm sure! He has no idea yet of what the road between here and Carragh will be like very soon now.'

If Dr Hegarty could only have been satisfied to remain as a friend and not wish for any dearer relationship, Carmen would have welcomed his visits gladly for he was the only human being for miles around with whom she could enjoy an intelligent conversation. Her servant was a local girl – no other would stay there, and Carmen often thought of how fortunate Marcella had been in having Ellen – and although she was useful in that she knew the locality and the people, still for that very reason Carmen could not talk much to her, as she would surely gossip to the neighbours. The schoolmistress was a sour, hard-featured spinster, who did not at all approve of Carmen – a fact of which indeed she made no secret and, with the exception of the fisher-folks' cabins, a few coastguards' houses, and 'Arabella's' emporium at the crossroads, there was no other society of any kind nearer than Carragh – Ardglen and Glenbeg being second editions of Glenmore. And Carragh itself, as we have seen, had lost all attraction for Carmen and indeed – except that the houses were more numerous and the shops something better, and that it contained the church and the priest's house – it also was very little different to Glenmore. And so Carmen Cavanagh sat at the fire one dull evening in November and looked forward to the next few months with a very weary heart. And yet it had been her own wish to remain there. She could, as Cis Bourke had observed, probably have got away before now if she had asked to be removed. But she had not done so, and the reason, of course, was because she had promised Victor Walpole to wait in Glenmore until Christmas – to wait for his promised return visit, and in the interval to make up her mind definitely as to what her answer to him was to be.

And this was just what she found herself unable to do. Heartsick and weary, wretched in soul and mind she was, while the great fight between the powers of Good and Evil went on within her spirit. For Carmen was completely honest with herself; she did not attempt to use sophistry or to pretend that she would only be 'sensible' or 'logical' or like other people if she did this thing. No she knew perfectly that she still had, and she firmly believed that she always would have, the Faith and therefore she could not possibly blind herself to the consequences of that act which she contemplated. Yes, she knew all that quite well. The whole business simply resolved itself into this: Which did she put first? Which, in fact, held most possession of her heart – her religion or Victor Walpole? And again, to go to the depths of things. Who did she love the better – her Lord and Master or the other?

Such was the situation and as such Carmen understood it, and yet day by day passed and she was no nearer to a decision. Of course she had not been to Confession since September, and consequently had not received Holy Communion for some months now. She could not have gone to a priest without mentioning her present state of mind – the Sacrament of penance would have been a mere farce for her otherwise – and she knew what any priest would say in the circumstances. No, this was a battle which she falsely believed that she should fight alone; and so, instead of enlisting every heavenly aid that was possible, she deliberately turned her back on all such help and, unarmed and weakened, she felt her wishes and desires turning more and more towards the man she loved with such a great passion, and farther and farther from the Church of God and its teachings.

Victor wrote regularly to her – several times a week – and she wrote to him in return, but not so often. All his letters breathed unutterable love and he always spoke of their future life together as if it was a foregone conclusion, and he drew pen-pictures of that life which made Carmen's heart beat rapturously and her great eyes to shine like stars. He alluded seldom to the barrier between them, and then always with a sure certainty of its being swept aside – as if indeed it was very slight, barely worth mentioning. And so the weeks passed, and Christmas drew ever nearer and nearer. One evening in early December she went down the road to the little Post Office to get some stamps, and found Mrs McNelis talking to several of the neighbours, in what was evidently a state of pleasant excitement. She turned to greet Carmen as she entered, and, changing rapidly from the Gaelic to the English tongue, she said, 'oh Nurse, I'm just after getting a letter from Mary Ellen – and 'tis she's coming home, maybe, for the Christmas!'

Mary Ellen – as may be remembered – was the pretty, shy girl to whom Marcella had been introduced when she had first come to Glenmore and had gone on a curious tour of inspection around the village under Annabella Gillespie's able guidance. Mary Ellen McNelis had gone to Glasgow nearly two years previously – bitten suddenly with the desire to see life and earn money, consequent on the visit of some smart Glasgow cousins. And although her mother had been intensely averse to the idea at first, she was now apparently quite reconciled, and, according to her accounts, Mary Ellen had been 'doing fine over there – a waitress in a hotel no less – a hotel too, as big as twinty of Wilson's beyant in Carragh!' Now it seemed that she was coming home 'for a holiday' as Mrs McNelis grandly explained to the listening neighbours, 'for it's a bit sick and tired in herself she does be feeling, living so long in yon big town!'

The neighbours were all listening in respectful admiration, with the notable exception of Arabella Gillespie, who, standing rigidly with arms folded and nose rather high in the air, remarked disdainfully, 'yerra, what wud ail the girl? Is it a fine lady she's got to be that she must be needing holidays and change and the rest of it! Yerra, woman dear, have sinse!'

''Tis changed they do be, sure enough when they go to foreign parts,' said a meek little woman who, according to rumour, was ruled with a rod of iron by her daughter, 'a returned Yank.'

Mrs McNelis was about to retort to these dissentient voices in no mild manner, when Carmen interposed. 'I always liked Mary Ellen, Mrs McNelis, and I'm very glad she is coming home for a while. She is such a nice girl that I'm quite sure Glasgow has not spoilt her in the least!'

'Spoilt her?' said Mrs McNelis. 'And what way would it spoil her? And she the best daughter that ever drew a bucket of water from the well!'

'Them's the wans that often turn out the worst in the latter end!' said Arabella sourly.

But Carmen made some laughing rejoinder and was turning away when the postmistress called her back. 'There's a letter here for ye, Nurse,' she said. '"Paddy the Post" took it over to Glenbeg be an oversight, and he's just after sending one of the childer back with it.'

It bore the Dublin postmark, and was in Marcella's familiar and beloved hand. Carmen sped back along the bleak, wind-swept road to her own gate and, pushing it open, ran quickly up the garden path – sodden and with the dripping veronica bushes standing like ghostly sentinels on each side. She hated and dreaded those yards from the gate to the porch once the winter nights set in; she would have gladly gone a mile any other way rather than have to traverse that small bit after dark. The big bushes, towering over her on each side, always made her shudder with a weird dread which she could neither understand nor define. Halfway up the path there was a gap in those same bushes, and she continually expected to see some terrible face peering at her there, as with wildly beating heart and trembling limbs she would be returning in the early hours of a winter morning from some faraway case. She had always felt this terror for this particular spot. She was only affected this way in the winter or of a very dark summer's night, and she always afterwards believed that at some former time an evil deed must have been committed there and left its influence to be felt by anyone with psychic tendencies.

So even this evening, although it was only just dusk, she ran up the path and gained the porch with a feeling of relief. Then she sat down by the cheery turf fire in the queer, old-fashioned sitting room to read her letter hungrily – for, much as her mind might be distressed just then and occupied by another and greater passion, her love for Marcella and Peg was still very deep and real. But before she had read many lines she gave a smothered exclamation of surprise.

'You will be astonished to hear,' wrote Marcella:

that your cousins are gone – all off to Canada! Cis wrote to me a few hurried lines on the eve of their departure, and begged me to let you know and to send her dearest love, and the same from the girls – and poor Philip, of course – and to tell you that she will write at the very first opportunity. It seems that C.V. had been behaving in a perfectly atrocious manner lately, and one night a few weeks ago he actually turned Cis and the twins out into the street at 2am. Luckily Mrs Bateman next door – you remember her? – took them in. Philip was away for a few days or I don't think the old villain would have dared to go so far. However, that was the limit, Letty very properly remarked, and they at once started to make arrangements for leaving the country. Letty wrote to her friends in Canada to expect them and – that girl is really wonderful! – settled quietly for the sale of the furniture – you know nothing belongs to C.V but the things in his own room. When he was out in the afternoon the purchasers came and saw the furniture and arranged to call and remove it on the evening of the day on which your cousins left Dublin – the key of the house was to be left with Mrs Bateman for them. Their boxes were packed quietly and by degrees and carried away to the station, and at last everything was arranged. It is astonishing to me how they managed it all without arousing his suspicions. I knew nothing of what was happening, because I had not had the time to go and see them, and Cis, from what she said in her short note, evidently shrank terribly from any farewells. I think she feels very much leaving Ireland – far more so than the rest will do, for they are beginning life and will soon make a home in the new country. But she is longing for *peace*, poor soul, that she would never have unless the sea separated her from that wretch she married. Anywhere in Ireland he would find her – for, as you know, she practically supported him – and none of us can realise what she must have suffered from him; indeed I believe he is hardly human in his malignity. She told me in the note to call and see Mrs Bateman next door, and it was she told me all the details I have given you, and also described to me the climax – at which I laughed till I cried. It seems that C.V. was suffering from a bit of a cold, and, as usual, considered himself very ill indeed so that he kept his bed in his own room at the top of the house until night time, when he would get up for his usual nocturnal wanderings. Therefore when the new owners came with men and vans to remove the furniture he was still in bed. His astonishment and indignation when, on hearing strange and unaccountable noises, he descended in dressing gown – the famous magenta one of course! – and slippers and the awful nightcap, and saw the furniture being removed can be better imagined than described! Of course he would listen to no explanation, but shouted and raved – a very madman – Mrs Bateman told me – until a passing policeman was called. To him the new owners showed receipts, etc., from Mrs Bourke, and he refused to interfere with their removal. Whereupon C.V. seized an empty soda water bottle and attacked all and sundry with it – cutting the poor bobby rather badly over the eye. He was removed in custody – it took six policemen to do it! and I am sending you the newspaper, where you will see a ludicrous account of his appearance at the police court, and also – and be glad, I'm sure – that he has got a month, with hard labour! How I would love to see him; and how the girls and Philip will laugh when they hear it. But the best of the whole affair to my mind is that Cis has left him with the quarter's rent to pay. When they married he insisted on taking over the house in his name, although he only once paid the rent for it – but it left Cis free at the end, you see. Whether the landlord will ever get a farthing is another kettle of fish!

And now, dearest old girl, how are you keeping yourself? I have been worried at not hearing so frequently from you of late, but I suppose you are very busy – and always wet and tired and cold. I know what winter is like in Donegal. Oh I pity you, although as far as work goes, I am kept going myself but *I* have civilized means of getting about and civilized roads, Oh, that awful road between Glenmore and Carragh – and the big hole at the top of the first hill, where so many poor horses have come to grief – of course it is still there!

Peg, as usual, sends all kinds of love and heaps of kisses. She misses you very much and often asks for 'Tarmen'. She still speaks as strangely as ever. She had a new frock on the other day for the first time, and she said, as she surveyed herself in the glass 'Peg nice 'ittle girl – Peg a *wanks*.' *Swank*, of course, she meant, but at first until I had gone through the usual formula of transposing the *s* I could not think what she was trying to say.

Well, now dear, goodbye for the present, and write soon and tell me all your news and when you mean to ask for a transfer. How I wish you were near us!

Your every loving, Cella.

P.S. – Cis has actually taken Sarah to Canada. The poor soul refused to leave them.

Carmen sat in stunned surprise for several minutes when she had finished Marcella's graphic epistle; and although she smiled with grim pleasure at the picture of C.V. and his disgust when he found he had been so cleverly 'done' by his detested stepchildren, still her uppermost feeling was one of sorrow and loneliness. Cis Bourke had been her only living relative in Dublin, and she had always been as a very dear elder sister to Carmen. And now she was gone – she and the twins, and Eileen and Letty and even Philip, who had been so fond of her – gone without a word or a sign.

'Cis might at least have written!' Carmen said bitterly, and she let the letter drop from her hands and lay back in her chair watching the turf blaze and splutter. 'Yes, she might have written – she can't have cared for me much after all! Ah dear, but it's sad and wretched for anyone to be so lonely as I am now! So lonely and so unhappy! Oh, I wish I knew what I was going to do – I wish I knew what lay before me!'

But even as she meditated in such a manner she knew that the issue of it all lay with herself. In her own hands was the power to decide how she would act. And yet she felt no more able to make up her mind now, in the month of December, than she had been over three months ago, on that evening when Victor Walpole had told her his love, sitting beside her in the 'field of the fairies' at Carragh.

A week later Mary Ellen McNelis came home from Glasgow – and she did not come alone. She brought her baby with her – a tiny, miserable, unwanted child of shame.

She arrived at her mother's house – which she left so gaily two years ago, an innocent young girl eager to seek her fortune – about half-past eight on a dark, cold night. Carmen, driving homewards a few hours later on Young Andy's car, from a sick call to an old woman with rheumatism on the other side of Ardglen, heard a loud din of voices with what seemed like sounds of bitter crying and sobbing from the Glenmore Post Office. What could it be, she wondered? Somebody must be sick – or even dead.

'Put me down here, Andy,' she said, 'something must have happened – perhaps Mrs McNelis has hurt herself in some way.'

Andy obediently drew rein, and when Carmen left the car and walked up to the ray of light from the partly open half-door, he followed her in mild curiosity – he was possessed of a very stolid temperament.

She pushed open the door and stood for a moment, looking with puzzled bewilderment at the scene within.

The place was crowded to its utmost capacity with men and women. Arabella Gillespie, well to the front as usual, had a commanding position near the hearth, and was looking down with sternly virtuous disapproval – tempered with a sort of 'I-told-you-so!' expression – at the girl, who was crouching on a 'wee creepie' near the fire and hiding her face against a bundle wrapt in a shawl which she held in her arms. Mrs McNelis was sitting opposite to her, rocking herself backward and forwards, moaning now and again, and with the tears rolling down her face.

Her husband, tall and stern, well known in the district as a 'hard man' in every walk of life, and his two sons, both over twenty, and as tall and nearly as hard as their father, stood leaning against the Post Office counter. And the neighbours from all the houses near were hemmed into the small space of the little room, half-kitchen, half-post office; and all were gazing at the girl on the stool.

Carmen's entrance caused a temporary silence to fall on the gathering – a silence which was weirdly broken by the wailing cry of an infant.

Then with a sudden sickening realisation of what it all meant, Carmen gave a quick gasp, and Young Andy said '*by Gum!*' – his favourite expression – under his breath.

Carmen went forward then and over to Mrs McNelis. 'What is it?' she asked, stooping over her. 'Oh Mrs McNelis, what is the matter?'

She got no answer beyond a convulsive sob from the poor distraught woman, but John McNelis straightened himself and a hard, bitter look came into his keen fisherman's eyes.

'So ye have come like the rest to witness our disgrace,' he said, and he pointed to the girl, still sitting with hidden face. 'We have got more than we bargained for under our roof tonight. Aye – and more than there's room for, I'm thinkin'.'

Carmen moved to the girl's side.

'Mary Ellen!' she said softly. 'Mary Ellen, it is you? Won't you speak to me – you remember me?' There was no movement from the crouching figure, but Arabella Gillespie, with a dry cough, interposed.'Ye'll maybe not be knowing, Nurse,' she said primly, 'that yon girl is not fit for the like of ye to be speaking to now. She's not an honest woman and she's brought disgrace and shame till a respectable family.'

'Aye,' echoed the neighbours, 'Aye, a disgrace and a shame it is, God help us all!

A dark flush spread over the weather-beaten face of John McNelis; a cruel blow had been struck at his honest pride and self respect, and he was not his normal self for the time being.

'Aye! Shame and disgrace!' he said, 'That's what she has brought on us all! But she won't stay here to shame us for long. No, out of this house she goes – she and her brat – this very night!'

'Aye!' agreed the two boys, their faces curiously like their fathers in their hard bitterness. 'Aye, she must leave! Let her go back till the blayguard that shamed her!'

Mrs McNelis ceased her crying and her rocking for a moment and sprang to her husband's side. 'No, no, John! Ye don't mean it – ye don't mean it – ye don't mean to put her out tonight?' And she broke into a torrent of Gaelic, of which Carmen could only understand a few words, holding on to his arm and almost shaking him in her agony of mind.

All was in vain and Carmen, with incredulous dismay, saw that the furious man was determined on thrusting the girl out of his house that very night. And looking at him, standing rigid with clenched hands, his honest face convulsed with grief and outraged pride, she felt the tears coming to her eyes, for she remembered how fond he had been in the past of this only daughter of his – how proud of her then in her gentle modesty and shy loveliness. And now, instead of the happy, innocent girl of two years ago, there crouched by his hearth a ruined, shamed woman, at whom all might point the finger of scorn, and who could never again hold up her head in Glenmore.

Even as these thoughts flashed through her mind, John McNelis, with one stride reached the half-door, and, thrusting the intruding Andy unceremoniously out of his way, flung it wide open and, while the neighbours looked on with profound interest and a sort of pleasant awe – as at a play performed for their benefit, he shouted across the room to the girl by the fire.

'Now, then, let ye go! And let me niver set eyes on ye or yere brat agin!'

But this was more than Carmen could stand without protest.

'John McNelis!' she cried, perfectly aghast, 'You don't mean it *really?* You don't surely mean to turn your daughter out of the house at this hour of the night? Where will she go? Where will she seek shelter?'

Involuntarily she glanced questioningly at the assembled throng, but there was no response except from Arabella who remarked curtly. 'In no decent house anyways! The like of her have niver been sheltered in Glenmore – and niver will be!'

'Now, then, are ye goin',' shouted McNelis once more, 'or will I have to throw ye out?'

In sheer desperation Carmen put her hand on his arm. 'But where is she to go?' she said again. 'She and her poor baby?'

It was the worst thing she could have said, and McNelis flung off her restraining hand, as he answered savagely. 'She can lie in the ditch – fit bed for the likes of her!'

And at the same moment the unfortunate girl staggered to her feet, white-faced and wan, with the pitiful bundle of unwanted humanity in her arms.

'I'm goin', father,' she said dully.

Her mother took an impulsive step forward as if she would have taken her daughter in her arms once again, but her elder son, with a sharp reprimand, pushed her back in her chair.

Falteringly the girl came through the crowded kitchen towards the half-door and her father's rigid figure and Carmen noticed how unobtrusively, and yet how definitely, each woman drew back – the metaphorical drawing away of the skirts – as she passed. Old friends and neighbours – young women who had been her schoolfellows, old women who had loved and indulged her in the past – all drawing away now from her. Even the men, with stern brow and compressed lips, seemed to feel her presence a contamination.

There is no sterner code of morality anywhere in the world than that which is to be found in the remoter parts of rural Ireland – stern, rigid, uncompromising, and utterly and completely merciless.

And so in the silence of utter condemnation Mary Ellen McNelis walked to the door of her old home.

'Neither do I condemn thee!'

It was as if a whisper – a breath – had carried the word to Carmen and she saw as in a flash, another of long ago standing in her shame and degradation before a Presence Human and yet Divine, who wrote with His finger on the ground.

'Mary Ellen!' she cried. 'Mary Ellen, come home with me. I'll look after you, and the baby, too. Oh, you poor thing. *You poor thing!*'

And moving swiftly to the girl's side, she put her arm round her shoulder and led her through the half-door and out on the dark road before the astonished and scandalised people could say anything.

Needless to say, Arabella was the first to recover her tongue. Crossing herself piously, she raised her eyes to the ceiling. 'Well, God help us all!' she cried. 'And who would have ever thought to see the like of yon! There's conduct for you! Not that I iver had much regard for Nurse Cavanagh, as I often told my mon!'

'God bless her!' cried Mrs McNelis, suddenly brave. 'God bless her for taking in me poor girl this cruel night!'

'Yerra! Hould yer whist!' said her husband, coming back to the hearth and savagely clamping down the blazing sods with his great boot.

A general babble of voices arose now, discussing the event in all its various aspects, and, as is customary in those parts, speaking as freely and unreservedly amongst themselves as if the unfortunate girl's relatives were not there to hear.

'Fr McGinley will be over airly in the mornin' fer sure,' said one of them. 'Paddy McShane is after drivin' over Carragh for male, and he's sure to tell his riverence.'

'He'll have a word to spake to the Nurse, I'm thinkin', and they don't be very great at anny time.'

Gradually the chattering crowd slipped away home until only Arabella was left.

'Well, I must be goin' too!' she remarked at last, to her hearer's relief, 'and I'm gey sorry for yere trouble John – God knows I am! But it's only a week past that I was sayin' to Mary that I hoped nawthing was wrong with the girl! Och, aye! but it's a pity! It's the fine wee girl she used to be – fine – I mind the time she made her First Communion, and she lookin' so happy and –'

'Blast ye, woman! Will ye hould yere tongue, for God's sake, and get home to yere own house out av this!' burst out John McNelis in sudden fury.

Arabella, casting a withering look on him, moved to depart but, as she reached the half-door, she turned and glanced back at the stricken family round their desolate hearth. ''Tis a true sayin' that pride goes before a fall!' she said venomously, 'and iverywann knows that ye all thought a sight too much of yon girl. Well, well, God help ye for poor creatures this night!' and so departed in virtuous triumph.

And in the meantime poor Mary Ellen was sitting by Carmen's fire, drinking tea and eating toast; the unfortunate creature had not tasted a morsel of anything since she had left Kilbeg early in the day.

Her wondering gratitude to Carmen brought tears to the latter's eyes. The girl seemed to consider her humiliation and ostracism as perfectly just and only what she had half expected, and that Carmen should treat in this friendly fashion seemed like a miracle.

' Oh Miss, dear! I'm not fit to be near ye! Sure I know fine I'm not,' was the burden of her refrain.

Carmen asked her no questions and the girl said little, but she mentioned that she was left alone and nearly penniless in Glasgow – her cousins had gone to Liverpool many months ago – and that her baby being sick – to Carmen's eyes indeed it seemed nearly dying – she had thought that perhaps her parents might have taken her in – 'for a wee while, just till the bairn got strong and I could get work, for I wouldn't look to stay at home now of course, Miss. But, ye see, me father he's an awful stern man and I was afeard to let on the way things were with me before I came, and so when he saw me sudden and the baby, he asked me where me husband was and – and –'

And Carmen could only try to soothe her and give her a little hope and courage, and as soon as she had finished her meal she took her to the spare room, where a bed had been made ready – to the intense indignation of Maggie, the maid – and settled her comfortably for the night. The poor creature was worn out absolutely, mentally and physically, and dropped into a sleep of exhaustion almost as soon as her head touched the pillow.

And then Carmen too went to bed, for it was nearly midnight – to bed but not to sleep.

Over and over again she saw once more the sordid tragedy in the McNelis cabin; saw the girl with the humiliated, shamed face, and watched the drawing away of the other women as she passed through them. And another thing she felt again, too, and that was the slight but definite feeling of repulsion which had run through her own body when she put her arm round the poor girl to help her. Unkind and hard like the others, Carmen knew that she personally could never have been. She knew too that she felt a very real pity for the unfortunate being whom she had befriended that night, but the feeling of repulsion remained. She could not help it, and realised that she could not. There is a gulf fixed between the soiled and the unsoiled that nothing in this world can bridge; for, no matter how liberal-minded and tolerant a 'good woman' may feel – and sincerely feel – with regard to her erring sister, that gulf still and always will remain – one of the fixed, unmovable laws against which there is no appeal.

Carmen tossed and turned in her bed, trying vainly to sleep, trying to forget the scenes of that night – to think that they did not concern her. All in vain, for another voice was speaking – an insistent, compelling voice which she could not stifle.

'Just so will all good people look at me bye-and-bye if I do as Victor wishes!' said this voice – 'all good Catholics anyway! Just so will they draw away from me; they would say I was living with him in sin; and if I had a child –'

She buried her face in the pillow, which was wet with her tears. 'God is trying to frighten me again,' she muttered. 'He tried before – the time Dr Murray killed himself! Trying to make me think of my soul – and I don't want to – it terrifies me! And now again the same way He is trying – making me see myself like that girl! But I don't care – I *won't* care! Oh what will I do? What will I do?'

And so hour after hour went by in sore conflict to the soul of Carmen Cavanagh, and it was only when the pale dawn of a winter's day was stealing over distant Slieve-na-Carragh that she slept at last.

XIV

TEMPTATION

Temptation – in which the Odds Greatly Please the Devil

Towards noon the following day Fr McGinley pushed open Carmen's front gate and wheeled his bicycle along the veronica-bordered path to the porch. Carmen had seen him coming – she was just preparing to go out – and came herself to let him in. She thought he looked sterner even than usual, but he shook hands with her in a friendly if somewhat perfunctory manner, and followed her into the sitting room.

'Won't you sit down, Father?' she said somewhat nervously. 'Take this chair near the fire – it's so cold. I suppose you have come about this sad affair of Mary Ellen?'

'Yes – I have come over about this disgraceful business,' the curate replied, and although he seated himself in response to Carmen's invitation, he sat very stiff and upright in his chair. 'I could hardly believe that it was really true when I heard it last night! But I suppose there is no doubt about the matter?'

'No – it's all true enough unfortunately,' replied Carmen, adding impulsively. 'Oh Father! Don't – don't be hard on her – she has suffered so much already!'

The priest's eyes flashed. 'She deserved to suffer,' he said. 'Reared a decent Irish Catholic girl, and to disgrace herself and her family in such a manner! No wonder John McNelis acted harshly towards her. I hear he ordered her out of the house last night?'

'Yes – at eleven o'clock!' said Carmen indignantly, 'and the poor girl had nowhere to go – not one of the neighbours would take her in!'

'No, so I would expect,' was the calm reply. 'Of course, Nurse, you hardly understand how the people around here feel about such things. However, I am thankful you gave her a night's lodging – it was a Christian act, and I hope she is grateful for your kindness.'

'Oh, yes, yes, poor thing!' cried Carmen, adding, 'I am quite willing to keep her for a while, Father, until something else can be arranged for her.'

'There is no need for you to burden yourself longer,' was the reply. 'It must be far from pleasant for you to have such a person in the house. I have arranged for her to stay in Carragh, with a woman who will take her to oblige me, and I am writing at once to people I know in New York who have a large institution there for such girls, and who will receive her and find her work.'

Carmen was silent – a great pity was filling her heart for the girl who was about to be driven forth, across the Atlantic, to eat the bitter bread of philanthropic charity in a strange land.

'Could she not stay in Ireland, Father?' she ventured.

'Stay in Ireland?' he repeated. 'No – certainly not. She must go where she is unknown. Besides we have no room for such as she in Holy Ireland!'

'But oh Father, there are many such,' said Carmen involuntarily. 'Don't you know what Belfast is like in that respect? And in a less degree the other towns and cities – yes, and even in the country I know.'

But he interrupted her unceremoniously. 'Yes – such a state of morals may exist – and I know it does – in all those towns where anglicisation has been at work to undermine the Faith and purity of our race, but it is different – very different, thank God – in our really Irish districts.'

Carmen smiled to herself as she thought how much she would prefer to live in dear old Dublin, with all its supposed sin and follies, than in this bleak corner of North-West Ulster. However, she said nothing more – she recognised that it was useless.

'About the child?' the priest asked curtly. 'I suppose she had it baptised?'

'Oh yes! She told me it had been baptised in Glasgow. Poor little mite! It looks very ill. I don't think it will live long!'

'So much the better, if it should be the Will of God to take it,' was the reply. 'What is before it but a life of sin and shame? And now if you will send the girl to me I'll speak to her.'

Carmen went with very unwilling steps to summon Mary Ellen to the sitting room, and she was not surprised to notice that the girl was white and trembling when she heard by whom she was wanted.

'Oh Nurse, dear, but I be afeared!' she whispered, with dilated eyes, 'Aye, 'tis in dread I be to face him!'

The curate was standing on the hearthrug, looking very tall and stern, when Carmen gently pushed the reluctant Mary Ellen over the threshold. She had just time to hear the girl's dry whisper 'Oh Father!' and the priest's sudden torrent of Gaelic before she fled and left them together.

She went upstairs to her bedroom, and stood at the window, idly watching the Atlantic as it foamed and dashed in winter fury against the rocky coast.

'And that is how he thinks and speaks about Mary Ellen,' she thought, 'a poor ignorant girl, a very child in worldly knowledge in comparison with me. And God only knows how she was tempted or why she fell! And yet she is paying the price, and it looks as if she would go on paying it to the last farthing! And if she is judged so hardly – so mercilessly – how will it be with me?'

She stood drumming her fingers on the window panes and gazing out with unseeing eyes upon the bleak winter scenery. And then the Devil, coming close to her, said complacently. 'Oh, but *you* need not fear – *you* will not have poverty or hardship to face, or the scorn of relations. And you will have a wealthy home waiting for you and the love of the man you adore! And as to the *Church* – well! After all – '

She heard the sitting room door open and the priest's firm step in the hall. He called to her, and she went down reluctantly – somehow she did not want to meet his eyes just then. But he was occupied with Mary Ellen's affairs and did not notice her.

'It is all settled,' he said. 'I am sending a car over for her after dusk this evening – naturally, she shrinks from driving to Carragh in daylight – and she will stay with Mrs McKenna till she leaves for America.'

Carmen only said quietly, 'Very well, Father. I'll see she is ready this evening'; but as she watched him mount his bicycle and ride away – towards the Post Office, as she had guessed he would – she felt for the moment in hot rebellion against his calm assertion of authority, and his matter-of-fact way of arranging everything, as if no one would dream of objecting to any plans which he might make.

'And of course they won't,' she said. 'Even poor Mrs McNelis, I suppose, is thanking him now, with tears of gratitude for packing off her poor girl to America. And she will always bless him for it and believe that it was quite the best course to take – just because "his reverence" said so! It would do him a world of good if some people would go their own way in spite of him. I know one individual who means to do so anyway!'

Mary Ellen McNelis and her baby drove away to Carragh in the evening, and Carmen was left all alone and for the following week she was fearfully – pitifully alone. Even the people, or so it seemed to her, were rather less friendly in their intercourse with her – it was plainly evident that they had resented, because they had not understood, her action in giving shelter to the girl who had brought such disgrace to her native village. Only Mrs McNelis was grateful, and slipped over many times from her own house to thank Carmen again and again, with tears in her eyes, and bringing with her some little gift – eggs, butter or a fowl. And Carmen, knowing how a refusal would have hurt the poor woman, accepted them with a grateful smile.

Christmas Day would fall on a Friday, and on the Tuesday before the great festival, Victor Walpole arrived in Carragh. He had written telling Carmen that he was coming on that day, but also telling her that he would arrive too late that night to come over to Glenmore. So she was not to expect him until the Wednesday, when he would be over early in the day to spend a long time with her. Carmen's work on the district was not heavy and, unless some fresh and unexpected calls turned up, she would be able to spend Christmas Day and the day following as complete holidays, and on the other days to spend a good deal of her time with Victor. On the Tuesday night she hardly slept at all, but was up the next morning and dressed earlier than usual, and, after a hasty breakfast, set off to see the cases she had on hand – they were not many and all fairly near. She hurried as much as she could, and when she reached home again went up to her room to change out of uniform. She had sent to Dublin – casting economy to the winds – for some new frocks, but even as she stood inspecting the contents of her wardrobe, and wondering which she would wear, she heard a car coming down the road and stopping at the gate. Hiding behind the window curtains, she looked out, watching him with all her heart in her lovely eyes as he jumped from the car, paid the driver, and then pushing open the gate, swung up the path in a few long strides. As he did so he swept the house front with his eyes and Carmen drew back for fear he should see her in loose wrapper and flying hair, while she continued to devour his beloved face from afar.

Maggie knocked at the door a minute later.

'It's the gentleman to see ye, Nurse.'

'All right, Maggie! Ask him to wait and I'll be down in a few moments.'

With shaking hands and flushed cheeks, she piled her hair on top of her head and slipped into a pretty afternoon frock of a soft grey material. Over this she wore a scarlet sports coat – and the combination, in Carmen's case, was simply perfect. Her heart seemed to be beating so loudly as she went downstairs that she thought even Maggie, in the kitchen, must hear it! And then she stood for a breathless moment with her hand on the sitting room door before she could find courage to turn the handle. He was standing restless and impatient on the hearthrug, gazing into the turf fire, but he swung round as the door opened, and in a flash was beside her. It was his hand that closed the door and then drew her into the shelter of his arms, and, as their lips met at last, it seemed to Carmen that not only would this world but even Heaven itself be well lost for love.

'Oh my dearest!' she said, when at last prosaic speech came back to them and they were beginning to descend to earth again. 'My dearest! How I have missed you! Oh Victor, I have been simply *hungry – starving* for the sound of your voice and the sight of your dear face!'

Victor Walpole smiled as he looked down on the lovely face against his shoulder. 'I'm glad I was not the only sufferer then!' he said, 'for, do you know, Carmen, I could really hardly attend to my work properly these last few weeks. Counting days – and even hours! – and tearing off the leaves of calendars was all I was fit for!'

It was not until evening that he approached the other matter. They had gone for a brisk walk together – watched with lynx eyes by Arabella as they passed the crossroads, Carmen, for once, being oblivious of her criticising glances, having forgotten indeed the woman's very existence – down by the shore, toward Glenbeg, the sea breezes painting a vivid colour on the girl's cheeks and stimulating the jaded Londoner's lungs, making them almost gasp for breath at times. Then they returned to a plain but delightful little dinner, the menu of which Carmen had carefully gone over with Maggie for days before. A town cook would have fainted at the idea of preparing *any* dinner at a turf fire and with a collection of 'pot ovens' but the roast fowl and apple tart which were baked in these primitive cooking utensils were done to a turn; the potatoes were as floury and dry as only Donegal potatoes can be, while Carmen herself saw to the sauce and gravies and other details which go to make an enjoyable dinner. Then they drew chairs up to the fire and prepared for a long, cosy chat, and Carmen knew that the moment she dreaded, although she tried not to admit the fact even to herself, was upon her.

'Well, now, sweetheart of mine!' said Victor, as they lit their cigarettes – Carmen was an inveterate smoker, and she used to laughingly excuse herself by saying that she must have inherited the habit from her Spanish ancestors. 'I suppose you have got over your prejudices against my former marriage and are going to be a sensible person and marry me – "soon and sudden" as the patients say, at the Registry Office?'

Carmen did not speak immediately; she was trying to find words in which to answer him, and, thinking she was still hesitating, he leant forward and laid one of his hands over hers.

'Surely you know, darling,' he said, 'that I would never have asked you to become my wife if there had been a fraction of doubt of any illegality in the matter. But there is none. Although I was certain myself, still – to make absolutely sure for your sake – I consulted a barrister when I was in London, and everything is all right. Your religion makes no difference in the eyes of the law; my divorce is absolute – my former wife has already re-married, as I told you before, and our marriage at the Registry Office will fulfil all that the law requires and make us man and wife hard and fast in the sight of man.'

'Yes – but not in the sight of God,' replied Carmen. The words had been wrung from her involuntarily – she had not wanted to speak them at all.

'Oh now, my dear girl,' Victor interposed, but before he could say anything more she interrupted him.

'As I told you before, Victor,' she said, *'there is no divorce in the Catholic Church.* In the view of Catholics you are still a married man and will be until your wife dies. The fact that she has "married again" doesn't alter anything. As a Catholic I have been taught this and – I believe it.'

He turned white in spite of his self-control. He was going to lose her after all, then! But her next words reassured him, although they immensely surprised him too.

'Yes – I believe all that,' said Carmen again; her hands were idly clasped on her lap, while her eyes gazed straight before her, and she spoke in a cold, even voice as though she talked of some trivial, unimportant matter. To Victor she seemed almost a stranger for the moment.

'I know it and believe it, but – I am going to go through the form of marriage with you.' Victor's handsome face lit up.

'Then you *will* marry me, beloved!' he cried, 'you will be my wife?'

'No,' said the cold, strange voice – 'I cannot *marry* you – no marriage is possible between us. I will go through the mock ceremony at the Registry Office because you wish it, but it has no power to unite us, and I will be your – mistress and not your wife.'

'*Carmen!*' cried the man in shocked and angry protest, 'don't talk like that, it's horrible! Oh my dear, my dear, do you think for one moment that I would have asked you – you whom I love and respect above all women – to become what you say! You will be my dear and honoured wife. Oh Carmen, my darling – don't look like that!'

Getting up from her chair, she came over and knelt beside him, and reaching up her arms she clasped them round his neck. 'Don't argue any more, *please*, Victor,' she said. 'All the talking in the world won't alter the facts. I am giving up everything that I once held dearer than life itself for you and your love – then take me, and oh, Victor, my dearest – love me, and be – be good to me!'

He calmed and soothed her with all the love and devotion of his heart, and after a while she partly recovered her gay spirits, and the evening passed in talk of plans out their future. He told her that he could arrange with another surgeon to take over his practice for a few months in the spring, and that as soon as they were married he intended to take her to Spain – the sunny land of her mother's people, and which she had never seen.

'We could be married in February, dearest – couldn't we?' he said. 'Give your Committee a month's notice at the beginning of the year and go and stay with Mrs Adair for part of February – until you are ready to come to me! And we will have a honeymoon to remember!'

She assented, but rather more soberly than he liked; however, as he began telling her about Spain, where he had once stayed for some time with friends, her cheeks flushed and her eyes shone.

'Victor! I will love to see it!' she cried 'I have always the greatest wish to go to Spain – my own dear Spain I call it to myself, for I feel that I will be quite at home there!'

'Do you know, sweetheart,' he said, 'you put me in mind of the Spanish women the first day I saw you. Do you remember that day last May when I arrived at Carragh and saw you wheeling your bike down the hill?'

Ah, yes, she remembered, and smiled and sighed at the thought of the change in her life since then – only a few short months ago.

'Do you know anything about your mother's people,' asked Victor then, 'or in what part of Spain they lived?'

Carmen shook her head.

'Teresa Perez was my mother's name,' she replied, 'but I don't know her social position or anything like that. She was very beautiful, with a lovely voice, and sang for a while in Grand Opera in Paris and London. It was in Paris she met my father – a poor, struggling artist – and they fell in love with each other almost at once and were married very soon. I have heard that they were devoted to each other and were perfectly happy, but my mother was never strong, and after my birth she simply got weaker and weaker until she died.'

'And your father?' asked Victor.

'My father had been painting a picture of her as "Carmen", her favourite character – she called me after her – and everyone who saw it said that it would have made a fortune and a name for him – it was so lifelike and every detail was perfect. But after her death he put down his brush and said he would never paint again – fame and fortune were worthless to him without the one who had inspired him. And also he could not bear to finish the picture from memory when *she* had been the model for so long. He only lived seven months, and then I, a poor little wretch of not quite four years, was sent off to a convent boarding school in the South of France. When I got older, as you know, I came to my Irish cousins in Dublin.'

'I have often wondered,' said Victor suddenly, 'that you never thought of going on the boards yourself?'

'Oh, but I would certainly have trained for the stage,' cried the girl, 'if I had been allowed, but my mother, for some unknown reason of her own, made my father promise faithfully that I would never follow her profession. I often felt it very hard lines – not that I think for one moment that I would ever have been fit for the opera – for my voice although fairly good and well trained is not good enough for *that!* but I know could have *acted.* I have sang in an amateur concert as "Carmen" too. Did you ever see me dressed for the part? But of course you didn't. We had no time for such frivolities during that terrible time at Carragh. Would you like to see me in my national costume?'

'I should think so!' he cried. 'Why? Have you got one here?' But Carmen was gone even as he was speaking.

Left alone, Victor Walpole sat smoking and gazing into the turf fire. Although feeling on the whole as happy as an accepted lover should feel, still Carmen's remarks earlier in the evening left, so to speak, an unpleasant taste in his mouth. She had spoken in such an extraordinary way, and then that insisting that she would not really be his wife – no matter what ceremony they went through – was both distressing and annoying to Victor Walpole.

He loved her very deeply and as he had never loved before. His first marriage, with a shallow, vain Society woman had been a 'fiasco' from the very beginning, and various other 'affairs' in which he had indulged, more from boredom than any other deeper feeling, had been of fleeting duration. But Carmen was another matter. He not only loved but respected – idealised – her and then that she should insist, in spite of all this, that she would not – in a moral or religious sense – be his wife was a very real thorn in the flesh to him. Not that he was religious – he was not even Orthodox, believing that somewhere there probably existed a First Cause, constituted his creed – but he wanted the woman he loved and respected to occupy an honoured position, and such could only be obtained by the marriage ceremony. He would put her on a pedestal for all his world to revere; she would be, in his eyes, like 'Caesar's wife' without stain or spot. And yet in her own eyes what would she be? And he remembered her bitter shame-shadowed words of a short while ago.

Well, he was a wealthy man, with private means besides his large West End practice, and he could and would give her everything that would make for happiness in this world. And as for her religious scruples – surely they would fade away before the reality of his great love. A clash of a tambourine, a flick of a cigarette ash blown across the room to him, a lilting laugh, and looking up, he saw Carmen – Carmen of the immortal song and story – standing on the threshold.

Yes, she made an ideal picture of the alluring Spanish beauty: there was no doubt of that, with her frock of scarlet and gold, its wide, frilly skirt standing out from her slight figure as she twisted around on her toes, a mantilla of old Spanish lace, an ivory fan, and a red rose stuck coquettishly over her ear. Before he could speak she clashed the tambourine and began to sing and dance – the Carmen of the popular opera was there before his eyes.

'Where did you get the rig-out? It's capital!' he said, when she had finished and was sitting, resting on the hearthrug.

She looked up at him, her face still flushed, her big eyes shining, and a look of gay abandon all about her. 'Oh, this is an old creation,' she answered, laughingly. 'I've had it for years, got it first for a fancy dress affair at the Mansion House and kept it ever since. Cis made the dress, it's worth nothing, but the mantilla was my mother's. Isn't the lace lovely?'

'Yes, and worth something, too,' he said, examining the dainty gossamer-like fabric carefully. 'Your mother must have had either family or wealth to possess this!'

Carmen only laughed.

'Neither of them have descended to me anyway,' she said. 'And now, my beloved Don Jose, we must say – Addio! Your car has arrived to take you back to Madrid – or Carragh – and it's after nine o'clock; you won't be back at your hotel till nearly eleven, and the very good and proper Mr Wilson would be scandalised if you were any later!'

'Until tomorrow, then, sweetheart of mine! It will be Christmas Eve – I'll try and get over fairly early.'

'Christmas Eve!' repeated Carmen quietly, her gaiety suddenly gone, quenched in a moment. 'Christmas Eve! *I had forgotten!*'

'Oh well, we must not forget Christmas!' said the man laughingly as he pulled on his great coat – not noticing her sudden gravity. 'It's a good old English custom you know to keep Christmas! Although I'm afraid for myself and a good many more of my countrymen its religious significance has gone out of date. It doesn't mean much to me now!'

After he was gone, Carmen sat by the dying fire for a long time, sitting motionless, a strange figure in her quaint dress, while the little clock on the chimney-piece ticked the moments away. Then she got up suddenly and, running her fingers through her hair with an almost distracted gesture, she said, 'Oh I mustn't think! I mustn't *think!* If I think I'll go mad! Christmas Eve, and no Confession – Christmas Day, and no Mass! For I won't be a hypocrite – on that point I'm determined. I won't keep on going to Mass while I'm here, just for the sake of appearances and to prevent talk. No! I have decided now – I have chosen my future life, and from this day forward I will give up all Catholic practices. Would to God that I could give up my *belief* too, and then I might have some peace of mind. But I can't do that – I'm like the devils – I believe and tremble!'

She paused for a moment and idly kicked a sod of turf with her pretty little foot.

'After all,' she said defiantly, 'I'm going to be happy – yes, I *am!* And Christmas – what is it after all?'

But even as she spoke, the Catholic soul of her – which was not dead yet – saw again the Manger and the dear little Christ Child with His tiny hands outstretched to comfort and bless, and a dry sob rose in her throat. She shook herself angrily as if she would get away from the haunting memories. 'Christmas doesn't mean much to me now!' she repeated as she remembered her lover's words, and went slowly upstairs to bed.

Christmas came and passed – the first Christmas without the Christ Child for Carmen Cavanagh – the first one she could remember without Mass – without the real joy and peace of that blessed time.

Of course Victor spent the day with her, and she put on her prettiest frock and talked and sang to him with feverish gaiety; and they had turkey and mince pies – one could get a large turkey for five shillings in Donegal in pre-war days! – and Victor brought some champagne over, and they toasted their future life together and apparently were as merry and carefree as it was possible for two people to be.

But Carmen carried her secret sorrow and care all the time – aye, and her shame, too, for she could not forget the wondering, frightened look in Maggie's eyes when she informed the girl, without making any excuse about it, that she was not going to Mass. And she knew, too, that gossip was already hard at work about her for, meeting some of the people from around on the roads when she and Victor were taking a walk, it had seemed to her that they avoided her – almost drew to one side as she passed with her lover, 'drawing away the skirts already – and they don't even know the worst of it yet!' she thought in bitter irony.

She had agreed to Victor's arrangements and would hand in her notice on January 1st. He had to return to London on December 30th, so they were making the most of their few remaining days together, and Carmen dreaded getting a call which might take her away to the mountains for a day or a night.

Walpole had made no secret of his approaching marriage and Carmen, once she had taken the plunge, which she now looked upon as irrevocable, did not care if he published the facts from the housetops.

So Mr Wilson of the Carragh Hotel, being a Protestant – and a Northern one at that – meeting Fr McGinley wheeling his bicycle one morning past the hotel, could not resist imparting the news to him, which, although partly guessed at in Glenmore, had not reached the priest's ears as yet.

'Good morning, sir,' he said – he would not say 'Father' but compromised with 'sir' on account of the priest-ridden district in which he had to live just then! 'Fine morning for this time of year!'

The curate, with a brief reply, was passing on, but Mr Wilson's next remark arrested his attention.

'So I hear you're going to have a wedding over at Glenmore! It will be a bit of excitement for the people there!' He knew perfectly well that there would be no 'wedding' from the priest's point of view, but he looked all innocence as Fr McGinley swung round.

'You know more than I do then, Mr Wilson,' he said. 'I've heard of no wedding among my people.'

'Indeed, sir – you surprise me! But doubtless you will be informed directly. Mr Walpole, the well-known London specialist – a guest with me at present – is about to marry Miss Cavanagh.'

The priest's face hardened; so she was going to marry a Protestant – it was only what he might have expected of her. But even as he was standing in annoyed silence Mr Wilson continued in suave accents. 'It is to be hoped that this will prove a happier marriage for Mr Walpole than his first one – most disastrous that was, I believe!'

'Oh, so the man's a widower,' said the curate.

'Oh, no, not exactly a widower,' replied Mr Wilson. He was really enjoying himself at the moment. 'Let us say rather a bachelor once again! Ha! ha! It's easy to see that you don't read the English papers. But, of course, we know you don't ...'

'No, I don't read the dirty rags,' agreed the other curtly.

'Just so,' said Mr Wilson, 'for had you done so you would have seen – but of course it's nearly two years ago – a full account of Mr Walpole's divorce case against his wife – she has married the co-respondent since, by the way!'

'What!' exclaimed the priest. 'What! Are you certain of what you are saying, man? Is this true?'

'Oh! Quite true, sir! But if you doubt my word I am sure Miss Cavanagh, who knows and accepts all the details, will corroborate my words – or Mr Walpole himself. He is still in the hotel, not having started on his daily visit to Glenmore yet. Shall I call him?'

'No!' the curt reply, 'my business is not with *him*!'

And mounting his bicycle he rode at a breakneck pace along the road to Glenmore.

'Put that in your pipe and smoke it, me brave boyo! Your domineering ways will get a back set for once, I'm thinking! Not that I should care to be in Miss Cavanagh's shoes just now. No, I don't fancy I should,' said Mr Wilson, with a chuckle, as he entered his hotel.

Carmen was upstairs when Maggie, looking rather scared, told her that 'his Riverence was below and waiting to spake to her.'

So it had come, she thought. Well, the sooner it was over – the sooner she made the final break with the Church – the better.

He was standing straight and rigid as she entered the sitting room, and if he had looked vexed and annoyed on that morning a few weeks ago when he had called to see Mary Ellen – now on her way to America, leaving a nameless grave behind her in Carragh – he looked terrible now. He did not offer to shake hands, and Carmen made no advance to him, nor did she ask him to sit down.

'Is this thing true?' he asked at once, his keen eyes fixed on her as if he would read her very soul.

She braced herself and answered so quietly as to surprise herself.

'If you mean my – marriage with Mr Walpole,' she said. 'Yes – it is true.'

'You may well hesitate – as I noticed you did – before the word *marriage*,' said the priest. 'I have been told that the man was divorced from his first wife and that she is still living. Is that correct?'

She nodded her head.

'Then you know, of course, that there can be no marriage between you and this man?'

'Yes – I know.'

'You know? You say you know this! And yet you intend to go through this farce of a so-called marriage – at the Registry Office, I suppose? Are you mad?'

'Perhaps.'

Something in the dull answer, in the haggard look, caught the curate's attention, and his voice changed. 'Look here, my child,' he said. 'Why are you doing this terrible thing. This dreadful act that will cut you adrift from the Church and the sacraments, and will destroy your soul for ever? Are you in trouble? Can I help you? Perhaps, God forgive me, I may have been hard, ungenerous to you, but ...'

'Stop, stop, Father!' cried Carmen. 'Don't – don't be *kind* to me – I can't stand that! I am going through with this mock ceremony at the Registry Office because Victor wishes it and believes it will make our union legal. I know, of course, that I might just as well go to him without any ceremony, for any good it is! But I am going to live with him – going to follow him to the ends of the earth if he asks me – because I love him – love him better than my life and my soul – better than my Faith – aye, and better than my God! I know *all – all* you would say to me! Oh, don't think I haven't suffered in the long nights and in the days, too – but I have decided now, and nothing – *nothing* will change me!'

She sank into a chair exhausted and dropped her face in her hands.

'Oh, but it is impossible – impossible! Not to be thought of!' cried the priest. 'You must listen to me – you don't know what you are doing!'

For an hour he talked, using every conceivable argument of which he could think. But it was useless, and a cold horror came upon him as if he were fighting something very tangible and evil. As if some abominable presence was near – mocking at him and his pitiful efforts to win back the soul of the girl who sat so quietly and listened without another word, but who was influenced not one bit by all he had to say.

He left her at last and mounting his bicycle, white-faced and haggard-looking with the thought of it all, he rode back towards Carragh. When about halfway he met Victor Walpole coming to Glenmore. The surgeon raised his cap courteously – he had always had a very real liking and respect for the curate ever since he had seen his work amongst the people during the epidemic – but the priest looked straight ahead and passed him without glance or salutation.

'By Jove, he has been over to interview Carmen!' thought Victor, 'Poor girl! I hope he hasn't been upsetting her with any of his medieval matrimonial ideals.'

For the moment Fr McGinley had hesitated as to the advisability of stopping and speaking on the matter to Mr Walpole, but he considered – and rightly – that it would have been useless, and in any case he had neither the authority nor the right to speak to this man.

On reaching Carragh he burst in upon the old parish priest as he sat in his study, a well-worn volume upon his knee, his old-fashioned mother-of-pearl snuff box on the table beside him. Fr Devereux belonged to another era and another class, and his curate, with his nervous energy and numerous plans and schemes, sometimes tired him a little.

He looked up now as the latter entered but before he could even ask a question, the curate rushed into the subject and told him all – ending with an account of his interview with Carmen.

'She is quite hardened, Father,' he said. 'I despair of her! She is like one who is obsessed by the Evil One himself, and is bent on rushing to her own destruction.'

The old priest made no reply; he only idly tapped on his snuff box with his slender fingers, which were the colour of old ivory, and gazed quietly into the heart of the blazing turf fire.

'Well?' said Fr McGinley, impatiently – he really often thought that Fr Devereux should retire, he was so old and forgetful – and so slack at times. 'Well, Father, what is to be done? I have said all I could to her, and it's useless! I asked her to come and see you, but she refused most definitely. I am afraid I can do no more.'

'I'm afraid not, my son,' was the quiet reply. 'You have, as you say, done all that lay in your power.'

'But can *you* do nothing, Father?' urged the curate so terribly helpless in the matter, 'for she says plainly that she is quite willing to sever her connection with the Church – to leave it altogether. Oh,' suddenly breaking down and covering his face with his hands, 'it is too horrible! And we can do nothing – nothing.'

The old priest rose slowly to his feet – he was very stiff, and walked with much difficulty, for he had been crippled by rheumatism for many years now.

'As you say, we can do nothing,' he said – 'so I am going to leave the matter in the Hands of the Only One who *can* help. Give me your arm across to the church my son, and leave me a while before the Tabernacle.'

XV

GOD'S VOICE

'I am Jesus whom thou persecutest.' *Acts*, chap. 9, v. 5
'She turning, saith to him: Rabboni (which is to say, Master)'
Gospel of St. John, chap. 20, v. 16

Victor Walpole cycled on quickly towards Glenmore; he was anxious to reach Carmen's side, for he was afraid that the priest's visit might have been upsetting to her and cause her to go over once again in her own mind all her scruples against their marriage. But when he reached the house Young Andy's car was standing outside and that individual himself saluted the surgeon with a beaming smile – for was he not a good Protestant? And if report spoke truly was going to be the means of 'turning' the nurse – for whom Andy had always had a sneaking regard – Papist though she was.

'Hallo Andy,' said Victor, a quick look of annoyance on his face, 'are you waiting on Miss Cavanagh? Has she a call?'

'Aye,' was the laconic answer. He was however about to add some more information, but at that moment Carmen appeared coming quickly down the garden path – a neat, sensible figure, with her mackintosh over her uniform coat, her storm cap well down on her head, and her bag in her hand.

'Oh Victor,' she said, stopping out of earshot of the jarvey, 'I'm so sorry, but I've just had a call to a maternity case – and it's away beyond Glen-na-Sheena.'

'Glen-na-Sheena, where on earth is the outlandish place?'

She laughed at his angry face, although she was vexed enough herself.

'Glen-na-Sheena is nearly twelve miles away – across the country from Ardglen. We will be several hours getting there – the roads are *terrible*, about the worst around here. And of course I don't know when I will be back – the last time I was up there I was three days away!'

'Good Lord!' he said, vexedly, 'and I have to be off the day after tomorrow!'

'Oh I know, dearest,' she said laying her hand caressingly on his arm, with a world of love in her glorious eyes, 'and of course I won't delay any longer than I can help – but it depends, as you know, on the patient – and on the *weather!* Andy says we are going to have *snow!* But goodbye now – I can't wait any longer!' and with a tight hand-clasp and a gay nod and smile, she jumped on the waiting car and was driven down the road in Andy's best style, leaving Victor feeling very disconsolate and ill-used by Fate, to drive back on the Carragh car to the deadly dullness of Wilson's.

'Just half-past twelve, Andy!' said Carmen, looking at her wristlet watch. 'How soon can we be there? The man who came for me was on horseback, and he said he came over in two hours.'

'It'll take us nearer three,' said her driver, as he pulled up the collar of his greatcoat, 'the wind's agin us, and the horse can't make much headway.'

It was an intensely cold drive, and when a little after three o'clock she saw the village street of Glen-na-Sheena – situated at the foot of a hill – Carmen felt very glad. The car could be seen by the villagers a good bit away as it carefully walked down the rocky hill, and as she came into the tiny street they came to the half doors and looked after her – one excited woman calling out, 'yerra – make haste, let ye! For the love of God! 'tis awful bad she be entirely!' But Young Andy, with the Protestant settler's supreme contempt for the 'mere Irish' – always plainly shown in Donegal – drove stolidly on as if he heard not.

Arriving at the house, however, Carmen found that she was not a moment too soon, and she had only time to evict eight 'wise women' and a few others from the patient's room and to make other necessary arrangements before the population of Glen-na-Sheena increased by one – and she congratulated herself that would get home that night after all. She made her patient comfortable and bathed the baby before the admiring gaze of the crowded kitchen, as many as possible of the neighbours having called in 'to see what God had sent.'

It was a clean, neat little cabin, and the cheery turf fire shone on the gleaming dresser of crockery and the spotless chairs and tables and on the patient's mother, in her scarlet petticoat and white frilled cap, as she deftly 'slapped up' a hot cake and 'wet the tay' – black and strong – while Carmen was putting the finishing touches to the toilet of the young gentleman on her lap.

'Ye'll take a cup of tay, Nurse darlint – the Lord bless ye!' said the patient, as Carmen smilingly deposited her 'bargain' in the bed by her side. ''Tis a could drive ye'll be havin' back – God bless us!' glancing through the tiny window at the darkness without. 'Is it snowing it is already?'

Carmen went over and peered out. Yes, snowflakes were falling from the leaden skies. They were not very big however, and she comforted herself with that.

'Oh, perhaps it won't be much!' she said. 'I'll drink a cup of tea quickly and then we can start.'

When she re-entered the kitchen she saw Andy drinking and devouring hot cake near the door; Carmen's table was spread in lonely grandeur for herself near the hearth and the enormous turf fire, 'as big as a haystack nearly' she thought, laughingly looking at the great pile of turf and backing her chair a little out of heat.

'Is the snow going to be much, Andy?' she asked, as the proud grandmother was excitedly pouring out the tea.

'Aye – I'm thinkin' it wull!'

'But we will get back to Glenmore tonight, surely?'

'Aye, if we can make the road, but I wouldn't say for certain.'

Half an hour later they started, speeded on their way by blessings, advice and instructions from the entire village as to their best route and the right way of driving the horse in the snow and other freely offered information – all of which was received in contemptuous silence by Andy.

It was now nearly six o'clock and quite dark, and the snow was coming quickly and silently down, blowing across their faces and into their eyes and causing the horse to shake and fidget. Andy had two good lamps and, as he knew the road well, they had hopes of getting back by ten or eleven o'clock that night – that it would take them fully that length of time they were sure, for their going could not be anything but slow under the circumstances.

They proceeded on their way for a couple of miles with increasing difficulty, for the snow was falling heavier and faster, making the journey very hard for the poor horse and stinging Carmen's face and almost blinding her. In vain she tried to keep her face buried in her wraps; the snow seemed to pierce through everything, and for the last half hour or so they had been uncomfortably aware that a blizzard was beginning to blow fiercely – and against them, too.

'I'm thinking it wull be quare and hard to make Glenmore the night,' said Andy – and he had to shout across the car so that Carmen would hear him above the noise of the ever-increasing storm. The horse was now only walking, for the snow was so deep about his feet that he was inclined to flounder, and the fierce gale was beating him with pitiless fury.

'Whereabouts are we, Andy?' asked Carmen,

'That's what I'm tryin' to find out,' and, drawing rein for a moment, he peered into the surrounding darkness – an impenetrable, inky blackness – and asked, 'What might the time be now, Nurse?'

Stooping down to the light of the lamp, Carmen with some difficulty discerned the hands of her watch. It was nine o'clock.

'We should be right be at McShane's crossroads be now,' said Andy, 'and I see no sign of them! Naw I do not, and I'm thinkin' I don't rightly know where we are at all!'

'Oh Andy!' wailed Carmen, the tears very near her eyes from sheer cold and physical discomfort. 'Are we lost then? And what will become of us?'

'By Gum! And that's what I don't know rightly myself!' was the dry answer.

He urged the willing but exhausted horse, and it floundered on for another while, but then stopped dead – deaf alike to pleading or scolding.

'It's no use,' said Carmen, 'he can't do any more, Andy, he's dead beat – the poor beast!'

'Aye – that's true for ye!' replied the horse's owner, adding. 'Would ye mind stayin' here for a wee while, Nurse, and I'll go forward with one of the lamps till I see can I find out where we are at all?'

'All right,' said Carmen wearily, 'but come back if you can, Andy, before the horse and myself are buried alive!

'Oh, I'll come back to ye! Never fear for that!' was the reply and, taking one of the car lamps in his hand, he took a few steps forward and was swallowed in the darkness.

Carmen sat in dull misery where he left her, only rousing herself now and again to speak a few encouraging words to the poor horse, as he shivered and floundered in the snow. She never remembered being so deadly cold in all her life before, and the pain caused by the snow blowing in her eyes was intense. She thought in a half-hearted way that she would get down off the car and walk about and so try to make her blood circulate better, but she gave up the idea and sat on trying to get some warmth from the rugs and wraps in which she was enveloped – but they might have been made of cotton for all the good they were.

How long she sat there she had no idea. Later she heard that Andy was away nearly an hour and a half. She was becoming more and more dazed and numb, and more indifferent to everything in the world – it was as though she had been sitting there for centuries and would go on sitting there still for centuries to come – when she heard voices approaching. She could hardly believe her ears, and thought it must be imagination, but presently she discerned a light coming in her direction and then she distinctly heard Andy's voice and several others talking also. 'Thank God! – Oh thank God!' she breathed.

It seemed that she and Andy had gone miles out of their right road, in the darkness and the blizzard, and were now quite close to the tiny hamlet of Glenavin – indeed had it been daylight they would have been able to see it – a mere handful of cabins with a school and a little further on, a small chapel – built on the rough mountain side.

Andy when he first started on his tour of discovery had gone away from it and so wasted much time and then, struggling back through the snow and not knowing where in the world he was, he had fortunately seen a light from a window and so found his way to help and shelter.

The horse was led by Andy and one of the men who had come with him as a rescue party, and the others walked beside the car and cheered and condoled with Carmen.

From the drift of their conversation, carried on in English out of politeness to the 'strangers' she learned that Andy was to be given shelter in the house of one Pat Doherty, where the horse would also be looked after, and that she herself was to sleep at the priest's house.

'Oh, but at this hour!' she faintly protested, her frozen lips speaking the words with difficulty. 'How could I disturb him!'

'Oh, that's no matter – none at all!' said the man beside her, "'tis the great reader his Reverence is – always at his books – 'tis little sleep does him! And he heard this man knocking beyant at Mary Gillespie's door and came out and talked to him. And he said then that we were to bring you to his house – and he called up his housekeeper to get things ready for ye.'

Carmen said no more, and in a short time she saw lights twinkling here and there and heard more voices, and then the car stopped and a very gentle voice – the voice of an old man – asked. 'Is this the young lady, boys? That's right! We are quite ready for her,' and Carmen, by the light of a lanthorn held by one of the men, saw the priest standing in the roadway by his house. He was wearing a rather rusty soutane, and she thought how like he was to an old French Abbe of her childhood's days, with the same longish white hair and clear-cut, cameo-like face.

She tried to speak – to thank him, and she also tried bravely to get off the car, but she had to be lifted down, for she was too stiff with the cold and her cramped position for so long to move. So Andy and another man lifted her between them and carried her into the priest's house, where they deposited her in a big easy chair before the blazing turf fire – and Andy said 'By Gum!' at which she laughed and felt better.

The priest's housekeeper, a stout, motherly person, helped her off with her snowy outer garments with many expressions of sympathy. Then drawing off boots and stockings, rubbed her frozen feet with a towel till they tingled again, and then brought her woollen stockings and carpet slippers of her own – about four times too large for Carmen's pretty feet – but which she was very glad to get. And in the background the priest was busy making delicious coffee – never was a cup of that beverage more enjoyed, and as Carmen sipped it, and partook of some oat cake and brown bread, she felt a different person to the frozen creature of a short while ago.

'How can I ever thank you, Father? How kind you are to me!'

The house was very small, and she glanced round it with interest as she began to feel herself again. The room she was in seemed to be the living room, and opposite was a door which led into the priest's tiny study. On the left was a room which was evidently the housekeeper's bedroom, and a narrow flight of bare wooden stairs, ladder-like in appearance, led to a room above. And in this room she presently heard the housekeeper moving about; evidently she was to sleep there and the woman was getting it ready for her.

'I hope I am not giving you much trouble, Father?' she said, 'but of course I know I must be! Oh what would I have done without you?'

'No trouble in the world, my child,' replied the priest, 'no trouble – only a great pleasure! And you may be sure that

Our Dear Lord would never let any harm come to you when you were doing your duty – such a useful person as you are, too!' with a twinkle in his kindly old eyes. The housekeeper came down the stairs at that moment, carrying some rugs over her arm.

'The room is all ready now for the young lady,' she said, 'and I'm after putting the hot jar in the bed.'

'Oh Father, am I taking your bedroom?' cried Carmen, in real distress. 'What a shame! *Please* don't let me put you out of your room! Why, I can sleep here in this chair quite easily – I could sleep on the floor this minute!'

The priest smiled as he answered, 'no, no, my child – you must go to bed and get a good rest and proper sleep after your hardship of tonight. As for me, I often sit up half the night reading, and with a couple of rugs and this good fire, I'll be as happy as a king! Let you go up now with Martha and she will see that you have all you need. Goodnight now, my child – God bless you!'

Carmen shivered a little; she felt she had no right to that blessing – that she had obtained it under false pretences. Supposing Fr O'Toole – as she had discovered his name to be – knew about the life which she intended to live for the future, what would he say, she wondered, and her cheeks burned at the thought.

She followed Martha up the steep stairs, and saw a bare, scrupulously clean room, with just a narrow bed, a table, and chairs, and at the far end a small altar with a Tabernacle and a lamp burning before it. A newly-lit fire was in the old-fashioned grate.

'Ye will be comfortable, I hope,' said the housekeeper. ''Tis dead beat ye must be! God save us! What a night!' as the blizzard raged round the house and the windows shook and rattled, and in the distance the terrible boom, boom, of the furious Atlantic could be heard.

'Oh I will be awfully comfortable, thank you so much,' replied Carmen, thinking how perfectly delicious it would be to lie down and sleep – sleep.

'I've left ye a nightdress of me own – mebbe not what ye're used to, but it's clean and warm – on the chair at the fire – the turf will soon light up.'

She paused a moment and glanced at the Tabernacle. 'The Blessed Sacrament is there,' she said, low crying her voice, 'this is the room where his Reverence sleeps ye know, and he keeps It there always in case of a sick call, for the Chapel is a bit out of the way these winter nights. I'll say goodnight to ye now – and sleep sound. '

She smiled at the girl, bent the knee reverently towards the Tabernacle, and left the room, closing the door after her – and Carmen Cavanagh was alone with her Lord.

For a few moments she stood horror-struck – terrified, gazing at the altar with dilated eyes. Then she drew in her breath sharply, and deliberately turning her back to it began to undress – and all the time she was feeling desperately angry, as if she had been tricked and deceived in some way, brought here on purpose. Just as if she could sleep with – *That!* The hands which were trying to unbutton her uniform shook pitifully, and she felt as if she was suffocating. Giving up the attempt to undress, she sat down on the bed, still with her back to the altar, but, in spite of herself, she felt her eyes drawn to it, and, turning her head slowly, and as if involuntarily, she looked again at the Tabernacle. A plain, simple receptacle of painted wood – very poor and ordinary – and a little lamp burning before it – that was all. But inside that little door – that locked door which no one might open but the priest of God himself – what was there! *What* lay within in loving humility – in Divine tenderness – in absolute love for mankind?

She covered her face with her hands as if to shut such thoughts away from her, and then back from the past came memories and scenes of other days – days when she was very different and when life was a happy, innocent thing to Carmen Cavanagh.

She saw the old garden of the French convent where her first remembered years had been passed, and, while the storm roared outside on the coast of bleak Donegal, Carmen seemed to be back once more in sunny France on a summer's evening. She could almost smell again the sweet Gloire de Dijon roses that climbed the old walls, and hear the soft tones of the Angelus ringing from the Nun's Chapel. And there was Sister Marie Therese coming so quietly across the grass to her to take her by the hand, with her gentle, 'come, then, my child – it is thy supper time.'

And then it was her First Communion – yes, there she was – a little thin thing with big staring eyes – with all the other children, all in white, and she had a wreath and veil too – and how proudly she held her candle and how happy – oh how happy she was *then!*

'Oh God, let me forget! Let me forget!' she cried in bitterness of soul.

But she could not – all her life seemed to pass before her. Her Confirmation, retreats and missions which she had attended from time to time; confessions, earnest and sincere, when she had made resolutions and meant to keep them. And then her life in Dublin, and later her gay, careless hospital days – her flirtations and amusements – innocent enough, and yet filling her life to the detriment of other and better things. Then came her friendship with Marcella – and then Peg – dear, dear little Peg o' Her heart – about whom she had lately thought so little and remembered so seldom!

And then she saw again that lonely house, with the weed-grown garden, where poor Dr Murray had said goodbye to this world and sent his soul forth to – what? Again she saw the dangling body and the staring eyes which had haunted her for many a day, but which lately had been receding into the background of her thoughts. She shut her eyes tightly as though in such manner she could shut the vision out, but she only saw it the clearer.

And then had come her meeting with Victor and the dawn of her great passion. Oh, how she loved him – how she loved him! – and the wretched thing he had to tell her in the 'field of the fairies' that evening in Carragh – that horrid story from his past which changed everything for Carmen.

And then she thought of Allan's death, and of Marcella and Peg going away to Dublin, and Victor back to London. Oh, how lonely she had been then – how lonely!

'But why were you lonely? Was not *I* always near?'

Had anyone spoken? Slowly uncovering her face, she looked almost fearfully around the room. There was no one there – No *one*? Involuntarily, in spite of herself – against her will as it seemed to her – her eyes were drawn back to the Tabernacle.

'I am Jesus, whom thou persecutest. It is hard for thee to kick against the goad.'

Carmen put out her hands as if to ward off the extraordinary sensation of which she was conscious – that of being quietly and slowly but irrevocably, surely, drawn towards the little wooden Tabernacle on the poor altar.

Someone was knocking at the door of her heart, a Voice, the tenderest, sweetest voice ever heard – was speaking to her. Twice before had God spoken to her erring soul, by warnings, but now He spoke for the third time in love.

Rising to her feet Carmen stumbled, with faltering feet, across the room and knelt prostrate before the Tabernacle.

Hours went by. Outside, the storm roared and blustered and tired itself out, and gradually became quieter, and away in the East the grey winter's dawn was slowly breaking. And still Carmen knelt on the bare floor before the Tabernacle, insensible to cold and fatigue – conscious only of her soul and the Divine Love which filled it to the exclusion of all else. Twice only had she spoken aloud. Once she said brokenly, 'My Lord and my God!' and again later, after hours of silent prayer, she had said half aloud, 'Master, what wilt Thou have me to do?'

At last, making the sign of the Cross, she slowly rose to her feet and bathed her face and hands and brushed her hair, and then, slipping out of her uniform, she put on Martha's warm nightdress and thought she would lie down and rest until she should be called, and, pulling the blankets over her, she was sound asleep in a few moments. So soundly did she sleep that she did not hear the housekeeper either knocking or entering the room, and so tired did she look that the good woman had not the heart to waken her, although she little guessed what reason the girl had to be tired.

So that it was nearly midday when at last Carmen descended the ladder-like stairs, and sat down to breakfast which, of course, she partook of alone – the priest always taking his at nine o'clock on his return from eight o'clock Mass. He was in his study now, the housekeeper informed her, and thither Carmen presently repaired, entering the room rather nervously, in answer to his gentle 'come in.'

He smiled at her over his glasses as she came to his side, and she suddenly smiled back – a radiant smile as if a flood of sunlight was filling her soul.

'I have come to you to hear my confession, Father,' she said, and knelt down.

XVI

GOD'S WAYS

Late that evening Victor Walpole was sitting impatiently and in rather a bad temper before the fire in the smoke room at Wilson's. He had the room to himself – there were seldom visitors to the hotel at that time of the year – and was not long back from Glenmore, where he had been for the second time that day, having driven over early in the morning and again in the afternoon in the hope that Carmen might have returned. But she had not, and he began to fear that he would not see her again before he left, which he had to do early the next morning – he could not stay a day longer, having a professional appointment in London which he must keep at any cost.

The snow – which had not been quite so severe in Carragh as in other parts near – had ceased, and the night was inclined to be dry and frosty.

'She ought to be able to drive back by now,' he thought, moodily, 'if the case is over, the weather won't keep her any longer. I wonder would it be any good to drive across to

Glenmore again tonight?' He glanced at his watch doubtfully. 'Eight o'clock! The car could be over there in two hours or less. By Jove, I'll chance it – in case she might have got back! Wilson will think I am absolutely mad – but what does it matter? What does anything matter if I can see her again before I leave?' Going out into the hall, which was big and roomy, with plenty of seats and a blazing fire, Victor saw Mr Wilson talking to a commercial traveller who had just arrived from a neighbouring village, and wanted a bed for the night.

'I want a car for Glenmore, Wilson,' said the surgeon, interrupting the conversation unceremoniously.

'A car for Glenmore!' repeated the hotel proprietor doubtfully. 'Is it another tonight?'

'Yes – and I want it at once. Hurry the man along, will you?'

But Mr Wilson still looked doubtful.

'I don't know, sir,' he said, 'whether there is a horse fit for that road again tonight; it's very heavy on them at this time of the year.'

'Oh, nonsense!' replied Victor impatiently. 'Get me a horse somehow, and as quick as you can!'

'Well, sir, I'll see what I can do,' said Wilson, and he walked away, resolving in his own mind to repay himself for all this extra trouble in the bill which he would present to the parting guest next morning.

'Seemingly he's made o' money!' he thought, 'and I may as well have me share as well as another!'

Just then there was the sound of a car stopping outside, and a moment afterwards a man entered the hotel and inquired if there was 'a party be the name of Walpole stopping there?'

'Yes, that's my name!' said Victor, coming forward, 'what do you want?'

'Fr O'Toole of Glenavin bid me give ye this,' said the man, and handed him a letter.

'Fr O'Toole? Glenavin?' murmured Victor in bewilderment, and then he saw that it was in Carmen's handwriting, and went into the smoke room to open it.

'She must be weather-bound somewhere, and has written to me,' he thought. 'I suppose I may give up all hope of seeing her in that case. What rotten bad luck!' but he forgot in the stress of the moment to countermand the order for the car and Mr Wilson, thinking it would still be wanted, went off to see if he could arrange for one.

Standing at the fire in the empty smoke room, Victor read Carmen's letter and as he did so his face changed like that of one who had received a mortal wound.

The letter was not long, but he was quick to realise its absolute finality. She told him how sorry she was that she had ever agreed to do what he asked, and that he was to forgive her for causing him pain, but that God had opened her eyes and saved her from terrible sin, and that she had been to confession and intended to live a different life from this on. She told him about the snow storm and how she had taken refuge in the priest's house at Glenavin, and about the Tabernacle in her room.

'Not that you will understand this,' she wrote:

I know you won't, but it is the only reason I can give you for what I am doing – and the true one. I believe Our Lord Himself spoke to me last night, and oh Victor, I can't refuse Him! I never realised before how great is His Love, but I am conquered at last! Fr O'Toole has been so good to me, and by his advice I am staying here until tomorrow, and then I will return to Glenmore, and you will be gone. Take my blessing with you, it is all I can give you now. I cannot write any more. Oh Victor, you *know*, you *know* what you were to me! Goodbye – or, rather, God be with you! – for that is the wish of CARMEN.

For some time after he had finished reading it Victor Walpole stood immovable like a figure carved from stone, with the note still in his hand, gazing unseeing into the fire. He was very pale and, cold as was the night, there were drops of sweat on his forehead. Mechanically he took out his handkerchief and wiped them away, noticing with faint surprise that his hands were shaking. The letter was final – absolutely final – and he knew that it was – knew that never again would he see the woman who meant so much to him, who had been to him more than life itself since the first day he had seen her wheeling her bicycle down the Carragh Hill, and trying in vain to keep the laughter from her lovely eyes as they met his. Never again might he kiss her beloved lips, never again feel the clinging caress of her arms, never hear her voice, never look again upon her adored face.

The man's shoulders were bent; he looked for the moment like an old man.

'*Carmen!*' he breathed in a dry whisper. '*Carmen,* my beloved!'

But he called to one who would never listen to his voice again; she had left him to walk this weary earth alone. Slowly and surely he tore her letter across and across, and dropped the tiny pieces into the flames.

'So ends my dream of happiness!' he said, 'it is over – gone for ever – the pale Nazarene has conquered once more.'

Hardly noticing where he was going, he walked back to the hall, and Mr Wilson came bustling forward.

'Your car is here, sir,' he announced.

'Car!' echoed Victor, stupidly. 'What car?'

'The car you wanted for Glenmore,' replied the other, noticing his guest's troubled appearance with much curiosity.

'Oh, damn you!' shouted Victor, suddenly losing control of himself. 'I want no car – it can go to the devil – and you with it!'

And he swung round on his heel and went out into the night, walking the lonely roads around until midnight, when he returned to the hotel and went to his room.

The next morning he was his usual self again, except that he appeared very pale and quiet with dark shadows under the eyes, telling of a sleepless night. He had to leave the hotel at eight o'clock, and was standing on the front step waiting while his car was brought round when he heard the bell of the little Catholic Church which was just beside Wilson's begin to ring for Mass, and immediately afterwards Fr McGinley came down the steps of the priest's house opposite.

As he was passing the hotel on his way to the church some impulse prompted Victor to go down to him and put out his hand.

'Shake hands with me, Father,' he said, with a smile that tried not to be bitter. 'I am going away from Ireland – and from the woman I love – for ever.'

The curate stood still on the road and stared at him. 'You mean?' he said.

'I mean,' replied Victor, 'that history repeats itself in the lives of individuals as well as nations, and so once more – Rome has spoken.'

The priest bared his head. 'My God, I thank Thee!' he said.

And as Victor Walpole jumped on the car and then turned for a farewell look at the little Donegal village where the greatest love and the greatest sorrow of his life had come to him, the picture which remained the clearest on his brain was the ivy-covered church and the curate on his way to celebrate Mass.

As he entered the porch, Fr McGinley turned and looked at the car which was just moving away, and something in the hopeless misery of Victor Walpole touched him to the heart. He felt now that he might have been unjust to this man at times – and he wished that he had spoken freely to him a moment ago, but his relief on hearing what the surgeon had said to him had made him forget that what was a subject for thanksgiving to himself might mean untold suffering for the other, who, agnostic – unbeliever though he might be – had spoken like a brave man when he had announced his defeat. And so, as the car drove down the village street, the curate waved his hat and called out, 'Goodbye, Mr Walpole and – and God bless you!' rather to his own surprise and very much to Mr Wilson's, who stared at him in sulky disapproval.

Returning from Mass, and passing the hotel door, he saw Mr Wilson standing there again.

'Good morning, Mr Wilson,' cried the curate, who was naturally in good humour with all the world that morning. 'So your visitor has gone!'

'Aye – he has,' was the rather curt reply.

'And there's not going to be any so-called "wedding" after all,' continued the curate.

'So I understand by a few words he let drop,' replied Mr Wilson, his curiosity overriding his dislike for the 'popish priest', 'but he gave me no reason for it, nor what had come between himself and Miss Cavanagh. Maybe it's only a lover's quarrel, although I must say that he looked as if it was pretty serious!'

'Very much so,' was the reply, 'and it is no lover's quarrel, Mr Wilson – they are as much attached to each other as ever – but Mr Walpole gave me the reason for Miss Cavanagh sending him away, and it is the most powerful one there could be – although he gave it to me in three words.'

'Indeed, sir!' cried Mr Wilson, almost trembling with his intense curiosity, 'and those were?'

'*Rome has spoken!* Good day Mr Wilson – a beautiful morning for this time of year!' and the curate went on to the priest's house with a very good appetite for his breakfast.

Fr McGinley, although reputed by his adoring flock to be 'the great saint entirely!' was very human after all!

A fortnight later Carmen developed a rather sharp attack of influenza, which, owing to her decidedly 'run down' condition at the time, left her very weak and prostrated. Of course Dr Hegarty was assiduous in his attention, going over to Glenmore every day, in all weathers, and the winter storms and gales were playing havoc round the Donegal coast just then.

Mr Wilson looked after him one day with cold contempt as he drove by in a perfect hurricane of wind and rain. The yard boy of the hotel, who was standing near, followed the direction of his master's glance.

'Yerra, there's the docthor off to Glenmore again!' he said, "tis very attintive entirely he is over there since the London surgeon wint away!'

'Aye – he is that!' said Mr Wilson, adding sourly, 'but it doesn't follow that he's going to step into the other's shoes be any manner of means!'

He detested the young doctor, whom he designated as a domineering young whipster with no respect for his betters – in which category, of course, he placed himself.

Arriving at Glenmore, the doctor divested himself of mackintosh and leggings from which the rain was dripping and entered the sitting room, where Carmen – now convalescent – was sitting in a low chair by the fire. She was very pale and thin – 'like a broken lily' Dr Hegarty used to think in his poetical moments – there was a look of peace on her face now to which it had been a stranger for some months past. Today, too, as he was quick to observe, she seemed to be aroused out of herself more than usual – almost excited, indeed.

She made a movement to rise, but he pushed her gently back amongst her cushions.

'No – no, don't stir,' he said. 'How are you feeling today? You *look* a lot better and quite *interested* about something – which you haven't been lately, you know. Is anything up?'

'Oh, Dr Hegarty!' cried Carmen, 'I've come in for a fortune.'

'*What!*' he cried, wondering if by any chance her mind could be wandering. But her next words undeceived him. 'No, I'm not dotty,' she said with a laugh. 'I have really inherited a fortune. It's from Spain, left to me by my mother's brother – and I didn't even know that such a person ever existed! The solicitor's letter is here – they traced me from one place to another and they got my address here from the Superintendent at the Dublin Home,' – and she thrust the letter into his hands as she spoke.

Yes it was all real enough, as he soon discerned. The Spanish legal firm had communicated with a Dublin solicitor known to them, and enquiries were set on foot which resulted in Carmen becoming the owner of a fortune which would bring her in about £5,000 a year. This Spanish uncle of hers had idolised her mother when they were young together, and, although he had quarrelled with her later on because she went on the stage – his pride being hurt thereby – during his last illness he had repented and had left directions in his Will to find her and if she still lived she was to inherit his wealth. If she was dead and had left any children, the fortune was to be divided amongst them. So Carmen, being the only one, inherited all. There were various legal requirements to be fulfilled, and the solicitors were anxious for her presence in Dublin; but there was no doubt about the fortune, and Carmen Cavanagh, who had never known what it was to have a spare pound in her life, was now a rich woman.

Dr Hegarty smiled at her bravely. He had known for some time that his love was not returned, but there had always been a tiny flicker of hope – especially since the affair with Victor Walpole had ended – and that had been a time of such misery to Martin Hegarty that he could not bear to recall it. But now, as he saw at once, he must stand aside and let her go without a word – for he was a very honourable gentleman, although only a dispensary doctor working in the wild places of Donegal.

'Congratulations!' he said heartily, patting her hand as he gave back the letter. 'It's simply wonderful – like a fairytale! And what are you going to do? I suppose you will be off to Dublin as soon as possible.'

'Yes – as soon as I feel able for the journey,' she said, 'and I'm sure I will get strong very soon now!'

'Will you live in Dublin altogether now? I mean make your real home there? Of course you will probably travel and see the world a bit – I should if I could afford it, like you can now!'

She hesitated for a moment, and her face flushed and paled. 'I – don't know,' she said, 'but I'll certainly live there for awhile at present. I'll take a house and have Marcella and Peg to live with me. Oh how glad I'll be to see them again!'

'And they to see you, I'm sure,' he said, adding, 'How is little Peg o' My Heart – what a dear she is! – and Mrs Adair?'

'They are both fairly well,' answered Carmen, 'but Peg is growing fast and has never really been the same since her illness, and Marcella is working too hard – she doesn't actually say so, but I can read between the lines of her letters. But now I'll give them both the time of their lives! Oh Doctor, when do you think I'll be able to leave here?'

He hesitated a moment. Perhaps he was tempted to delay her going – even by a few days. But commonsense stepped in and asked where was the good of putting off the inevitable, however painful it might be.

'Eat and sleep all you can – drink a gallon of milk a day! And you can travel in a week.'

Carmen clapped her hands with a flash of her old gaiety, and then something in Martin Hegarty's honest eyes caused her own to fill with sudden tears, for she was weak still.

'You have been so good to me – so awfully good,' she said, 'and I am sorry that – that I couldn't –'

'Oh, it's all right, dear Carmen, let me call you so for once. Don't worry about me at all! I'll get over it!' and, stooping, he kissed the small, perfectly formed hand which he loved so much, and left her.

XVII

CURTAIN FALLS ON CARMEN

It is three months later and instead of cold, grey February, it is May, with lovely June near at hand; and instead of wild, bleak Donegal, we are in that most beautiful of all the counties of Ireland, no matter what the natives of the other thirty one may say, dear County Dublin. And there, in a delightful old house near Killiney, we find our two friends again.

They are in the garden this warm evening, Carmen idly swinging in a hammock, her hands clasped behind her head and her great dark eyes staring up at the blue skies above her; Marcella, sitting beside her with a book on her knees, but her thoughts are somewhere else, and she presently gives up all attempt at reading and looks at her friend with a speculative look as if she was debating some knotty point in her own mind, and Carmen, catching the look, gives a little laugh as she says, 'well! What is it, Cella? You want to ask me something, don't you? I can see you are simply dying to put me through my catechism!'

'Yes,' admitted the other, 'I am. Tell me, Carmen – and don't be vexed with me for asking – but lately I have thought that perhaps you were going to make some change in your life? You have so often gone into Dublin to see Fr Black and the solicitors, and you know if – if Peg or I are in the way at all, or if ...'

But she was interrupted by Carmen slipping out of the hammock and giving her a warm kiss as she cried, 'oh, you old goose! it wouldn't be you if you weren't worrying over something. However, I *am* going to make a change and a very big change, in my life, and you may as well hear all about it now.'

She sat down beside Marcella and remained in silence for a short while, staring straight in front of her at the house in the distance and the beautiful old garden, which already she loved so dearly.

And the garden was very lovely just now in this month of May. Everywhere was the scent of lilac and the blaze of the golden rain of the laburnum – Carmen had often said in the days of her poverty that if ever she *could* choose a house of her own, and how very unlikely such a possibility seemed then, there should be plenty of those trees around, and certainly Pook's Hill, as the house was called, was surrounded by them. And there were hedges of hawthorn and, in the orchard behind the house, the apple trees were a mass of exquisite pink and white. The house itself was built of grey stone, with a terrace running round the front of it, upon which opened the French windows of the dining room and drawing room, and also the pretty breakfast room, one of the daintiest places in the house. It was a good-sized building, with more than enough rooms and, Carmen having left all the domestic affairs in Marcella's hands, the household was smoothly worked by capable servants under Ellen's supervision.

Carmen had chosen this house with a thought of Peg,

always first in her mind, and only for Marcella putting her foot firmly down the child would have been certainly spoilt at last. But her mother would not allow much difference to be made in the child's mode of life, Carmen's ideas of a day and night nursery, furnished most extravagantly and with a head nurse and under nurse, were swept aside by Marcella.

'No, Carmen,' she said quietly but firmly, 'the child has never been used to that kind of life, and it wouldn't suit her now, and I don't think she would be happy in it, she would feel too much cut away from you and I. Let her have the dressing room off my room furnished for herself, and a young girl to take her out when I am busy, and that's all until it's time for her to go to school or to have a governess.'

And so it was settled, and Peg was as happy as a little queen. She had toys and picture books by the score and dolls of every description. It was useless for Marcella to try and curb Carmen's shopping where the little one was concerned, and the sweetest frocks and clothes of all kinds. She had her own 'garden' too, where she dug and planted and sowed seeds which she generally washed out of the ground immediately afterwards by copious watering, upon which she would sadly remark to the sympathetic gardener's boy, 'Peg's 'eeds won't tays down!'

And she had a delightful donkey and trap to drive her down to the beach, with the same boy – her abject slave – to look after it for her.

Marcella's eyes often filled with tears of joy as she looked at the child getting so fat and rosy once more, and so happy and unspoilt. Both she and Peg had known the pinch of poverty – that genteel poverty, which is the hardest of all – since leaving Carragh, and both of them could not but enjoy their life now.

But Marcella, dearly as she loved Carmen, was still a rather proud and decidedly independent individual, so that at times she often felt that her present life could not go on for ever. How could she remain idly living on Carmen's bounty? And yet she shrank from saying so to her old chum, dreading to hurt the girl who loved her so much and who had been through sorrow and suffering before her prosperity came to her. And Marcella, having 'loved and lost' herself, knew that there are some wounds which no amount of money can heal. However, during the last month she had thought that Carmen had seemed restless and preoccupied, as though she were making some definite decision, and Marcella knew, too, that she had been consulting her confessor frequently and had several interviews with her solicitors.

And now Carmen had admitted that she was going to make a change in her life. What was that change to be?

As if in answer to her unspoken question, Carmen moved slightly and slipped her hand through Marcella's arm.

'Cella, dearest,' she said, 'I am going to enter religion.'

Marcella started and gave a little exclamation, but for the minute she could not speak. But her attitude towards this resolve of Carmen's was very different from what it would have been a short time ago, for Marcella had been received into the Catholic Church a month ago, and Peg was to be Baptised on the following day to this of which we are writing. So Marcella Adair sat very quietly for a few moments and then turned and kissed Carmen.

'Oh, Carmen!' she said, 'I never thought of *that*. And – and I am glad – *glad* for your sake, but for mine and Peg's –' and she suddenly broke down and sobbed, for it seemed to her for the moment to be a hard trial that she who had lost Allan so recently should now have to give up her friend, too.

And Carmen understood and tried to comfort her with love and sympathy until Marcella dried her eyes and said, 'how selfish I am thinking of my own loss instead of your happiness and gain – for oh, Carmen, my dearest, I know you *will* be happy!'

'Yes, I will be happy,' said the other quietly, but her eyes were shining, 'and, Marcella, I could do no less for *Him*!'

There was silence between them for a little, and then Carmen, looking at her watch, said. 'It is nearly five o'clock. Mary will be bringing the tea shortly. I told her we would have it out here this evening. And now, Marcella, I want to talk *business* to you for a few minutes – it won't take long – but please attend,' and she smiled.

'Business!' echoed Marcella, adding. 'Oh yes, of course. You will be giving up this house, I suppose, and –'

'Be quiet, please, and let *me* talk,' interrupted Carmen, with mock severity. 'I will not be giving up this house; in fact, it's not mine to give up for I have bought it and made it over to Peg; she also gets half my money – the rest of course goes to the Convent. Now don't interrupt, please. You are her guardian, and I hope you will both live on here – it is a dear old place, and I would like to think of you and Peg happy together. Will you, dear?'

'Oh! Carmen!' cried Marcella through her tears. 'How can I take your money? How?'

'*You* are not taking any of my money,' was the answer. 'You will be allowed a suitable allowance for yourself and Peg until she is of age and – and mind and look after her well!' she ended with a laugh that was rather shaky, and then as her eyes strayed across the garden she cried, 'oh, here is the tea – and Peg herself!'

Ellen came across the grass, carrying a table, and followed by one of the maids, with the tray, and in the near distance Peg could be seen trotting as fast as her fat legs would go, and with some object clasped lovingly in her arms. She was followed by the gardener's boy and, as she came nearer, her burden proved to be a very fat collie pup which was wriggling for all its worth to get free.

'Oh Mums! Oh Tarmen! Yook what Ams' – the boy's name was *Sam* – 'dave Peg – a puppy – a yive puppy!'

Sam, looking very sheepish, was blushing under the cold stare of Mary, the housemaid, with whom he had a chronic feud, but his spirits were lifted sky high when the ladies praised the pup and promised Peg that she should keep it, but that Sam must take it away now during teatime.

'Here Ams!' said the young lady, imperiously, and then said to the pup, 'div Peg a kiss, will 'oo?'

The pup complied most fervently and enthusiastically to this request – licking Peg's face all over with great diligence to her huge delight, and then when he was borne away by Sam she turned her attention to the tea table, where she spotted several of her favourite kinds of 'bikkie.'

She munched in silence for a while until her mind reverted to another important event, of which she had heard much talk. 'Peg goin' be *Baptied* in de mornin'?' she asked presently.

Carmen and Marcella both laughed.

'Yes sweetheart, you will be baptised, please God, in the morning,' assented Carmen, while Marcella said whimsically, 'she doesn't in the least know what it means, of course, although she has some idea that it is to be in a church – but I'm afraid she is thinking more about her frock than anything else!'

'Peg be a yovely dirl,' said the little maiden complacently as she selected a very enticing 'sugary' biscuit under Carmen's guidance, quite impervious to Marcella's.

'Now, Peg, take the *plain* ones!'

But it was evident that her mind, as her mother had guessed, was on the new frock which Carmen had selected – a little dream of silk and lace – for she spoke again presently.

'Pegs be a wanks!' she said grandly.

The two who loved her so dearly laughed and kissed her – but Peg wondered why their eyes were wet.

There is an enclosed order of nuns who have a convent on the northside of Dublin, with a chapel which is celebrated for a beautiful shrine to Our Mother of Perpetual Succour. Benediction is at four o'clock every day and is generally crowded, for not only do people from the near neighbourhood attend but many from far parts of the city come – some to pray at the famous shrine for 'special intentions' and some to hear the singing of the choir.

Carmen – now Sister Mary Carmel – sings there, and there sometimes Marcella and Peg go to hear her voice again. And sometimes, but not often, they are allowed to speak to her, but they cannot touch her and the first few times there was a heart–breaking scene with Peg, who could not understand the partition between them and cried bitterly for Carmen to 'come out and kiss Peg.' But now she is quite used to it and goes cheerily away, blowing kisses towards the quiet figure in the white habit which once was the gay and laughing Carmen. And down in the chapel, before the shrine Peg folds her hands and prays, as Marcella has taught her, 'dod bess Tarmen, and make Peg a dood dirl. Amen.'

THE END